Muzzled

Books by Eileen Brady

A Kate Turner, D.V.M. Mystery
Muzzled

Muzzled

A Kate Turner, D.V.M. Mystery

Eileen Brady

Poisoned Pen Press

Copyright © 2014 by Eileen Brady

First Edition 2014

10 9 8 7 6 5 4 3 2 1

Library of Congress Catalog Card Number: 2013941468

ISBN: 9781464201844   Hardcover
      9781464201868   Trade Paperback

Poisoned Pen Press
6962 E. First Ave., Ste. 103
Scottsdale, AZ 85251
www.poisonedpenpress.com
info@poisonedpenpress.com

Printed in the United States of America

To my husband, Jon, the yang to my yin, whose support and confidence in me has never wavered.

Acknowledgments

I wouldn't be the writer I am today without the critiques (both good and bad) of my writer's group, the Sheridan Street Irregulars. Thanks to Sharon McGee, Art Kerns, Scott Andrews, Bill Butler and most of all my friend and mentor, the incomparable Betty Webb. See you on Tuesday, guys.

Working with the people at the Poisoned Pen Press has been a joy. Special kudos to my terrific editor, Barbara Peters, former publisher Jessica Tribble, Beth Deveny, Suzan Baroni, and Pete Zrioka for all their help. The cover art by Mike Hagelberg couldn't be more perfect.

To my daughters, Brittney and Amanda, thanks for the interruptions, reminding me that life goes on even while I'm sitting at my desk. Love you both.

My mom, Marie Brady, always told me that even as a child all kinds of animals would follow me home. A love of animals has been a constant in my life. Thanks to the encouragement of the staff at the Animal Medical Center in New York City while I was working as a technician, I pursued my dream by going to veterinary school. My husband, Jonathan Grant, also a veterinarian and I have been privileged to work at and own the Rosebank Veterinary Practice, in Staten Island, New York, Olive Animal Hospital near the Ashokan Reservoir in Olive, New York, and the Scaredy Cat Hospital in Scottsdale, Arizona.

Although I've been a veterinarian for over twenty years, this book is a work of fiction—inspired by all my wonderful clients and patients. Any errors or mistakes are completely mine.

watchful eyes, I searched for my bandage scissors and gauze pads. Even Damian reined in his imaginary horse, raised the Pop-Tart in the air like a sword, and stood next to his brother. Gingerly, I unplugged the vacuum from the wall outlet.

Their mom returned clutching a stack of newspapers and some garbage bags. After handing them to me she called to her daughter. "Come here, Angie." The girl ran over and pressed her face into Mary's waist.

With newspapers covering the rug, I opened the red plastic latch securing the vacuum bag, then reached in and pulled it free. Using the blunt side of my scissors, I slowly cut along the top with my finger as a guide. I reached inside. Like a magician, I pulled out a brown hamster covered in lint. The little guy's eyes were closed tight, but on quick exam he seemed to be okay. I picked all the lint off his fur and stroked his head. Suddenly his eyes popped open, black and bright. He looked around and squeaked.

"Hooray," the kids cheered.

Still holding the hamster in my hand, I glanced at Tommy. "Get Peanut's cage and bring it here. He needs a little quiet time."

"Dead, dead, dead," Damian called out gleefully, then, started to gallop again.

With Peanut safely stuffing his cheek pouches with food, I gathered the family together for a stern lecture on pocket pets and electrical appliances. It turned out Tommy wasn't a bad kid, just careless. I reminded them about supplementing Peanut's food with a hamster multivitamin, since hamsters, like people, don't make their own vitamin C. After Mary settled her bill over the phone, we looked at Peanut's habitat and I made some suggestions for improvements. The kids started talking about maybe getting a dog and Damian offered me the last bite of his squished Pop-Tart. A quick glance at my watch told me that I was already running late for my second appointment of the day.

"Thanks so much, Dr. Kate." Mary said taking the newspapers from my hand. "We'll be much more careful with Peanut in the future. I promise."

I followed her through the living room to the front door. "Make sure you observe him carefully the next few days and call me if there are any problems."

Out of the corner of my eye I saw her give me a speculative glance. Then she said, "Did anyone ever tell you that you look a little like Meryl Streep, except younger?"

Outside I gunned the office truck, set the GPS, and headed for my next appointment. As I drove along Hamilton Lane the skies darkened and rain began to fall. Spring in upstate New York could usher in sunny weather or buckets of rain. The windshield wipers barely kept up with the developing storm as lightning streaked above the trees, followed by booms of thunder. Fifteen minutes late stretched into a half hour as visibility worsened. Pooling water on the roads slowed everyone down. Finally, I turned into a long private driveway leading to an elegant brick mansion on five acres. Fat drops of rain pelted the windshield. Pulling my lab coat over my head, I jumped out of the truck and ran up the slippery front stairs to the front door. With twenty-seven dogs barking, rain blasting down—almost as loud—I stood drenched in the noisy downpour.

No, this wasn't an episode of animal hoarders—in fact, just the opposite. The dogs inside are pampered and fussed over like royalty, which they are. Vivian and Thomas Langthorne raise and show champion-quality Cavalier King Charles spaniels and each one was barking like crazy. Thunder boomed again as I lifted the dog-shaped brass knocker and banged it hard against the black-lacquered front door. The open porch with its six marble columns didn't do much to shelter me from the wind and rain.

Between the storm and my veterinary technician having injured her knee, my whole day's schedule was morphing into a disaster. I half expected to see Vivian Langthorne standing by the front door waiting for me, puffing a cigarette, and muttering to herself. At least that was the scenario two weeks ago during their last house call. She'd still been hopping mad at me for shaving the front leg of her champion stud dog, Lucky Eight's King Charles Too.

"Dr. Turner. How can I show him like that?" she'd asked touching the small shave mark on his left front leg. I reminded her that Charles Too had been extremely ill with symptoms of acute pancreatitis. Without intravenous fluids and medications, the dog could have died.

"Humph," had been her final word on the subject. Even in her eighties the tiny woman with wispy white hair and stern black eyes radiated that second-grade teacher authority. If she could have forced me into time-out, she would have.

I knocked on the door again and rang the doorbell. The buzzing sound was drowned out by the rainfall and roaring thunder above. My elderly clients probably couldn't hear anything over the din. Getting no answer again, I called the office.

"Hey, Sandy, I've got a little problem here."

"Running late again?" The raspy voice of Oak Falls Animal Hospital's chief receptionist and office manager, Sandy Hendrik, was a product of unfiltered cigarettes and rumored shots of Jack Daniels.

"I'm at the Langthornes' front door but no one is answering. Are you sure the appointment was for ten this morning?"

A lull in the storm let me hear computer keys clicking. After a moment Sandy came back on the line. "The appointment calendar says 'Langthorne recheck at ten.' Wait there and I'll call the numbers I have for them."

While I waited, the rain began to let up. A small rivulet of water meandered along the side of the cobblestone driveway, heading down the hill toward Little Silver Creek. The weather in the Hudson Valley during early April often changes by the minute, as witnessed by a ray of sun piercing the clearing gray clouds. Restless, I tried the front door handle. The door slid open.

"I think they left the door open for me."

"Nobody's answering." Sandy's voice crackled on speakerphone. "This happened once before, I think, when they were at the back of the house by the kennels. I say go ahead in."

"All right, but bail me out if they charge me with breaking-and-entering." The phone abruptly cut out. I wondered if Sandy had headed outside for a quick cigarette break. Carefully I wiped both feet on the doormat, picked up my battered leather medical bag, and walked in.

An overpowering odor, much worse than usual, hit me in the face. Mixed with the animal stench, I recognized the metallic smell of blood and saw a bloody pawprint.

Alarmed, I called out, "Mr. and Mrs. Langthorne? Are you here?" A sea of little dogs yapped at my feet. No lights shone in the dim foyer. Dodging the spaniels I made my way into the formal living room.

It looked like a horror movie tea party. Vivian slumped in a brocade armchair, her skin bluish white. A large dark stain over her heart ruined the yellow cashmere sweater set she wore. Thomas had fallen against the side of his chair, his head at a terrible angle. An identical stain covered his polo shirt. I checked each for a pulse, although I was sure they were dead, then, called 9-1-1.

Three Cavalier King Charles spaniels barked and decided to chase each other past the tea table. A massive Georgian silver tray held little sandwiches now sprinkled with blood. A plate of scones sat next to the teapot, the paired blue-and-white porcelain sugar bowl and milk pitcher nearby. In the center, a Chinese dish held thin lemon slices arranged in a circle. I'd been their guest for a similar tea each time I'd come to their house. Proper etiquette demanded it. My eyes strayed back to Thomas and his dropped teacup staining the Oriental carpet. A gun lay near the broken cup.

What happened here? Was this a murder-suicide?

One of the spaniels jumped up on my leg, stared at me with liquid brown eyes, and whimpered. I bent down to pet it. Why were the dogs out? Normally when visitors came over the Lang- thornes kept the dogs in the kennels attached to the house. As I stood there more dogs poured into the living room. Were all twenty-seven dogs loose? When the emergency responders came, some of the frightened dogs might escape into the neighborhood.

"Come here, babies," I crooned, mimicking Vivian's voice as best I could while trying to lead them into the kitchen. The bag of dog food and a box of treats on the countertop gave me an idea. Waving the treats in front of me, I led the dogs into the large office separated from the kitchen by glass-paned French doors. Like a canine pied piper I got the little dogs, eagerly anticipating food, to follow me. I dumped half a bag directly onto the wooden floor and watched as the stragglers ran over to join the crowd. After placing two giant bowls of water in the office, I closed the doors and walked outside to wait for the police. A profound sadness settled on my shoulders, weighing me down. What had happened in there?

Sirens wailed in the distance. Blue sky showed through the clouds signaling the end of the storm. The damp air, smelling of junipers and wet cedar chips, began to chase the smell of death away. I paced the porch, then called the office again.

"Oak Falls Animal Hospital," Sandy answered through a run of coughs.

"Hey, it's Kate again. Can you call my next appointments and tell them I might have to reschedule? There's an emergency here."

"What's up? Having problems with Vivian?"

I stared out at the holly lining the walkway, spiky leaves glistening from the rain.

"Sandy, I found the Langthornes dead inside the house. I'm waiting for the police to arrive."

Her stunned silence went on for almost twenty seconds, before I asked, "Are you okay?"

"Damn," she grumbled. "You lost another client. Doc won't be happy about this." She hung up the phone.

Please let her be joking.

The house went from empty of humans to full in less than five minutes. As the only witness, I was told to wait inside. Once more I stood in the living room, but turned away from the bodies. The EMTs brushed past as they moved back and forth from their truck, filling out paperwork with no sense of urgency. Between the smell of death, the sounds of the dogs yipping and barking, and someone who unwrapped an Italian submarine sandwich in the corner, I needed fresh air.

"I'm going outside for a moment," I told no one in particular.

A clean breeze welcomed me when I opened the front door and stepped out onto the porch. I followed the columns along the side of the house, away from the trucks and the still-flashing lights. My lungs pulled in big gulps of pine-scented air, pushing away the odors that lingered on my skin like a thin layer of sweat. Now in the silence so many questions occurred to me. Why were the dogs in the house? I couldn't imagine the Langthornes leaving all the dogs out, even during the heat of an argument. When the dogs came indoors they had to be segregated by gender, since only controlled mating was allowed. Sometimes it was difficult for owners to know if a female was about to go into heat. Male dogs had no such trouble.

Something else about finding the elderly couple was bothering me. That scene in the living room didn't look like the scene of an argument. I'd witnessed fights between the Langthornes before. They followed a predictable pattern—verbal abuse escalating to the point at which Thomas went into his office and slammed the door. Vivian usually hurled one last insult before stalking off to her space in the front parlor. Then ten minutes later it was as if nothing had happened.

I gazed out at the manicured grounds—such a contrast to the tragedy inside. I remembered my last visit, Thomas barking orders from his office while Vivian tried to cajole him into doing what she wanted. A nagging thought about something being different in the house fluttered around at the periphery of my brain. What it was escaped me.

◇◇◇

"Dr. Turner?" The officer had spotted me on the side of the house then came toward me. I could see big patches of gray under his dark brown eyes. "I'm Police Chief Robert Garcia. I believe you gave a statement to Sergeant Edwards?"

"Yes. He asked me to wait." I'd never given a statement to the police before.

"We're almost done here. If you don't mind, I'd like to go back over the events with you." He took a notebook out of his pocket and flipped a page before looking up at me. "I understand you had an appointment with the deceased couple."

"Yes." My hands started to shake. I jammed them into the pockets of my lab coat.

"Are you cold? We can do this inside."

Just the suggestion made my skin jump. "No, I'm okay. Delayed reaction, I think."

"That's very common," he said, his voice softening. "Take your time."

I leaned against the pillar at the corner of the porch. It felt good to have something solid across my back.

"Now," he continued, "what time was your appointment?"

"Ten o'clock, but it was closer to ten-thirty by the time I got here. I was running late this morning. Normally I work with a technician, but she called in sick today." I stopped to take a breath. "When I got here no one answered the door. I called Sandy, the office manager, to make sure I had the date and time right."

"Did you see anyone else around the property? Any cars?"

"No. It was completely quiet except for the rain, the same as always."

He looked up. "You've been here before?" His sleepy eyes woke up.

"Yes, several times. I saw the Langthornes about two weeks ago for a recheck on one of their dogs."

"How did it go?"

Why did I think he wasn't really interested in the dog's health? "He did fine."

The baleful eyes stared at me.

"There were a few bumps in the road, but everything got resolved." I heard myself open Pandora's box.

He was on it like a mouse on cheese. "What bumps in the road?"

I sighed. How to explain dog show people to people from the real world? "Well, they were a little upset with me." Upset as in screaming and vowing to report me to the New York State Veterinary Medical Board. Not to mention threatening to take away my license to practice medicine.

He flipped his little notebook to a new page. "Why were they upset with you?"

"Their dog was dehydrated, so I put in an intravenous line for fluids and took bloods."

He frowned, which pulled his two black eyebrows into one black line. "What's the matter with that?"

"I shaved a patch of hair on Charles Too's leg for the IV. Charles Too is the dog's name."

"I don't understand."

My hands popped out of my pockets like they had a life of their own. "Lucky Eight's Charles Too is a retired grand champion Cavalier King Charles spaniel. The Langthornes' kennel name is Lucky Eight. His name is a play on words." That passes for humor on the dog show circuit."

"What about the patch of hair?"

"I didn't know they were going to Westminster this year."

The look of disbelief on his face intensified.

"I shaved off part of his coat." My voice rose precipitously as I tried to explain. "It would have grown back by then, but they were worried it would look uneven, or come in a different color." I hesitated.

"Okay."

"Today was a final recheck appointment. Plus they wanted me to take a look at one of the females they were trying to breed."

"I see." Again, more notes in the notebook. While he wrote, he moved his head, which set his jowls swaying.

"Of course, I didn't get a chance to examine him today, what with discovering the…ah…bodies. It was a murder-suicide, right?"

He cleared his throat and ignored my question. "Did you hear anyone in the house?"

"No."

"See anything suspicious?"

"No." Again a memory of something unusual danced away in the back of my mind.

"Did you touch anything?"

I thought for a moment. "Obviously, the front door. Then I checked Vivian and Thomas to make sure they were…gone. That's when I called 9-1-1." I tried to remember the exact sequence of events. "Oh, I went into the kitchen to get some dog food and herded all the dogs into one room. They normally aren't allowed to run around like this."

"Was there some animosity between you and the Langthornes?"

"I think they were still…perturbed." I watched him stop for a moment, continue to write, then, flip over to a new page.

"When we arrived, you were on the porch."

"Yes. Once I had secured the dogs, I thought it best not to disturb anything else."

"Now, the Langthornes knew you were coming here today. Correct?"

"Correct. They scheduled the appointment with Sandy, our office manager. Someone from the office usually calls the day before to confirm."

He closed the notebook and put it back into his pocket. "We'll need a statement from her. What is the office number?"

I gave it to him, but I had some questions of my own. "Chief Garcia, those dogs inside are technically my patients. Someone said Animal Control would hold them for the next of kin?"

"That's right, until legal ownership is determined."

"Well, if it's okay with you, I want to stay here and help secure all the dogs. The Langthornes loved their pets very much. They centered their lives around them, as far as I could tell. Honestly, I feel an obligation to them."

"Fine, just stay out of everyone's way." With a quick gesture he guided me back inside.

After contacting Animal Control I went into the office with the dogs, determined to calm them down a bit and take a quick head count. That proved impossible; I'd have to wait until Animal Control got here to help. On the other side of the French doors cameras flashed. Turning away I looked back at the office. Two walls lined in bookshelves; Thomas Langthorne's huge mahogany desk took up the rest of the space. I noticed it was cluttered with paperwork, but a big manila envelope marked "Last Will and Testament" was positioned against his desk lamp—obviously placed there for everyone to see. An appointment book open to a weekly schedule lay by the phone. Sure enough, I saw a note in his spidery handwriting that read "vet at ten" written on today's date. Being careful not to touch anything, I noticed the edge of a scratch pad poking out from under a dog magazine. With a pencil I lifted the magazine to reveal a yellow-lined notebook filled with doodles. Mixed in with the dollar signs, cartoon figures, and sketches of airplanes were several phone numbers with an unfamiliar area code.

A knock on the door started all the dogs barking. One of the officers gestured for me to join her. Careful to not let any dogs out, I squeezed through the office French doors.

"We'd like you to wait outside for Animal Control," the officer said politely, then pointed me toward the front door. When I gazed back over my shoulder I saw her standing guard, arms crossed over her chest, her eyes still following me.

It took over two hours for the Animal Control Unit to arrive. After the senior officer coordinated with the police, we organized into three teams. I checked each dog before handing it over to be walked outside to the van. I didn't like the whole thing, but the dogs enjoyed the new experience, especially since they were traveling with their doggy relatives. The workers assured me that as soon as the custody details were worked out, the dogs would be released. When we got the clearance to leave, I waited in my truck, head pounding, hands on the wheel, until they were safely on their way.

Raindrops from the storm had made splatter patterns on my windshield. The engine whined before it turned over on the second try. Exhaustion and hunger weighed me down, made my brain fuzzy. Then I realized with a start what was wrong.

I'd put my hands on each and every dog in the house. Not one of them had a shave mark on its leg.

Grand Champion Charles Too was missing.

By the time I got back to the office it was eight-thirty, my twelve-hour day finally over. Sandy was long gone, but she'd printed out tomorrow's list of appointments and stuck it on the cork message board.

Because I'd learned that a complete search of the Langthornes' house by the Animal Control team under the supervision of the police had produced no more pets, I left a message for Animal Control to please check all the dogs carefully and call back. No one but me seemed concerned. There were twenty-seven dogs living in the house and twenty-seven were recovered. Obviously, they thought I'd made a mistake.

After a long shower and a quick frozen dinner, I fell into bed. A glass of white wine helped convince me I had probably overlooked Charles Too in the bedlam. Tomorrow was Saturday with appointments scheduled until noon. I needed my sleep.

My last thoughts revolved around Thomas and Vivian Langthorne. I tried not to think of that final tea party, tried to think of them in happier times. I hadn't known them that well or that long—just a few months. Now I would never forget them.

Chapter Two

Saturday turned into a nightmare. The office was suddenly besieged with calls for emergency appointments. Sandy complained up and down and squeezed in as many as she could, after putting the rest off until Monday. It turned out none constituted an emergency for me. The real emergency was that Doc's house-call clients were dying to find out all the details about the Langthornes' deaths. One sweet old lady after another gently asked me if the dogs had disturbed the bodies in any way.

When I got out of the truck at my last appointment, what I saw surprised me. The small house with a white picket fence could have been on the cover of a home magazine. Tulips and daffodils lined the walkway, while early annuals and cascading ivy filled the window boxes. When I pressed the doorbell it greeted me with the tune of "How Much is That Doggy in the Window?"

I wasn't prepared for the couple that opened the door.

The canine and his owner came to the door dressed in identical outfits. Although definitely a male Chihuahua, my patient today wore a peach-and-green plaid shirt with a matching green-trimmed beret. His full-toothed growl indicated he wasn't happy about it. Neither was I. How the heck could I examine him like that?

"Mrs. Davidsen?" I asked the gentle-faced elderly lady also in plaid, her beret perched at a jaunty angle. "I'm Dr. Kate Turner from Oak Falls Animal Hospital.

"Come in my dear," she said, while the Chihuahua increased his growl to threatening level. "Nicey-nicey," she cooed to the pissed-off dog who kept on barking.

One thing about house calls is you learn a lot about your clients while visiting their homes. Every inch of Mrs. Davidsen's compact house was crammed with tiny statues, magazines, and ornamental doodads. Hand-crocheted doilies decorated the arms of all her upholstered chairs and sofa. In spite of the clutter, the floors and walls shone, scrubbed scrupulously clean.

I followed her into the kitchen. Gleaming copper pots hung from an iron rack above the island.

"Doc Anderson, bless his soul, always examined my baby here." She pointed to a small patch of empty countertop before placing the grumpy Chihuahua gently on the tiled surface.

My furry patient and I locked eyes. Even under perfect conditions it's hard to examine an uncooperative small dog. A Chihuahua is basically a big head with teeth on top of four matchstick legs. They can hurt themselves struggling to get away from you.

"Can you please take off his…outfit?" I tried to figure out what to do next. Mrs. Davidsen didn't seem surprised and proceeded to remove his shirt and both their hats. Thankfully she kept her own shirt on.

"So you're taking over while Doc Anderson is away. Is he enjoying his round-the-world cruise?" She folded the tiny dog shirt neatly and topped the pile with both their berets.

"Sounds like it. He's updating everyone on his Facebook page. The staff and clients get a big kick out of it." I reached into my pocket and pulled out a roll of thin gauze, my weapon of choice. After making a small loop, I approached my patient. As expected, his barking escalated, but he had backed himself between a Crock-Pot and a large blender.

"Good boy," I said in a soft voice. "No one's going to hurt you."

Mrs. Davidsen held out her hands. "Come on, angel, be good for mommy."

The little dog turned away from me, distracted by his owner's voice. Fast as a snake I slipped the noose over his pointy nose and tied the ends around the back of his head. Surprised, he went to remove the muzzle with his front feet, but I'd already picked him up and held him tightly against my body.

"Okay, let's see what's going on." As I examined the wiggling dog I asked Mrs. Davidsen what the problem was.

"He's having problems down there."

Now, down there is code for only two places. Delicately I broached the subject. "Is he licking at himself? Going in the house?"

"No. No. My Little Man is the bestest. Aren't you baby?"

I patted the thin skin on the dog's head, then, ran my hand down his entire body. "Little Man" seemed to be a misnomer. His testicles were the size of golf balls.

"Is he scooting?" I'd detected a funky odor when I lifted his tail. It came wafting up at us overpowering the scent of vanilla from a burning candle.

"Yes. He's been rubbing his—you know—his bottom, like it itches."

I flipped the dog around and examined his rear end. Sure enough, it looked like the beginning of a painful anal gland abscess. He'd rubbed one side raw trying to relieve the discomfort.

I turned the dog again and stared into his bulging eyes. You could see the veins in his almost transparent bat ears. Little Man was cute, the kind of cute only a mother or a veterinarian could love.

"Hey, little guy." I cuddled the dog and stroked his side. "I'm going to take care of you so you won't hurt anymore." Deftly, I untied the muzzle and handed him to his mom. He blinked at me and stayed quiet.

"Mrs. Davidsen, Little Man needs to come in to the office so I can take care of that sore under his tail." I gathered up my things. "He'll need some pre-op blood tests to make sure the anesthesia we use won't be a problem for him. Could you call Sandy and bring him in this afternoon? She'll give you an estimate."

With a concerned look on her face she shook her head.

"This abscess can rupture," I explained sternly, "so the sooner I take care of this, the better."

"I'll do just what you said, Dr. Kate," her voice upset. "Thank you for being so gentle with him. I didn't know what to expect. If you need anything, you come straight to me, all right? I'm on the town board."

Not being sure what that meant, I told her thanks and turned to leave.

"Don't worry about the murders. I'm sure no one blames you," she continued.

I paused with my hand still on the door, confused. "If you are referring to the Langthorne tragedy, the police believe it was a murder-suicide."

"That's what they say now, my dear." She lowered her voice conspiratorially. "But we have our suspicions." Not to be outdone, Little Man managed a couple of half-hearted yips and another growl.

Stunned, I stood there, the screen door and my mouth open. Was she overdramatizing the situation?

"I'll keep that in mind." I tried to be non-committal

After a moment she continued, "Did anyone ever tell you that you look a bit like that actress, what's her name?"

Glad to be on a lighter subject I said, "As a matter of fact, I've heard the Meryl Streep thing before." I gave her my best Academy Award-winning smile.

"No, not her my dear." Mrs. Davidsen's brown eyes scrunched up in concentration. "You're not that pretty." She lifted Little Man's paw and waved bye-bye with it.

I waved back, definitely put in my place. "He really likes you," she called out in amazement as I started down the front stairs. "He always bites Doc Anderson."

Back at the hospital, finished for the day, I sank exhausted into Doc's worn office chair and closed my eyes. I was tempted to take a hit off the Jack Daniels bottle I knew lay hidden behind the huge Ettinger's Veterinary Medicine reference book on the shelf above his desk. Rumors were that many a night he and Sandy, the office manager, shared a drink together after the clinic closed. People speculated about what else they shared after-hours.

When I bent down to loosen my shoes, a sharp pain cramped my back muscles and started my head pounding. Four months as a relief vet in upstate New York and I needed a vacation. My thoughts wandered back to Mrs. Davidsen implying that the Langthornes had been murdered. Tomorrow I would call the chief of police and ask him about it.

The smell of my Chinese takeout chased away thoughts of murder. I cleared the desktop to start unpacking my order of spareribs and vegetable fried rice when my cell phone rang.

"Kate, is that you?"

As soon as I heard that familiar voice I wished I'd let it go to voice mail.

"Hey, Jason."

"Having fun in the boondocks?" I could just see my former boss' smile and the cute way he crinkled up his face when he made a joke. Why did I have to remember it so clearly?

"Not really," I maneuver the fried rice in its aluminum container out of the bag. "Yesterday was murder, literally."

"Tell me about it." He skipped right over my news. "Give me city life any day."

"How's Tiffany?" I didn't add *that little tramp you're sleeping with*. That was implied.

"She's great. She sends her love."

Yeah, right, like I could give a damn. But I had only myself to blame. I'd been silently mooning over Jason for eight months while he finalized his divorce; going out to dinner and listening to his rants about alimony and splitting their weekend place in the Hamptons. While I worked overtime without pay, he took time off for the lawyer, the therapist, the life coach, the masseuse—time off for everyone except me. Like a fool I believed him when he confessed how much he needed me, depended on me, couldn't live without me.

Then Tiffany brought her Pomeranian in for vaccinations. One look at her gigantic chest, short-shorts, and pouty glossed lips, and he flipped. Never mind that the Pomeranian was smarter than she was. She got knocked up and I got knocked out of the game.

I half-listened as he told me about their long weekend in the Bahamas, munching on shrimp with lobster sauce through all the places they visited, but started yawning when he got to the moonlight dinners on the beach.

Interrupting his reverie, I said, "Sounds great, but I've still got some work to do. Say hi to the gang for me."

"Oh." There was a pause and then, "Sure, we'll catch up some other time."

"Good night." I hung up then tossed the phone on the desk. The thump made a definite statement in the quiet room.

A deep bark echoed in the building. "Be right there, Bullet," I called out to the black lab, my sleepover companion for the night.

Why didn't I visit Doc's place before I accepted this job? I knew the answer. I was in too much of a hurry to get away from Jason and the girlfriend.

Doc's setup was unusual to say the least. When he'd told me I could use the furnished apartment attached to the clinic for free while he was away on the cruise, I naturally thought of a rustic one- or two-bedroom place, comfortable chairs, maybe a fireplace for those chilly nights. No such luck. After his wife passed away from breast cancer almost twenty years ago, Doc sold their home and temporarily moved into what must have been the garage of the old house he'd converted into his clinic. He'd lived there ever since. It suited him fine.

All he needed was a laminate countertop with an electric cooktop, some cabinets, a small refrigerator, and a microwave. The apartment basically consists of one room, so a few steps from the kitchen is the living room, decorated with a sagging flowered couch and Doc's navy blue La-Z-Boy recliner. An ancient rear-projection big-screen TV sits in the corner like Jabba the Hut. If you turned too quickly you might tumble into the double bed, an oak desk serving double-duty as a headboard. Unfortunately if you needed to go to the bathroom in the middle of the night you were out of luck. The toilet, shower, and tub are in the other building.

I decided to spend the weekend watching old movies and fixing up the apartment. Stacked in the corner by the TV were boxes I still hadn't unpacked. Maybe I'd buy some new sheets or a pretty comforter to cheer the place up. After all, I had a year contract.

Another woof and I jumped up. I could hear the Labrador retriever's tail thumping on the wall of the dog run as I entered the treatment room.

"Hey, big guy," I said to the smiling dog. "You look like you're feeling better." His owner had accidentally hit his ninety-five-pound pet in the driveway when the Labrador retriever had run out to greet him. Luckily, Bullet ricocheted off the sub-compact's fender.

"Good thing you've got some extra padding," I told the chunky dog while I listened to his heart and lungs and checked his vital signs. His injuries consisted of a scrape and a dislocated shoulder that I'd put back in the socket.

"Let's see if you have an appetite." Sitting down in front of the cage, I slowly handed him some canned food that would be easy on his intestinal tract. His appetite hadn't been affected at all. He nearly sucked down my fingers with it. After checking his IV drip and adjusting the metered flow, I turned off the lights and went back to my own little cage.

Chapter Three

I first got an inkling of trouble on Sunday morning while shopping at the country store, conveniently located across from the historic cemetery at the end of town. Set in a converted farmhouse, The Oak Falls General Store features a picturesque porch running the length of the building with antiques and collectibles for sale clustered at every turn. Inside, tourists could feast on homemade ice cream and fudge or spend their money on all kinds of gadgets, trinkets, pottery, and t-shirts.

"Who do you think killed them?" asked a strident voice. I poked my head out from behind the greeting card rack to see the cashier conversing with someone swathed in layers of hand-knit and a big hat.

"Only new person around is that lady vet working at Doc Anderson's place," answered the hat, her voice muffled. "Maybe she's got rabies."

I burst out laughing, then tried to disguise it with a cough. Afraid they would turn my way, I picked up some blueberry syrup and pretended to be fascinated with the label. Before I was found out, a group of tourists flooded into the store chattering away about how quaint and old-fashioned it looked, oblivious to the fact that most of the stuff for sale was made in China. The open door momentarily let in fresh air that cut through the overwhelming scent of cinnamon candles and potpourri.

Taking advantage of the opportunity, I snuck out to the jingling of sleigh bells on the door.

Another carful of weekend tourists pulled in as I picked my way toward the beat-up F-150 truck Doc had loaned me—part of the deal for taking care of the clinic. Spring had sprung almost overnight, encouraging everyone to get outside and enjoy the weather. Daffodils and crocuses bloomed along the iron gates of the cemetery entrance. Dodging the rainwater-filled potholes dotting the asphalt parking lot, I called my friend Gracie to share the rabies joke.

She didn't find someone accusing me of murder particularly funny.

"Lighten up," I told her as I climbed into the Ford. "Wouldn't you like to brag that your Syracuse University college roommate turned out to be a vicious killer?"

"Listen to me, Kate. You've got to be careful in a small town. I grew up in one." Her voice reflected her concern. "They've got nothing to do all day but gossip and spread rumors. Before you know it you'll be caught in the middle of it."

I started up the truck. It sputtered and coughed and finally turned over. Sitting in the driver's seat felt like sitting in a blender.

"I've got to go," I interrupted her lecture. "I need two hands to drive this thing." The engine wheezed and farted out a burst of black smoke, definitely overdue for a tune up.

"Okay. But call me later."

Sliding into reverse I glanced up at my rearview mirror. Parked directly behind me blocking my path, blue and red lights glaring in the sunlight, sat one of the five Oak Falls police vehicles. In the mirror, like in some weird Fellini movie, I saw the country store door open and people pour out to see what was going on. Big-hat lady elbowed her way to the front, a multicolored loosely knit scarf draped over her shoulder.

Being a suspect didn't seem so funny after all.

◇◇◇

"You're not a suspect at this time," Police Chief Garcia said again, taking a bite from his sandwich.

The Oak Falls station house looked and smelled more like a McDonald's than a police station. Molded plastic seating and laminate countertops in shades of brown and mustard littered the new town hall and the police station building.

Piled on the desk in front of me were several books filled with pictures of felons. "Why again am I looking at these pictures when I didn't see anyone?" I finished studying the page in front of me then turned to the next. They looked almost identical.

"In case any of them seem familiar, like you might have passed them on the street or spotted them in the victims' neighborhood. Or maybe you knew them when you worked in New York City."

"Long Island, big difference."

The look on his face didn't change.

"But what has this got to do with the Langthornes' deaths? I thought you said it was a murder-suicide."

Garcia took a hearty swig of soda, lightly belched, and replied, "Never said that. You take care of the animals and let the law enforcement professionals handle the rest."

Heard that already.

It was downhill from there. An hour later, all the felons' faces blurred into one nasty guy with tattoos and piercings.

"Chief Garcia," I called over to him, "have you contacted the next of kin yet?"

He rolled his chair toward me. So many things—gun, night-stick, handcuffs—dangled from his belt that he looked like a human charm bracelet.

"Did that right away. There's a daughter, and two distant nephews, I believe."

"Do you know what they're going to do about the dogs? Animal Control won't be able to keep the little guys for too long."

"The lawyer took care of that. They've already been picked up by the daughter. She told them that the Charles Too dog you were worried about was there after all." He reached for his sub sandwich again. When he bit into it dressing ran down his chin. He blotted it with a napkin and kept on chewing.

"That's great," I rubbed my eyes. "Listen, I'm going to have to take a food break here." Between the fluorescent lights and lack of sleep the last two days, my mind was mush and the tang of salami and Italian dressing was making me hungry. "Can I finish these some other time?"

"Sure. Sure." He picked up the book I'd just closed and moved it to the far side of the desk. "You're free to go."

"Thanks." Stiff from sitting in the chair for so long, I stretched my shoulders, then slowly walked toward the exit. I stopped to say good night to the dispatcher at the reception desk.

"Remember, you're not a suspect at this time," Garcia called after me.

I heard it but I wasn't so sure I believed it.

"You're not a suspect at this time?"

"That's what he said, Gramps. I don't get it." Rain had started up again, pinging against the converted garage's old metal roof above me. After I'd left the police station I'd filled up the truck and bought a banana and an iced tea for dinner. There wasn't much in the refrigerator. Utilitarian best described the apartment that came with the job. I put my feet up on the coffee table and broke out the Tostitos and salsa.

Heavy breathing came through on the phone. A bad case of emphysema made stealth impossible now for my grandfather, a retired New York City fire marshal, who'd worked for the Bureau of Fire Investigation. Even walking up the stairs of his brownstone in Bay Ridge, Brooklyn, took a toll on him. Some days were better than others.

"They got nothing, honey, so they're taking a look at you. Do you want me to make a phone call?"

"No, thanks. So far so good." I decided to hold off involving Gramps until I had to. Any kind of excitement made his breathing worse. We were a small but tight little family now, Gramps and me. My mom and brother were killed by a drunk driver when I was fifteen. Four months later my dad, a vascular surgeon, married his pregnant secretary. I've been holding a grudge since.

A hissing noise sounded in the background. "Took a hit of my inhaler," he said, breathing slightly better. "Now, was there a note?"

"I didn't see one."

"Any history of violence?"

I held the phone away from my mouth as I crunched another chip. "Not that I know. The husband, Thomas, bossed her around a lot, but the wife held her own. They were always yelling about something. I thought that kind of stuff stopped when you hit your eighties."

"Age doesn't matter. We had a one-hundred-year-old guy kill someone for sitting on his bed in a nursing home. What about money?"

"They lived in a big house on five acres, but I have no idea how much they were worth. Competing in the dog show circuit costs quite a lot of money. I think the daughter inherited everything, but the will hasn't been made public, yet. "

"People get killed for the price of a pack of cigarettes these days." He changed the subject. "So, how do you like your new job?"

"It's good. The office manager runs a tight ship, but Doc left her in charge of everything except the medical cases while he's gone."

"So, is she the boss?" Leave it to my grandpa to cut right to the chase.

I thought about my answer for a moment. "Well, she definitely runs the clinic and I guess that includes me. Sandy's worked there for twenty-five years and I've only been on board for four months as a relief vet, so I understand Doc's logic. But with anything medical, I'm in charge."

He huffed in agreement. "Never knew anyone who went on a world cruise. Where is the old Doc now?

"I think he's still in China. We have his itinerary posted so we know where the ship is."

"One of these weekends I'll come up and you can show me around."

"Sure, Gramps, anytime." We both pretended that was still possible.

After taking a few last chips, I folded the bag and put it on top of the refrigerator so I wouldn't be tempted to eat any more.

Walking back to the sofa, I plopped down, put my feet up, and remembered.

"Oh, there's something I forgot to tell the police. Something they said during my last visit."

"What's that?" His voice sounded carefully inquisitive.

"Vivian told me that Thomas never helped with the dogs because he fainted at the sight of blood. So how does someone like that shoot his wife in the chest?"

"Nothing surprises me anymore, Katie." His breathing was much better. "Maybe he didn't look."

Feeling restless after talking to Gramps, I decided to make a diner run. Oak Falls was famous for its diner, run by Mama G, otherwise known as Maria Gianetti. She and her husband, Antonio, had moved from Staten Island almost thirty years earlier along with their stainless steel 1950s diner. Featured on the Food Network and in countless food guides, their claim to fame was Mama G's homemade apple pie, voted the best on the East Coast. Each day they made two kinds of pie, one apple and the other a seasonal fruit or nut. When they had sold out for the day, patrons were out of luck. Personally, I needed to stay away or begin rationing my pastry intake.

If you put the pedal to the metal, and if there wasn't too much traffic, you could make it up to Oak Falls from Manhattan in under two and a half hours. That proximity made it a favorite spot for second homes. Tired power couples could leave the frantic city and be in bucolic upstate in the time it took to watch a movie. The locals had a love/hate relationship with the weekenders. They resented them pouring into town on the weekends, but needed the money they brought. Increased popularity drove home prices up, making it hard for young people born here to find affordable housing. Some of the younger staff couldn't afford to move out of their parents' homes.

But I changed my mind about going out and sat back down on the sofa. I didn't have the energy and didn't need the calories. Instead I thought about the Langthornes, Charles Too, and how I almost made a mountain out of a big pile of dog poop.

It was natural for the police to concentrate on me for a while. They didn't have anyone else, nothing to get paranoid about. I'd only been in town for four months. Now was not the time to make waves. Plus people in town were getting used to me now, instead of always asking for Doc. The last thing I wanted was to nose around in the elderly couple's personal business and make enemies doing it.

I breathed a sigh of relief that Charles Too was safe and sound, poured a glass of white wine, picked up my well-read copy of *Sleeping Murder* by Agatha Christie and went to bed.

Chapter Four

The next week passed like a blur. A sex scandal involving a conservative local congressman and his pretty young intern captured the headlines and replaced the Langthornes as the topic of the day. Still short-staffed on the house calls since my technician Mari had twisted her knee, I scrambled to do double-duty. Trained as a technician, Sandy worked both the front desk and the back treatment area. Each day presented a new challenge, from diagnosing an active case of heartworms to an accidental antifreeze poisoning. I started to feel like I lived in the hospital—which, technically, I did. Slowing down to attend the staff meeting at lunchtime almost felt like a vacation.

On the first Friday of the month, the office manager scheduled a monthly staff meeting to discuss any problems or issues that have come up, but mostly to eat huge quantities of free pizza. I sat in the back trying to decide between a slice with everything on it or the old reliable pepperoni. Since I was a temporary replacement for Doc Anderson I didn't think it was my job to change his practice. Not that Sandy would have let me. She still reigned with an iron fist. I don't know if it was the responsibility of running the practice all by herself, but Sandy saw no reason to hide her grumpy side.

Today Sandy took the opportunity to haul Cindy, our part-time receptionist, out on the carpet. "Please make sure all the fees are entered properly into the computer, especially the house calls. Dr. Kate sends her invoice estimate to the office first, so we can check it for accuracy. The ball is being dropped here at reception." She eyeballed Cindy, leaving no doubt in anyone's mind who she was talking about. Thankfully she didn't single me out because without my field tech this past week, it had taken twice as long as usual to do my paperwork. I couldn't wait for Mari to be back to work.

Cindy, being blessed with a happy-go-lucky personality, naturally blond hair, and a pixie face, just nodded and shoved another piece of pizza into her mouth.

"Nick. We had a complaint that one of the dogs went home smelling like poop." All eyes turned to our part-time tech and kennel help, Nickolas Pappadapolis. Only nineteen, he worked on the weekends and went to the community college during the week. Cindy and Mari fussed over him, plying him with cookies and advice on his many romances. With his dark hair and contagious grin, he got constant texts from girls.

"Was that Mrs. Rarjedam's Bernese mountain dog?" he replied quickly, not missing a beat.

Sandy gave him the evil eye. "Yes."

"Well, the dog took a huge dump in the waiting room after I handed him to his owner. Then he jumped up and stepped in his own poop. I told her I would take him back to the kennel and wash him, but she declined."

I smiled, hearing this exchange become more business-like on his part. I'd found Nick to be a smart and resourceful kid.

"Well, you should have made a note in the record."

Nick snuck a look at Cindy.

"Oh, that might be my fault," she volunteered, wiping her mouth with a stained paper napkin. "Nick had to clean up the mess so he asked me to put it into the record. I guess I forgot." Her answer to everything was to smile and shrug her shoulders. Which she did.

"That's exactly what I am talking about." Sandy's voice cut like a sharp blade but it was lost on Cindy.

Of all the employees, Cindy caught the most reprimands from Sandy. Sure, sometimes she messed up, but never in a major way.

In her defense, the clients loved her, she had endless patience with the more difficult owners, never called in sick, and always had a smile on her face even when the day was a frantic one. To me she was worth her weight in gold. Since Sandy made a big point about entering all charges, from habit I always checked the invoices after they were posted. I was confident mistakes didn't happen that often.

"Mari," she continued, turning to face my technician sporting an open cast, "how is the knee doing?"

"Much better, the swelling is way down." Another happy personality, Mari combined enthusiasm with impressive upper-body strength, a plus for a veterinary technician. A part-time weight lifter, she'd pulled a ligament cross-training for an iron man event. "My orthopedist said I could be back to work on Monday with a knee brace." Her no-nonsense look masked a tender heart.

I led a spontaneous round of applause.

But Sandy hadn't finished with us yet. "Please watch your consumption of paper goods. We are running through them like crazy. That's including toilet paper. Remember we're on a septic out here, not city sewer."

I was going to ask how many squares of toilet paper we were allowed per visit to the john but decided not to be a smart ass. Sandy wouldn't have appreciated it, and when Sandy was unhappy, no one was happy. Recent dental implant surgery probably didn't help her mood.

"Anyone have anything else to discuss?" As usual no one said a word.

The rest of the meeting dealt with housekeeping issues, work schedules, and tracking the prescription foods we stock for clients. Sandy did most of the talking. Nick reminded everyone of his upcoming vacation, making a point of pulling up the work schedule on the computer and entering it in front of the entire staff. Cindy detoured off point with a lively discussion of the rock concert she and her husband saw the previous weekend. When she began giving us the playlist, Sandy stood up.

"Okay, let's get back to work."

I stretched a moment by my chair and glanced at the afternoon schedule. Not too bad. Appointments didn't start again until two-thirty, which gave me an hour of downtime. Maybe I'd check on Doc Anderson's whereabouts and live vicariously through him. Taking my coffee with me and resisting another slice of pizza, I went into the doctor's office and shut the door.

The best place to follow Doc's travels was Facebook. I logged in and scanned his postings. By now his chair felt pretty comfortable. I saw picture after picture of Doc loaded down with camera equipment waving in Tiananmen Square under the picture of Mao, bowing in the Forbidden City, and posing with a clay warrior from Xian. By his side, wearing sunglasses, a hat, and a big smile, stood his sister. A cancer survivor and recent widow, this was her second remission in five years. When she decided it was time to see the world she'd asked her big brother to join her. I could only imagine how difficult it was for Doc Anderson to drop everything and turn his practice over to a stranger. I admired him for it. There was no reason to spoil his well-deserved vacation with the clinic's petty problems.

Before I knew it, time was up. I finished my cold coffee and started all over again.

◇◇◇

At the end of the day, I couldn't get the Langthornes out of my mind. Finding two people shot dead had affected me more than I let on to anyone. I'd rationalized the scene at their home by assuming Thomas killed Vivian for any of a million crazy reasons, then feeling remorseful, took his own life. But now two people had mentioned murder. Was there some truth behind the gossip? And why were the police still questioning me?

Obviously I needed some help here. With most of the staff gone, I turned to the most efficient source of Oak Falls information available.

"Hey, Sandy," I tried to keep my voice casual. "I'm finished for the day. Do you want to meet me for supper? I'd like to pick your brain about something."

"Is it about the receipts because...?"

I interrupted her. "This is personal, not work-related." To cinch the deal I said the magic words, "My treat."

I heard her clear her throat before she agreed to meet me at the diner in half an hour. After changing my scrubs for regular clothes and washing up, I climbed into the truck and arrived exactly on time. Sandy, of course, had beat me, parking her blue Chevy truck with the double grill next to the entrance. I noticed a large rug held on to her roof rack with bungee cords.

The diner was packed and noisy. Harried waitresses walked double-time, zipping past customers, trays loaded with food carried at half-mast. I'd worked as a waitress in high school and college and knew how heavy those plates could be. You'd never find me tipping less than twenty percent, even if the server was having a bad day.

A raised arm waved at me. Sandy sat at a booth, coffeepot and cup in front of her. It didn't matter what time of the day it was, she always made room for coffee. My intake of java had increased as well.

"Hi." I slid my fanny across the worn vinyl. "Boy, they're busy tonight."

"I already ordered pie for both of us," she said with a weak smile. "They might run out."

"Smart woman."

"Running the practice takes a lot out of me these days."

She leaned into the space between us, her watery blue eyes embedded in folds of wrinkles studying me. I felt like a ninth-grader caught cheating in French class. Come to think of it, Sandy reminded me of my old French teacher, Mrs. Dumois. Both wore their gray hair twisted into a tiny bun with stray hairs springing out like prisoners running for freedom.

"What do you want to talk about, Kate?"

I picked up the salt shaker and twirled it around in my hand. "Someone told me today that the Langthornes were murdered."

She snatched the salt away and moved it out of my reach.

"In other words, maybe it's not a murder-suicide." I shook the pepper for emphasis.

"Did the police tell you that?" She removed the pepper from my hand.

I was running out of condiments. Sighing, I told her everything that happened at the country store, the police station, even Mrs. Davidsen's weird remarks, interrupting myself only to order tonight's special, Brunswick stew, a decaf tea, and asked for my pie to go.

Within minutes the table jammed up with plates. Sandy dug into her pot roast dinner, pausing to chew carefully on the side of her mouth with the new dental implants. "Listen, I can't imagine the police think you have anything to do with this. You went there for a scheduled appointment. I sent you and they know you're filling in for Doc. The whole county knows he's on vacation. I wouldn't pay attention to gossip. Chief Garcia's is the only opinion that counts."

Already feeling a little better, I put milk and sugar into my English Breakfast tea, then reached for some bread and butter. "People talk in situations like this. Thomas and Vivian made lots of enemies in this town," she continued between bites.

"That old couple?" I could hardly believe it. They seemed concerned only for their dogs and the dog show circuit.

Mopping up the gravy with her biscuit, Sandy laughed. "Being old doesn't mean suddenly being nice. Take the Tube Depot on Main Street. Randy Molinari leases the building and land that the tube rental store is on. I heard Thomas decided not to renew the lease because he didn't like the tube crowd in his town."

Finishing up the last morsel of stew I put down my fork and pushed the plate away. Something she said didn't make sense. "What do you mean his town?"

The waitress came over and began to clear the table. "Your desserts will be out in a moment." "More coffee, tea?"

"We're good, Jill. Looks like you're earning your money tonight."

"You know the weekenders, stingy on the tips." After loading the last plate, she took off in the direction of the kitchen.

"Do you know everyone in this town?" I sat back, pretty full from racing through my food in under ten minutes.

"After forty-nine years living here I should know everyone, or if I don't, I know someone who does.

Not wanting to get off the subject, I returned to my question. "Why is it Thomas Langthorne's town?"

Sandy checked to make sure no one was eavesdropping, then leaned in again. "It's his town because at one time he owned almost all of the land it's built on. Every time something came up for sale he bought it. He also went after specific pieces of land and offered the owners two or three times the market value."

Jill returned with the bill and our deserts, strawberry rhubarb pie for me, classic apple for Sandy.

"I'm so full. I don't know if I have room for dessert." Sandy sounded exasperated.

"This is my comfort food. There's always room for pie plus a slice to go." We were both quiet for a while as she dug into a juicy apple slice. "So are there people here in town who might be considered suspects? Someone mad enough to kill them?"

"Let's see." She began to count under her breath, fingers popping up until all ten were extended in my direction. "I can count at least ten."

"Ten?"

"At least." She put on her reading glasses to double-check the bill, even though I'd told her I'd pay.

"I find that hard to believe." The noise level hit a new crescendo as the baby in the next booth began to wail.

"Believe it." She drained her coffee, the cup clinking on the plate. "Out of that list of ten, I figure I'm number eight."

"What do you mean?"

"Let's go outside. You're bound to hear about it anyway." She stood up and gathered her things.

I left enough cash to cover the bill and tip, picked up my takeout pie, and followed her outside.

The air smelled like exhaust from all the cars going in and out of the parking lot. Sandy leaned against her truck and beckoned me closer. "This is a touchy subject." She put a finger to her mouth. "You have to promise to keep this quiet."

"I promise." What could possibly be this important?

Clearing her throat she looked down at her hands. "I had a knock-down-drag-out fight with the Langthornes a few years ago about a private matter."

I could barely hear her.

"Thomas Langthorne and his wife went to Doc and insisted he fire me. There was name-calling and back and forth. Somehow they found out I had a prescription drug problem."

"What happened?" I knew her veterinary technician license could be suspended.

"I'd already gone into a rehab program on my own. Doc told them my problem didn't influence my work and to butt out." She shuffled her feet and continued to look down, not meeting my eyes. "But the Langthornes made Doc and me go through hell, just for spite."

"Some people are like that." I leaned against the Chevy's shiny hood. "You can't always tell who's going to give you the shaft until they stick it in."

"You won't find me mourning them." She glanced around the parking lot again. "In fact, there are a few more people I wouldn't miss in this town."

The look on her face made me step back. For a moment it seemed Sandy had disappeared and someone else had taken her place.

Chapter Five

After a relaxing weekend, Monday appointments rolled smoothly all day long until dinnertime. On my way to Tony's Deli for a food run, I received an emergency call.

"Dr. Turner here," I spoke to the wireless headset.

"What are you up to?" Sandy's voice rumbled around the cab of the truck.

"I'm on a lasagna run for Mari and me, with a side salad and garlic bread." I pulled onto the side of the road next to maple tree. "What's up?"

"Pippi Langthorne wants to talk to you."

For a crazy moment I thought she'd said Pippi Longstocking, the pig-tailed heroine from the Swedish children's books.

"Is this for real, or are you joking with me?"

Sandy made a disapproving sound then cleared her throat. "I told her you were busy today, but she became pretty insistent."

A silver colored SUV rumbled by, shaking the driver's side window. It was just past five. Curiosity got the better of me. I could probably squeeze in one more appointment, especially with the daughter of my deceased clients.

"Did she tell you what she wanted?"

"The lady wants health certificates. I can't believe how cheap she is. Wouldn't pay for a recheck on Charles Too and wants you to use the info from your previous exams so she doesn't have to pay for a new one. I got tired of arguing with her. Just write the certificates and get out of there."

"Is that what you want me to do?" With a quick glance in the rearview mirror I pulled back onto the road.

"Yep, don't make waves over the small stuff is what Doc always said."

"You're the office manager." What Sandy didn't know wouldn't hurt her. No way would I write up a health certificate without examining the animal. Pippi must be something if she wore down our tough-as-nails office manager. I leaned over and plotted Thomas and Vivian Langthorne's address into my GPS.

"I hate rich people," Sandy snarled before she hung up the phone.

The waves of distress that washed over me when I spied the Langthornes' house again surprised me. Sorrow, fear, anger, you name it. A little over ten days ago I had arrived at this address in the pouring rain, with no idea of how my life would change just by walking through the front door.

This time I noticed everything. Sunshine cast the landscape in high relief. The azaleas and holly that formed a mixed border lining the walkway already bloomed in shades of pink and red. The granite steps up to the porch had been swept clean. The dark pines like sentinels on the property line pointed to the sky. I paused for a moment, waiting for something else, the sounds of barking. Why weren't the dogs barking this time?

I wondered why Pippi Langthorne insisted on meeting me here instead of coming to the clinic. What was this appointment really about? Before I could gather my thoughts, the door swung open.

Fifteen minutes later I was trapped in the small sitting room to the left of the front door, a cup of tea in one hand and a cheese biscuit in the other, listening to Pippi's nasal voice droning on and on about her problems, her home in Virginia, and how she hated estate lawyers. The room felt claustrophobic with too much French provincial furniture crammed into the space. Gold-printed wallpaper on all four walls matched the fabric on the chairs, but looked grimy at dog-level around the room. A scented floral candle burned on a side table next to an ornate silver tea set, contributing to the heavy formal feeling. I stared at the tea set. Could that be the one I saw that awful day? I had to pull my eyes away from it to concentrate on my hostess.

The only thing Pippi seemed to have in common with her Scandinavian namesake was her red hair, sleek and shining in a simple blunt cut. Slim as a whippet, she had distinctive angular features that were carefully made up. Her total package declared Rich Lady From The Country.

We hadn't talked about the dogs at all, or her parents. If she was one of those people who hid their feeling, she was doing a great job.

"Excuse me, Ms. Langthorne…"

"Call me Pippi, please."

Reluctantly I began again, "Pippi…"

"Can I get you more tea, or perhaps another biscuit, although it's hard to find anything good in this godforsaken town. I still have no idea why Viv and Tom lived here."

I'd been polite long enough.

"Pippi," I stood up and put my teacup down on the coffee table. "What exactly did you want me to do for you today?"

An odd look passed across her face and was gone so fast I thought I'd imagined it. She turned away for a moment, her red hair a flash of bright color among the subdued antique golds and silvers of the sitting room. When she walked toward the fireplace her footsteps were silent, swallowed up in the dense Oriental carpet under our feet.

"I'd like you to give me a health certificate for Charles Too. I'm going to take him back to Virginia with me."

Finally an answer. "Are you taking all of the dogs with you?" I mentally added up the paperwork to do on twenty-seven dogs.

"No. I've got Charles Too, one of his sons and a pair of his pregnant bitches."

I frowned. "What about the others?"

Pippi smoothed her already smooth hair. A discrete diamond stud earring twinkled briefly under a curtain of red hair. "I got rid of them."

Her tone said it all. She had no use for the dogs that had meant so much to her parents.

"Did you…" I didn't want to say it, especially in this house.

"I sold some to Maybelle Guzzman, and some went to a kennel in New Jersey. The old ones no one wanted I brought to the pound."

Stunned, I didn't say anything. The Langthornes had kept all their elderly champions and retired breeding stock together, here at their Lucky Eight Kennel. Their daughter was heartless. "You know there are rescue groups for different breeds that would have been happy to help you, not to mention your parents' friends in the show ring."

She yawned. I couldn't decide if it was deliberate or not.

"So, where are the dogs I'm supposed to see today?" My tone was less than sympathetic. I was tired and she got on my nerves.

"They're in cages off the kitchen."

That's strange, I thought. Why aren't they barking? The last time I was here I could barely hear the doorbell over all the noise.

I followed her through the living room. The rugs had recently been cleaned and a tang of pine cleaning fluid hung in the air. Memories of that day flickered in my mind. The gruesome tea party, dogs scooting past me—a gun on the floor in the center of a tea stain. The two brocade armchairs were gone.

The kitchen gleamed, spotless and scented with lemon. Sunlight streamed through the skylight and windows over the sink. Pippi rinsed our teacups and put them in the dish rack to dry. Through the glass doors to the study I could glimpse brown and black fur poking through the bars of four plastic dog crates lined up in a row. A hoarse sound, like a cough, greeted us when she opened the doors.

Now I knew why the house was so still. These dogs had been debarked.

"Nice and quiet," Pippi gestured me inside the office. "Dogs, like children, should be seen and not heard. It's so much more pleasant for everyone."

I guessed she didn't give the dogs a vote. Unfortunately, it wasn't illegal. The dogs were her property to do as she wished.

"Okay, this is…" She started searching her pants pocket until she found a folded piece of paper. "Let me see…"

"She's Queen Guinevere," I interrupted. "The largest of your parents' females but with the most refined head. Your mother's favorite." A pink tongue stuck out of the carrier and licked my fingers. I bent down and clicked it open. A rush of wiggling dog burst into the room, a very pregnant, happy dog.

Pippi made a big deal out of checking the silver tag hanging from the thin leather collar around her neck. "Yes, that's correct. I don't see how you can tell them apart."

The dog stood in front of me wagging her tail, so I reached down and began a quick exam, even though Sandy told me Pippi wouldn't pay for it. There was no way I was sending these spaniels, especially a pregnant one, on a plane without making sure no physical problems had surfaced since I'd seen them last. Then I would sign a health certificate, not before.

"When are they flying?" My hands traveled along the expanded abdomen and mammary glands of the soon-to-be-mommy dog.

"Tomorrow," she said. "I've got them booked for an early flight."

I'd last examined this dog four weeks ago for a pregnancy check. At the temporary shelter the workers had separated the males from the females. "Do you have a breeding date?"

"Somewhere, Viv had notebooks with everything in them. You don't need to concern yourself. Just finish the health certificates."

The impatience in her voice signaled again her disdain for the creatures in front of her. They seemed more like a commodity to Pippi. "I have some reservations about this dog flying. All the excitement and pressure changes she might encounter could be detrimental to the puppies. She could even suffer a miscarriage or stillbirth." I stood up and stared at Pippi who shrugged her shoulders at the news.

"That's not what my breeder in Virginia thinks. It's a short flight down there. Believe me I wouldn't take a chance on anything happening. With Charles Too as their father, those puppies are worth thousands of dollars." Unceremoniously she pushed the dog back into its kennel. "One down, three to go."

Victoria Regina, the next dog, was a quiet, somewhat nervous small female, not terribly socialized. I believe the Langthornes had planned to use her to introduce smaller stature into their breeding stock. After my exam I gave her a reassuring pat on her head and ears and gently guided her back into the kennel.

Next bounded out a rambunctious young male about nine months old named Charlie's Angel Too. Through the entire exam he wiggled in delight.

"You know they need to be uncrated until the flight," I reminded her.

"Yes. I know. I'm putting them in the runs in the back as soon as you are done with them. See?" Pippi pointed to the leashes sitting on the desk.

Not trusting her one bit, I decided to help her move them to the runs when I finished. It would be on my mind all night if I didn't.

"Okay. Now for Charles Too." Pippi struggled with the sliding bolt on the front of the crate. "Damn, I hate all this," she muttered as the locking device held, then abruptly swung open after she frantically jiggled it. Again she made a big point of checking his tag and collar. "Look for yourself," she told me, her voice snippy. Out stepped a calm black and tan male, his large head and body conformation confirming him as an intact male, an experienced show dog, confident, with a well-balanced personality. Charles Too was an American and European champion stud dog worth his weight in gold.

His right front leg showed evidence of being shaved for a catheter, but was growing in nicely. In three months you probably wouldn't be able to tell it from the other normal leg. I'd been the one to shave it weeks ago when Charles Too had come down with a an acute episode of pancreatitis after an appearance at a dog show. Unable to hold anything down, he'd needed IV fluids for three days before he bounced back to his normal self. Instead of being happy for his recovery, the Langthornes had screamed at Mari and me, and threatened to sue us for damaging his coat. After several conciliatory phone calls the whole thing died down. His last recheck was the reason I had come to their house that terrible day.

Only one problem.

I had shaved the other leg.

This wasn't Charles Too.

Chapter Six

If this wasn't Charles Too, then who was it? Did I have any proof this wasn't him? He looked identical to the famous show dog. The Langthornes didn't believe in identification tattoos commonly used in kennels. They also scorned chip technology, relying instead on their identification collars and their own memories. Unfortunately, that's all I had, a memory of shaving the other leg. Would it be noted in my medical record? Not necessarily. Unless there was a problem with the catheter I usually didn't write down what leg we used. Was I positive, certain enough of my memory to take on Pippi? Not without some kind of backup. Maybe the shelter mixed up the collars? Maybe I remembered wrong?

I didn't think so.

Excusing myself for a moment I stepped outside and called the office.

"How did it go?" Sandy's voice crackled a bit.

"Fine." There was no point in blurting out all my suspicions at this point. I didn't need any more people thinking I was a traveling nut job.

"We need to update the medical records since Pippi said someone's picking up the paperwork in the morning. Which dogs did you see?" It sounded like Sandy was taking a cigarette break while talking to me.

How should I put this? "She said they were Victoria Regina, Lady Gwen, Charlie's Angel Too, and Charles Too. I'll supply all of them with health certificates. Their vaccinations are up-to-date."

"Okay, everything all right? Your voice sounds a bit funny."

"It's nothing, just a little creepy going back there. I'll update my records in the computer and scan copies of the health certificates in there just in case." I hesitated for a moment, trying to keep my voice casual. "Sandy, can I talk to Mari for a minute?"

"Sure." Music blared in my ear as the on-hold tape played.

"Hey," Mari said, "where's my lasagna? I'm starving." Mari took her food seriously.

"I had to do some last-minute health certificates, but I'll be back in about half an hour."

My technician groaned into the phone.

"Mari, you were my tech when I put the catheter into Charles Too, the Cavalier King Charles with pancreatitis. Do you remember which leg I used? "

"What, are you kidding? I don't remember what I ate for breakfast today."

"If you had to guess?"

"I don't know. The right leg, maybe?"

Wrong answer.

◇◇◇

When I'd finished the exams, I put the dogs in the indoor/outdoor runs myself, and made sure they had food and water, then hightailed it out of there, away from the loathsome Pippi and that house filled with sad memories. I took a sharp turn onto Elm Street. Low branches hanging from overgrown trees on the corner scraped the roof. Doc's truck had a million scratches on it and I could see why.

By the time I got back to the hospital the truck smelled like an Italian restaurant. Mari and I started in on our feast, barely pausing between bites.

Sandy came in and watched us for a moment. "So, you're done for the day. Just double-check the certificates before you print them up and sign them."

"Okay. See you tomorrow. I'll leave a copy of Pippi's paper-work on the reception desk."

"Hate to eat and run but I've got to meet my sister." Mari finished the last few bites of her dinner before getting up. "See you later, 'gator."

The visit with Pippi had left a bad taste in my mouth and a huge unanswered question. I needed time and quiet to think. I changed out of my scrubs, stuffed some water bottles and the rest of the Doritos into my backpack and drove to one of my favorite places, a little-used picnic area near one of the many trailheads leading into the national forest reserve.

Unfortunately, a baseball game complete with cheering parents, occupied the first picnic tables next to the athletic field. I kept on driving, remembering that the forest service had placed benches for hikers all along this trail. The road emptied into a second gravel parking lot, blissfully away from all the noise. I turned off the truck, opened the door, and let the sharp tang of pine soothe me. Only one other vehicle sat in the parking lot. Normally that might bother me, but today I welcomed it. I slipped on my backpack and headed along the path toward a long bench I'd discovered on one of my trips along this trail. Shaded by the tall canopy of the trees, I sat on the wood-and-metal bench and tried to forget about all the craziness I had stumbled into. Resting my head on the wooden cross-slats, I shut my eyes and listened to the birds singing. How nice it would be to sit here forever.

My fantasy of running away and living in the woods full time was interrupted when two standard poodles, one black, one white, bounded around the corner, and then gave me an enthusiastic—and wet—hello.

"Jazz. Jewel." A smiling, middle-aged women made her way along the path, two long dog leashes in her hands. Her pink cheeks and round face with a sprinkling of freckles were very familiar. Rosie Gianetti lived up to her complexion and happened to be my favorite waitress at the Oak Falls Diner.

After thoroughly bathing my hands in dog saliva, the poodles turned their attention to a squirrel that had wisely run up a tree.

"Hi Rosie. Going for a hike with the girls?" Jazz and Jewel briefly ran over, checked in with their owner, then took off after another squirrel.

"No, I don't have that much time today. I thought I'd let them run around here for a bit to burn off some energy." As she spoke to me she focused her eyes fondly on the two large dogs. "This is one of our favorite spots."

"Mine, too. Please, sit down."

She settled herself next to me on the roomy bench and placed her carryall on the ground by her feet. I could see a large water bottle and some jerky treats sticking out of the top.

"So, how's life at the diner?" I picked up a long stick and began to draw in the dirt.

Rosie turned even rosier. "It's in an uproar. There's talk of a developer buying the land the diner sits on and building condos along the river."

"What?"

"Well, the family has been leasing the property from the Langthornes for the last twenty-five years. When they hauled the diner up from Staten Island there was nothing much here so they didn't want to buy the property. Papa insisted on a long lease from Thomas Langthorne but the latest one is up in six months. Mama G meant to renegotiate with them, but seeing as she and Vivian played bridge together every week, no one thought anything of it. Now we don't know what's going to happen."

"But if they wanted to, they could move it again."

"Except they built an addition to it and created that patio area along the creek. None of that can be moved, I don't think." She took a quick look to check on the dogs, shifting her weight on the bench.

"How is Mama G taking it?" Although I had only been in town a few months even I had heard about the famous matriarch of the Gianetti family.

"She's fit to be tied. It's all because of that Pippi Langthorne."

I drew a face in the dirt with a stick and put devil horns on it.

"Well, most of you must know her from growing up around here."

"I've never seen her before in my life. When Pippi was little the Langthornes very rarely came up here, and then only for the weekend. By the time they moved here full time almost twenty years ago, Pippi had graduated and headed for California."

"Was she estranged from her parents?"

"That I don't know. But no one here remembers them talking about her or any visits."

"Interesting." Carefully I drew a question mark in the middle of the face on the ground. Who was Pippi Langthorne?

Suddenly the dogs came running up and obliterated it.

The Internet can be a wonderful thing. I sat in front of my computer with a hot cup of tea, nice and comfortable in sweatpants and my oldest t-shirt, getting the dirt on Pippi. After plenty of false starts my search skills paid off. My screen displayed an old *National Enquirer* story. Fifteen years ago a dentist's wife tried to run over her husband and his twenty-year-old mistress in his office parking lot. The mistress turned out to be our own Pippi Langthorne, who crawled under a parked car to get away from one truly pissed-off spouse. Some of the items the enamored dentist had purchased for his new red-haired girlfriend included a Mercedes, a diamond-and-emerald choker with matching earrings, and a two-bedroom apartment in Boca Raton, Florida. Unfortunately, the only picture of her in the article showed a slim young woman in big sunglasses with golden streaks in her strawberry hair.

She next popped up five years later as a codefendant with her husband, Karl Yevtushenko, in a real estate development scam, also in Florida. Several photos showed her again concealed behind a huge pair of sunglasses walking into court with a short, heavyset man. The prosecution claimed building lots were sold to hundreds of investors in a luxury oceanfront community that was never built. When the company went bankrupt, buyers lost their deposits, some in the six-figure range. Her lawyer argued that although her husband put her on the books as an officer of the corporation, Mrs. Yevtushenko was never involved in the project. He went to jail and she walked after turning State's evidence against him. Then she divorced him and relocated to the Cayman Islands.

Pippi was a pip.

There was something else bothering me. No one seemed to remember Pippi visiting her parents in the last twenty years, after the Langthornes moved permanently to their Oak Falls home. I didn't remember seeing any pictures of her in their house, nor did she pop up in conversations I had with Vivian and Thomas. Her natural coloring certainly was unusual, that pale red hair, hazel eyes with golden flecks, and very white skin. Neither of the Langthornes looked like her.

Was this con artist really their daughter? Confused and frustrated about everything, I decided to cheer myself up. Instead of meditating, taking cleansing breaths, or striking a yoga pose, I resorted to instant gratification. I'd indulge in a piece of pie. As a concession to fashion, I changed my t-shirt.

I made it to the restaurant in record time. After nine minutes gravel spun under my wheels from an abrupt stop in the Oak Falls Diner's parking lot. Surprisingly, it wasn't that crowded. I must have arrived between rush groups. Thankful for a bit of quiet with my baked goods I hustled inside and snagged a booth by the window. The place smelled of coffee, fries, apple pie, and bacon. Some company should make a perfume out of that. I dropped my backpack on the seat and craned my neck to read the daily specials on the blackboard by the counter.

"Hey Kate." Rosie took her pen and pad out of her apron pocket.

"Talking to you made me hungry," I confessed, "that, and the fresh air."

"Is this early dinner or late lunch?" Her dark brown curls threaded with silver threatened to escape from the period hat that was part of the diner's uniform. A fifties-style dress and apron in white and gray with deep pockets and a button-up front completed the retro look.

"I'm just here for a pick-me-up. So a piece of today's pie and the Italian blend coffee will do me fine."

She made a quick note. "Be back in a jiffy."

My obsession with pie had begun to show in the increasing tightness of my jeans. But since it provided most of the pleasure in my life lately, I decided to increase my exercise to even everything out. And no second helpings or take-home allowed.

I looked around the room. It may have been a small crowd but it sounded lively, especially the family a few booths down from me. The young mom had given up controlling her two young children who were standing on the booth cushions engaged in a pushing contest. The youngest, head covered by a Yankees cap, seemed more aggressive, finally shoving his brother on the floor, spilling a soft drink on him and the table. This time the mom jumped up, separated them, and muttering under her breath, began to escort both kids back to the restrooms.

As the trio passed by my table I noticed the little one stick out his tongue at his sibling. Quick as a rabbit the older brother got his revenge as he reached behind his mother's back and knocked the cap off the troublemaker. It sailed through the air and slid across my table.

"Go and apologize to the nice lady," the woman told her youngest, not realizing what had taken place behind her back.

"But Ma..."

"Just do it, Melody," the words spoken in an exasperated tone to be obeyed. So the younger kid was a girl? Dressed like a boy... you could have fooled me.

"Sorry lady." Melody stood in front of me, her hair plastered to her head except for the fine wisps of bright red hair escaping behind her ears. The young girl's hazel eyes with golden specks met mine for a moment. A jolt of recognition hit me.

Melody was the spitting image of Pippi Langthorne.

What the heck did that mean?

Chapter Seven

Tuesday night the staff took Mari out for drinks after work to celebrate her twenty-fifth birthday. Nick, the nineteen-year-old kennel boy, would be our designated driver if necessary, since the legal drinking age in New York is twenty-one.

Our destination was the Red Lion Pub, a family-style restaurant and bar nearby. By the time we got there the parking lot was packed. The red neon sign cast an electronic glow over the first row of cars and the smokers leaning against the wooden building. The original restaurant bar area had been expanded, the add-on resembling a small barn. That's where the music and the tables for large groups were. We met by the front door, then proceeded straight to the back to get away from the country-rock band playing at full volume. Sandy barreled ahead while Cindy stopped at practically every booth to say hello to someone. Finally, after being waylaid by a client, I slid my butt along the beat-up vinyl seat of the combination booth and table. Here at the far end of the room, the music allowed conversation without shouting. Mari corralled our waitress and ordered a pitcher of beer and a plate of nachos. The alcohol made us even hungrier and the nachos disappeared instantly, followed by a big plate of wings with extra ranch dressing. The celery that came with the wings was the only green thing on the table.

"How does it feel to be twenty-five?" Nick asked over the crowd noise. "That's almost thirty."

A roar of disapproval rose from the women at the table. "You could have gone all night without saying that," Cindy told him. She threw a half-eaten piece of chicken at him for emphasis.

"Bring it on," said the birthday girl, already leading the pack in number of glasses consumed. The Red Lion Pub catered to families, parties, or anybody looking for a good time—but not a wild time. The place dated from the 1960s and looked every inch of it. Most local high school students at one time tried to carve their name into its dark wood. Sawdust gave a slippery edge to the floor and each inch of wall space was covered with a picture, stuffed animal, or keepsake the owner liked. The stale smell of beer oozed from every surface. The total effect ended up being noisy but strangely comfortable.

"Hey, Kate," Cindy fluffed her blond bangs. "How was your meeting with Pippi Langthorne?"

All eyes swung my way. Nick seemed particularly interested in what I had to say.

I'd been backed into a corner. "Good, I guess. She's not the nicest person in the world."

"That's no surprise," Mari said, her voice rising to compensate for the noise around us. "Everybody in town hated her parents."

"Mari," Sandy quickly said, "please don't exaggerate."

"No, she's right," Cindy disagreed. "I can think of plenty of people who disliked them. Randy Molinari for one. I heard he leased the building and land that the tube rental is on from Mr. Langthorne. Well, his lease is up in a few months and Mr. Langthorne decided not to renew. Instead, he was going to sign with that tube company from Phoenicia for twice as much money. Randy was furious."

"See Sandy," Mari said with a little slur in her voice. "It's no secret. I'm not letting the cat out of the bag."

Sandy's face looked like a thundercloud, but that didn't deter our technician who took another gulp of her beer and continued. "Remember the problems they caused after you hurt your back and had that drug problem?"

Now the little group looked embarrassed. It came a bit too late.

Nick jumped in innocently. "How did you hurt your back?"

Resigned to telling the story Sandy tried to make it quick. "A car accident left me in a lot of pain. I developed a prescription drug problem and the Langthornes threatened to report me to the state."

"They seemed to do that a lot," I said. The waitress arrived with another pitcher and a second round of nachos, this time with taco meat which made me a little queasy. The black olives looked like eyeballs. No one else seemed to notice because they all started eating and crunching like crazy.

Nick spoke up again from the corner of the booth. "So what happened?" Overcoming her initial reticence with a sigh, our office manager continued. "Doc told them it didn't interfere with my work. He told them to mind their own business. After some surgery I took time off, went to rehab, and got straight."

Cindy put more nachos on her plate. At five-foot three-inches tall, and about one hundred pounds, she ate more than anyone else and never gained an ounce. "Didn't they turn you in anyway? Doc too?"

"Yep. It took three years of hell before the board ruled in our favor. Anyway," she glanced around the table, "let's change the subject."

"You bet," Mari agreed boisterously. "Anyone want more wings?"

We talked and laughed for over an hour, but when the staff started talking about their sorry-assed boyfriends, Cindy and I called it a night

"Nick. You better make sure these girls keep eating and slow down the drinking. Remember, some of you have to work tomorrow." Cindy threw everyone air kisses and followed me out through the heavy wooden front door.

The cool night air revived me a bit. I hadn't realized how hot it was inside. After only one beer Cindy and I both had switched to Diet Coke so we'd be good to drive. Having Nick on hand to get the girls home safely proved a smart idea.

"That was fun." Cindy smoothed down her skirt.

"It sure was. Where's your car?"

She pointed to the left. "It's over by your truck."

"I needed a night out," I confided to her as we walked across the asphalt parking lot together. We had to concentrate on dodging the cars and trucks, not always lined up in neat rows, plus the potholes. Behind us the band broke into a boot-stomping favorite.

"I hear you've been talking to Bobby." Cindy reached into her handbag and took out a big wad of keys.

"Who?" I searched my memory but didn't come up with a Bobby.

She laughed. "Police Chief Robert Garcia. Bobby is my brother-in-law. My sister mentioned he'd talked to you about the day you found the bodies."

"The chief of police is your brother-in-law?"

"Sure. And the coroner is my best girlfriend's uncle. If he gives you any grief, let me know. Don't forget," she lectured me, "it's a small town and there isn't much to do here in the winter, especially when you're snowed in."

At first I didn't know what she meant, then I figured it out and grinned at her. "Have sex?"

She clicked the remote on her Subaru, then opened the car door. A sly smile lit her face.

"That's right. Husbands not always with their wives, and wives, well, you get the picture. Some people around here would be surprised if they ran a paternity test." She winked, smiled, then closed the door and drove away.

Although it was only nine-thirty, I made my way home and got into my pajamas, too tired to concentrate on anything. My stomach churned from all of the bar food I'd stuffed into it. I started thinking about what Cindy had said. Pippi could be Thomas' illegitimate daughter that they adopted. That might explain some things. Perhaps I would approach Chief Garcia through Cindy and find out the latest discoveries in the Langthorne case.

The phone rang before I put my mind on hold watching television.

"Hey, Katie," a familiar voice said. "I hear you're over there in Oak Falls killing off clients." Tim Shapiro, my lab partner all through vet school, laughed into the phone. "Just kidding, of course. How are you doing?"

Used to his sense of humor I didn't take offense. "Truthfully, I need a vacation."

"Don't we all. Did you know we moved to Rhinebeck?"

"I remember something like that from your last Christmas card," I said.

"Well, we'd love to see you. We'll be at a dog show this weekend. Why don't you join us for dinner?" His enthusiasm began to wake me up. I'd forgotten that Tim and his wife Tina showed the elegant toy breed called papillon. This would be a good opportunity to experience the show world that the Langthornes moved in.

"I'd love to. In fact, I'll meet you at the show."

"Kate," Tina interrupted on speakerphone. "I can't believe it. We were just talking about you."

I leaned back while Tina told me about their new house, her prized line of papillons, the length of ear fringe on her breeding female, her new grooming parlor, and how crazy the current extreme dog hair-coloring contests are. Then she said something that made me sit back up.

"What do you call them?"

"Cavapoos. Crosses between a King Charles spaniel and a poodle. I tell you, Maybelle Guzzman is ready to kill someone."

That name sounded familiar. "Who is Maybelle?"

"Only one of the grande dames of the dog show circuit. Big friends with the Langthornes, well, friends or enemies depending on the day. She shows pugs and Cavalier King Charles spaniels."

My interest piqued, I wanted more information. "Is she going to be at the Rhinebeck show?"

"Of, course. She seems to be having a revival of sorts recently." I could hear Tina reprimand one of the dogs.

"What do you mean by a revival?" I wanted to keep her talking.

A melodious giggle floated out of the phone. "Why her Cavaliers, dear. Her new Cavalier King Charles spaniels are to die for. If Thomas and Vivian were still alive they'd be throwing daggers at each other."

Still tired, I felt I was missing something. "Why do you say that?"

"Honey, they've had a rivalry between them for a prize at Westminster since before I was born. Not to speak ill of the dead, but they would have done anything to kill one another's chances." She lowered her voice for effect.

"Don't you know there are more bitches outside the ring than in the ring at dog shows?"

Chapter Eight

Saturday afternoon on my way to the dog show, cruising over the Kingston-Rhinecliff Bridge in the truck playing Doc's Beach Boys CD, I felt so good I indulged in some discreet car-dancing complete with shoulder moves.

Looking forward to the show and dinner with my pals, I decided to put Oak Falls and all the town gossip on the shelf for now. The sun shone full and strong, promising a glorious spring day. I rolled down the windows and listened to the Hudson River lapping against the bridge supports. A two-mast schooner slid directly under the bridge below. Rays of sunlight glinted off the blue-green water dotted with sailboats and small fishing vessels. Over the past thirty years environmentalists and locals devoted to the river had turned it around from a polluted mess to a living home for fish and wildlife.

Even the toll collector had a smile on his face.

I made a right at the base of the bridge and headed for the Ulster County Central High School. The preliminary judging started at nine, with the finals scheduled to wrap up by four in the afternoon. It was already a quarter to one.

Going to a dog show is like watching models strut their stuff during New York's Fashion Week, only these models wear fur, not fashion. Show dogs are the supermodels of the canine world—beautiful, expensive, and catered to. For the breeds with long coats, hours are spent on grooming and styling. Bleaching, coloring, curling, and powdering are all part of the bag of tricks in the show ring. This particular show was a major event that often predicted the winners of the Westminster Dog Show, the Academy Awards of the dog world, held every February in New York City. Breeders and handlers would be out in force hoping to add points to their animals' quests for a championship.

After paying my fee and receiving a map and schedule of events at the gate, I parked the truck in the parking lot and hiked to the main building. Two police cars and a fire truck had pulled up next to the entrance, I guessed to provide crowd control for the raucous dog show fans.

There were dogs everywhere. From the largest Irish wolfhound to a diminutive Yorkshire terrier and everything in between, beautiful examples of the American Kennel Club's recognized breeds strutting their stuff in this group show. The more experienced dogs took the attention in stride while others started at all the noise and pulled at their leashes. A mixed chorus of dog barks, from the highest yipping to the lowest bass, floated in the air.

I checked my map looking for the Toy Group area. The show organizers had divided the football field into sections with canvas tents. The largest tent was reserved for the Best in Show judging. According to the schedule the Toy Group showed in Tent B. I found the tent and angling through the portable bleacher seats I watched the competing groups of toy dogs. Little dogs have big personalities and today's group was no exception. In front of me nine flame-colored Pomeranians pranced in the ring, ready to take on the world. Brushed into living fur-balls you could barely see their teensy feet as the dogs trotted on their leads past the judge.

The audience showed as much variety as the dogs, with men and women elegantly dressed in suits and cashmere next to spectators in shorts and clinging t-shirts. One fellow taking photos from the aisle wore a red shirt that said "Bite This." In fact, if it weren't for all the dog paraphernalia everywhere it could have been any sporting event. Families hunkered down in clumps, devouring pizza, hot dogs, and huge sodas, and parking infant strollers next to the bleachers to cause minor traffic jams.

But why were the handlers of most tiny dogs rather large ladies? Was it on purpose, an optical illusion so the canines would look even smaller? I tried not to giggle as a wire-coated affenpinscher moved past me, the massive shelf of its handler's bosom at least twice the size of the dog bouncing along behind.

My eye caught something waving directly across from me. When I looked closer I realized someone was waving two silky haired papillons, one in each hand, like flags.

It could only be Tina.

Sure enough, in a moment I saw her dark mane of fine hair, swept off her face much like that of the dogs she held. She gestured with one of the papillons, pointing off to the back behind the stands. Following her lead I got up and made my way through the crowd, almost colliding with a small boy, his vision obstructed by a huge pink cone of cotton candy held directly in front of his face.

"Kate, it's so good to see you again," Tina shifted the little dogs onto one arm and hugged me with the other. "I'm so excited. Maurice won Best in Breed and Bardot got her first point." With that she planted a delicate kiss on each of the slender dog's noses. They responded by licking her face with tiny pink tongues.

I gathered Maurice and Bardot were the dogs.

"When do you have to go back in the ring?"

"In about an hour." She pressed one of the dogs into my hands and said, "Follow me. They've got us set up in the locker room."

We wound our way toward the door in the marked exhibitors' entrance until we were stopped by a security officer. After I showed my American Veterinary Medical Association membership card and ID to the guard and explained that I was one of Tina's veterinarians he gave me a temporary pass and we plunged into dog show heaven…or hell, depending on your point of view.

"Gail," screamed a thin woman just inside the door, wearing a tool belt filled with combs, picks, brushes, and objects I couldn't identify. "Where is my powder? I need it right now." Her voice went up another octave after she dropped on all fours and started to search through several canvas bags on the floor.

At first glance it seemed as though we had stumbled into a drug deal, but I realized the crisis probably centered around a bottle of unscented baby powder. The stoic standard poodle on the grooming table needed to be white-white without a hint of yellow. That's where the baby powder came in. Sprinkled into the coat and combed through, it helps the coat reflect light and look as perfect as freshly fallen snow. It was anyone's guess if the shiny black nose pad on this dog was due to Mother Nature or to a little dab of shoe polish.

Tina zipped through aisles and breeds, and it was all I could do to keep up with her. The smell of mousse and hair spray punctuated the air. Abruptly we moved from more poodles to a bevy of tricolored papillons.

"I'm over here, Katie," said a familiar voice. I looked up to see my veterinary school classmate Tim Shapiro waving scissors at me.

"Let me take her," he said, reaching for the dog. Again, more French kissing between species. "What a crazy morning for us."

Tim looked good, more relaxed than when we were in school and definitely at home in the dog show world. His curly black hair was cropped stylishly close to his scalp, and he'd traded his old black glasses for designer frames. A baby blue sweater was loosely tied around his shoulders, the color repeated in his turquoise belt buckle. I wondered if Tina picked out his clothes for him. He handed Bardot to Tina then checked his watch.

"You've got forty-five minutes, Honey."

Tina scrunched up her lips. "Don't tell me again."

"Do you want us to leave you alone?"

"Yes." She continued to comb the dog's silky coat, paying close attention to the frill on Maurice's chest. "Wait. No."

"How about we stand right next to the column, in case you need us?" I offered. Tina's normally friendly face shone tight with tension.

"Honey, it's going to be fine. The judge really liked him." Tim crooned to his wife.

"I don't know how you can make this dog look any more stunning," I said, truthfully. "He's got the most gorgeous ear fringes."

"Oh, thanks so much, Kate. I have a special conditioner from France that I use so they stay silky but don't drag down." Tina continued to comb the flowing fur while Maurice held still like the champ he was.

We walked over to the column but kept in clear eyesight of her in case she needed us.

"It's like flipping prom night all over again," Tim said ruefully. "But we love it. The dogs are our babies."

"You seem happy." I had babysat him through two bad relationships before he met Tina.

"I am. So, what about you, Katie? Still carrying a torch for Dr. Perfect?"

"Dr. Perfect" referred to Jason. I thought a moment before I answered. "I'm way better than I was."

"What did you see in that guy?"

"Damned if I know." We both laughed. The heart wants what it wants.

"Sorry about the joke last night."

"No you're not." Tim was nothing if not a jokester. I watched him carefully.

"You know me too well, partner. I think I breathed in too much formaldehyde in anatomy lab. It scrambled my sense of humor." He kept glancing over at Tina who was trying to improve on perfection, then, waved to her. "Honey, we're going to get seats. Do you need anything?"

"Valium." She combed and primped the dog. Finally she released the grooming noose and carefully placed the dog on the cement floor.

"Kill them out there," I told her. "Break a leg and all that stuff."

After quick hugs all around, we walked back through the hall and made our way out to the tent where the Best of Toy Breed judging would be held. Tim led me to bleachers on the side, near the handlers' entrance but away from the judges' table.

"Is this close enough?" I was concerned we didn't have that great a view.

"It's fine. I'm too nervous to be up front." He glanced around at the audience. "There's the gang from Crosswinds Kennels. They breed fantastic affenpinschers and Brussels griffons. Can-Do Terriers are the kennel people in the red t-shirts up front. I've met some of them. Tina heard they're almost bankrupt."

Tim sat down but I said, "Listen, I'm going to run to the restroom before it starts."

"Okay. It begins in ten minutes."

"No problemo."

Scooting past two ladies wearing vests decorated with pictures of dogs, I made a beeline to the porta-potties set up on the side parking lot near the trees, about three minutes away. Everything was well marked and the line not that long. With any luck I'd probably only miss the opening announcements. After washing up I picked up my backpack and started toward the show ring. Leaning against a parking sign, his face turned away from me, some broad-shouldered guy lit up a cigar. Immediately the aromatic smoke rose in a cloud around his shaved head. A blonde woman wearing a long raincoat scurried by and covered her nose and mouth with her hand. Something about her looked familiar, but I couldn't place it. Maybe one of my pet-loving house-call clients out for the day? I cut across the parking lot toward the building thinking I could save some time, but instead I got turned around. As I entered the tent I heard the announcer welcome the audience. From the back I caught the names Maybelle Guzzman and Mu-Shu's Jinglebell Nights followed by Tina Shapiro with Double T Maurice's Chevalier. They must be introducing the competitors as they enter the ring.

Pushing past a gaggle of teenagers in Goth clothing I realized I'd come through a different entrance. I peered over the bleachers as the handlers made a circle around the judge. Tina looked elegant as she passed by, Maurice's silky fur and Tina's flowing locks swaying in unison with every movement.

I began walking toward my seat but stopped when I caught a glimpse of the pug's handler. Trotting toward me in the ring was the lady with the big hat, who watched me talk to the police in the country store parking lot. The same one who told the cashier I might have rabies. So that's Maybelle, I said to myself. What a surprise.

But that was nothing compared to my astonishment when two shots rang out in the tent.

I saw a red stain bloom on Maybelle's satin shirt. A puzzled look crossed her face then she stumbled and fell to her knees, leash still clutched in her fingers. Dogs began to howl as the crowd around her screamed and bolted toward the exits.

While everyone around me ducked down or tried to flee the tent, I dropped my backpack and ran toward the injured Maybelle. From the other side Tim maneuvered past people in the aisle and made his way into the ring. You might call it force of habit, but we were both trained in trauma medicine and until a human doctor showed up we were the next best thing. I detoured around a mother hugging her children and vaulted over the last two seats. Maybelle lay still, eyes closed, her left hand fluttering on the bright green indoor-outdoor carpeting.

Tim pushed Tina and the dogs down behind the judges' table, then ran to my side. He ripped off his blue sweater and pressed it to the wound. Together we fashioned a crude bandage from the cashmere and applied pressure.

"Her heart rate is okay for now, but she looks like she's in shock." I checked her vital signs. My hand slipped gently under the small of her back to check for an exit wound. It came back clean. Outside the tent we heard security yelling at the crowd. Almost immediately, sirens blared, followed by the muffled shouting of the emergency responders. Someone outside yelled, "Over here."

"Maybelle, don't worry. The EMTs are here. Everything will be all right." I held her hand and squeezed it. She didn't squeeze back.

I looked at Tim. "Did you see who shot her?"

"No. I was watching Tina. What about you?"

I shook my head.

"How can this be happening?" Tim continued to press down hard on the wound. Blood seeped through the sweater and bathed his fingers with red. A police officer followed by two EMTs burst into the tent, their feet pounding the ground as they made their way down to us.

"Hang on, Maybelle," I said. The show spotlights still shone on her pale face.

The pug whined and licked its owner's hand.

As I moved out of the way I heard Tim say, "This makes no sense. It's only a dog show."

Chapter Nine

The police closed the parking lot and herded everyone into the school gymnasium until they could get statements from the witnesses. Tim and I stood under the basketball hoop next to Tina and several of the other toy breed exhibitors and handlers.

"Why couldn't that damn gunman have waited until after the judge had made his decision?" whined the Brussels griffon handler in a patrician Southern accent. "I need that point for Scrunchy."

Sensitive he wasn't.

Tina rolled her eyes. "I think that's a moot point now."

"Ha ha. Well," he sniffed, "I know Maybelle would feel the same if she were here."

"That's for sure," chimed in another breeder standing nearby. "She could be ruthless when she wanted something. I believe her pug only needed one more point for a championship. This show would have given her that, bless her soul," she added.

"Has anyone heard anything?" someone asked Maybelle's assistant, who waited with the pug.

"No. The last time we saw her, the EMTs had wheeled her into the ambulance and were driving away."

Now that the hysteria had quieted down, people stood around chatting like they were waiting for a bus. They seemed grouped according to their dog breeds. The majority of them thought Maybelle would be fine. Tim and I weren't so sure.

Too restless to stand still, I wandered around. I recognized some of the people who were in the audience, but most were strangers to me. A cluster of Goth kids all with their phones in their hands sat on the floor with backs against a wall. One of them caught my eye, hesitated, then got up and came over to me.

"Hey. Aren't you the one who helped Mrs. Guzzman?" Her pale face sported a nose ring, a bar above her eyebrow, and multiple heavy silver earrings.

"Yes." Several others drifted over to us. In a desperate attempt to look different, they all now looked exactly alike.

"Do you think she's going to be okay?" asked a tall, very skinny boy with plugs in his earlobes.

"I honestly don't know. I'm sure we'll hear more news later tonight." I was about to leave but decided to ask them some questions. "Did you see who shot her?"

One girl rolled her eyes. "I wish. You can make some good cash if you had that on video." I suspected she'd said that for effect, but I was wrong.

"Look." Someone shoved a cell phone in front of my face. On the screen I saw myself looking at the stage. Audio accompanied the video. Suddenly a shot could be heard and the picture jiggled. I saw myself react to the gunshot, drop my backpack, and vault over the chairs in the direction of the stage. You could barely make out Maybelle crumpled on the floor.

"Isn't it massive?" the girl with the ring in her nose gushed at me. "I've already got it on YouTube, and I posted it on my Facebook page."

Something puzzled me. "Why were you focused on me before the shooting?"

An embarrassed look shot between the two girls. "We thought you might be Meryl Streep."

After an hour of waiting in the stuffy locked gymnasium that now smelled of dogs and angst, my head throbbed like a juicer making an orange-carrot smoothie. Tina sat on the floor with the tiny papillons in her lap and leaned on their heap of bags.

I reached for my backpack. Not there. Did I put it with their stuff? I bent down and searched, but it was gone.

"What's up?" Tim asked. He had spent most of the time playing solitaire on his phone.

"Have you seen my backpack?"

"No. Maybe you put it down?" His eyes never left the screen.

I tried to remember when I had last seen it. I'd definitely had it in the bathroom, because the space was so awkward I had taken it off and hung it on the porta-potty door hook, which sort of grossed me out. Then it came to me. In the Goth kid's video I'd dropped it on the ground before I vaulted over the seats and rushed toward the stage. How could I find it now? Before I could think clearly about what to do, someone called my name.

"Kate Turner? Is there a Kate Turner here?" A New York State Trooper in full uniform, a tan felt Stetson on his head, stood with his hand on the gymnasium door. He stared into the crowd; when I raised my hand, he glared at me.

Tim glanced up from his game, a surprised look on his face. Heads swiveled toward me.

"I'm Doctor Kate Turner." My voice sounded shaky even to me.

Our eyes locked and he stared at me as though taking an America's Most Wanted photo with his eyeballs. If he was trying to intimidate me, he was doing a good job. He gestured with his hand. "Follow me."

As I walked toward him I glanced back at Tim and Tina. They both mouthed and gestured *call me* before the door shut with an ominous metallic click.

"What is this about?" I hurried to keep up with him. For a big man he moved pretty fast. Then I noticed another trooper trailing us about ten feet behind me. Either he didn't hear or simply chose to ignore me. I put my head down and followed, noticing the concrete floors beneath us had webs of hairline cracks. The corridors stretched long and cold with few windows and not much sunlight. Finally, after doubling back, we stopped outside a door labeled "Employees Only." Without hesitation the officer pushed it open, revealing more muscles hiding under his shirtsleeves.

Inside, telephones were ringing and multiple laptop stations were in use. Someone pushed past me without taking a breather from his cell phone.

"Over here," the officer indicated with his index finger.

He knocked on the metal door, then opened it and ushered me inside. A gray-haired man in shirtsleeves sat behind a large mahogany desk and looked at me suspiciously. Either I was getting paranoid, or I was in serious trouble. A quick glance at the desktop and I knew without a doubt I wasn't paranoid. It was deep, deep trouble.

Resting on his desk in a large evidence bag lay my backpack. The barrel of a gun protruded from the front zip pocket, comfortably nestled next to an almond granola bar.

Chapter Ten

"What was in your backpack?" my friend Gracie screamed through the phone.

"This gun I'd never seen before, plus the usual stuff." I took another sip of white wine and sprawled on my sofa in front of the television trying to chill. After going over and over what happened before and after the shooting and viewing the Goth kid's video a hundred times, the State Police reluctantly let me go, advising me not to make any travel plans. Prudently I'd stopped myself from blurting out that I'd heard that before.

Gracie's voice brought me out of my little fog.

"What usual stuff do you carry around, Kate?"

I thought for a moment. "You know, my wallet and credit cards, duct tape, syringes, a bag of fluids, some sterile needles, epinephrine, dexamethasone, Advil, some extra socks…"

Her quick intake of breath warned me something was wrong.

"That sounds like the stuff serial killers carry around. No wonder they kept you so long." She made a funny smacking noise with her lips. "Why did you have all of that with you?"

I took another sip of wine. "That's my veterinary emergency kit. I always have some medical supplies with me."

"Why?"

I straightened up, put my glass down, and tried to explain. "A couple of summers ago I was hiking part of the Appalachian

Trail. The temperature hit ninety-five with really high humidity. On my way back down I came across an English bulldog suffering from heatstroke. The owner didn't know what to do. The only thing I had with me to help them was a half-empty water bottle."

I didn't need to close my eyes to remember.

"After that I vowed never to be without a small emergency kit. Believe me, it's come in handy over the years, from cuts and broken legs to stabilizing a golden retriever that had been hit by a car."

"What's the duct tape for?"

"You can use it for a whole bunch of things— making a splint, fashioning a stretcher with branches and tape, securing an IV bag, putting on a pressure bandage. It will even take off moles. Duct tape is great, and now it comes in colors." I silently toasted to duct tape by raising my glass.

I could almost hear Gracie thinking about my encounter over the phone lines.

"Did you use it on Maybelle?"

"No. By the time we put pressure on her gunshot wound the EMTs were there."

"I'm worried about you, Kate. What is this, the second time in a month you've been involved in a shooting?" Again that nervous teeth clicking sound came over the receiver.

"That's why I'm pouring another glass of wine," I said. "Someone planted that gun in my backpack, either deliberately or because it happened to be there on the floor. The police think it just presented an opportunity to get rid of the weapon, but I'm not so sure. It's too coincidental." Mari's two rottweilers lay at my feet. I didn't want to admit to Gracie that I was jumpy as hell and happy to babysit my technician's dogs for the weekend. I'd been questioned by law enforcement enough for a lifetime. Before I took this job, the closest I'd gotten to being in trouble with the police was a speeding ticket while trying to get to the airport on time.

"What about calling Gramps?"

"No."

"Listen, I'm sure he's got some friends in the NYPD who could help out."

Another sip of cold Pinot Grigio and I was ready to answer my oldest friend.

"That's a no. Look, I'm not under arrest. I'm not even a suspect. I don't want to get Gramps upset if I don't have to."

"Suit yourself," she said in an exasperated tone.

We were silent for a few moments, both thinking the same thing. Of course, she was right. I might have to get my grandfather involved. He was my ace in the hole, the only person I knew with contacts in law enforcement that I could trust. But just like in a game of poker, you don't want to pull out a hidden ace too often.

Someone might think things are fishy.

The conversation with Gracie made me restless. I walked back and forth aimlessly, followed by the dogs who dutifully padded along behind me. After my third stop at the refrigerator staring at the same stuff, I had to come to a decision. I called the dogs over and discussed it with them.

"So, Lucy," I told the tricolored dog, "I'm feeling pretty uncomfortable about this. Now I'm a witness at two shootings. Maybe I should contact a lawyer." The dog panted in agreement.

"But what would I tell a lawyer?" I talked while I scratched her massive head. "The police think my backpack on the floor presented an opportunity to hide the gun. Nothing directed at me." Ricky, the ninety-pound male shoved his head under my free hand. "But they look at me a whole different way. Who would believe I'm always in the wrong place at the wrong time?"

Two sets of brown eyes gazed at me with perfect understanding.

"Should I continue asking questions about the Langthorne deaths? Maybe I should shut up and mind my own business."

The dogs wisely kept their opinions to themselves.

"Why did someone switch another dog for Charles Too? What if Thomas didn't kill Vivian? Maybe someone staged their deaths to look like a murder-suicide?"

Lucy dismissed my barrage of questions with a yawn.

I finished my glass of wine, corked the bottle, and put it back in the refrigerator. Leaving a light on for the dogs, I climbed into bed. The sheets felt cold even though the room was warm.

"I'll think about it tomorrow," I said aloud.

The only response was the clicking of Lucy and Ricky's toenails on the wooden floor as they both circled in different directions, then lay down in their beds.

Chapter Eleven

I spent Sunday at home, eating leftovers and doing laundry—anything to make it seem like a normal day. After lunch while surfing the Internet I found a disturbing piece of publicity on the home page of MSNBC. A picture of Pippi Langthorne was plastered under the caption "Million Dollar Dog," showing her shaking hands with a man named Charles Too Yakimoto, the CEO of King Electronics in Hong Kong. Front and center, a Cavalier King Charles spaniel was identified as Charles Too. Pippi held an oversized phony check made out for one million dollars.

It turned out that Charles Too's pedigree traced back to the spaniels owned by the King of England, Charles the Second, also known as the Merry Monarch. The buyer, Charles Too Yakimoto, was the proud owner of a young female King Charles spaniel. An ad agency he hired to promote his Internet business came up with this crazy publicity campaign, taking advantage of the name similarities. They planned to televise the "wedding" of the two dogs and start a countdown for the first litter of puppies. Charles Too's babies were then scheduled to be adopted through a lottery for lucky customers who registered by email. Television ads were already running showing Yakimoto romping with his two dogs. His company's website bragged that over three hundred thousand dog-lovers had already entered the drawing. They estimated the puppies to be worth ten thousand dollars each. King Electronics had even kicked in a year of free food and veterinary care.

Free enterprise rules again. No wonder Pippi Langthorne didn't care about the rest of her parents' dogs, she'd hit pay dirt! But why did she substitute the look-alike son for the father? Did Charles Too somehow get away during the Langthorne murders? Was all this mystery caused by a lost dog?

On that thought I took a snack break from the computer and foraged around in the cabinets for a bag of potato chips. I'd splurged on fried, not baked. What's the fun of eating potato chips if you can't lick the salt off your oily fingers?

That reminded me. I propped the refrigerator door open to find mostly bare shelves. A jar of mustard, some extremely wilted celery, and two lonely Diet Cokes reminded me to go food shopping. From years of eating alone I'd developed a bad habit of either parking in front of the TV or munching at the computer, greasy keyboard and all. With my hands full I looked for a place to sit, but stacks of books, papers, and junk mail covered the kitchen table. Maybe tomorrow I'd eat like a grownup, I thought, making a beeline for the computer. Meanwhile I needed a laugh. What would it be, cats on a treadmill? Maybe that orangutan walking a dog? Luckily there were countless animal-related funny videos to watch and articles to read.

A story about cat teahouses in Japan, where customers paid to interact with the feline residents, caught my attention…until I was interrupted by a phone call.

"Kate? I'm so glad you're there." My technician Mari sounded upset. I knew she'd gone to visit her elderly mother and hoped she was all right.

"Is everything okay, Mari?" The dogs pricked their ears up at the sound of their master's name.

"I found a dog on the way back."

I wasn't surprised. Mari found dogs, cats, birds, rabbits, and all kind of creatures on a regular basis. Or should I say they found her.

"He looks pretty bad. Can I bring him over right now?"

"Of course, do we need a stretcher?"

"I'm afraid so. He's only about ten or twelve pounds and looks emaciated." She paused for a moment. "I'm worried about his spine and neck, plus his skin is all messed up."

My heart sunk. "I'll be waiting. Pull up into the front lot and I'll meet you."

"Thanks, Kate. I know it's your day off."

"It's yours, too, Mari. Don't worry about it."

I logged out of the computer and slipped into a pair of scrubs. After taking Lucy and Ricky for a quick walk, I went back into the hospital and pulled out our emergency crash kit. Not knowing what to expect, I also got out bandage materials and surgical scrub for the wounds.

I heard the gravel crunch in the parking lot as Mari's big SUV came to a stop. I quickly grabbed the hospital stretcher and went out to meet her.

"He's back here." She opened the tailgate.

I looked at the dog lying on a blanket. The hair on his legs and tail was matted and dirty. An injury to his side left a large open sore, very close to his kidney. His whiskers were singed. His tail hung down at a strange angle, obviously broken.

Crawling into the back of the SUV, I knelt next to the dog and slipped a stethoscope on his chest wall. I could count each rib. He immediately stirred from his sleep. Gingerly I examined the skin lesions.

"I think these are from being hit by a car. I can see where he slid across the gravel."

"The poor dog," Mari leaned the stretcher against the back of the SUV so we could slide him onto it.

"I'm sorry, buddy," I said to the dog. He slowly raised his head and placed his bristly muzzle into my hand. Sad brown eyes looked deep into mine. Then his left paw lifted up and touched my arm. The shave mark where I'd put the catheter in was growing back nicely.

It was Charles Too.

Although he looked terrible, his vital signs, X-rays, and blood work indicated he would suffer no permanent damage other than his tail. With nutritional support and treatment for his skin infection, I expected a full recovery. I didn't reveal to Mari who I thought this dog was since I had absolutely no proof. According to the Internet, Charles Too was heading for Hong Kong after earning his former owner, Pippi Langthorne, a cool million dollars.

I knew that many older show dogs sported blue tattoos on their inner thighs, but Charles Too had no such mark and no identification chip implanted near his shoulder blades. Vivian had made several appointments in the past, according to Doc's records, to insert chips into the dogs, but Thomas had always declined. He didn't want to pay registration fees for all the dogs, plus he was suspicious of the new technology. Absent any identifying marks, I couldn't prove my suspicions, especially since I'd already signed a health certificate for the phony Charles Too.

Mari gathered up Lucy and Ricky and all their stuff. She had a doctor's appointment tomorrow, a follow-up on her knee injury, so once again I'd be seeing patients by myself. Tired from her long drive and limping more than usual, she went out to her SUV and headed home.

After all he'd been through I couldn't let Charles Too sleep in a hospital cage tonight. I fed him several meals spaced out over the evening and settled him on a soft dog bed in my apartment. While he slept, his legs twitched like he was running in some crazy doggy dream. Right then I decided this dog was through being a pawn in a game we both didn't understand. No one looking at him now could guess he'd once been a show dog. I knew Thomas and Vivian Langthorne, wherever they were, would feel the same. He'd be safe with me.

The person or persons responsible had made a big mistake. They'd made me really angry.

No way would I stop asking questions now.

Chapter Twelve

I renamed the dog formerly known as Charles Too. I called him Buddy, and over the next week he and I fell into a comfortable routine. After a short morning walk I'd go to work, then, come home for lunch. Each day Buddy improved in strength and outlook, finally greeting me with an enthusiastic wag of his now stubby tail. He quickly became house-trained and stoically let me tend his skin wounds. His hair pattern probably wouldn't be the same as before because of the scars on his back, but I didn't care. I kept his coat short and told everyone he was a mixed-breed spaniel.

Spring now burst into full bloom. I climbed into the truck after spending lunchtime with Buddy and checked on my afternoon appointments. From the driver's window I could see a distant view of the mountains. A glimpse of bright blue sky shone between the treetops. How could anything go wrong on such a gorgeous day?

Little Man welcomed me profusely with ear-piercing yips when I arrived for his two-week checkup while Mrs. Davidsen and I talked between the barks.

"How is everything down there?" I asked diplomatically as I closed the door behind me. Today they were both dressed in black and white. Little Man wore a faux leather jacket that said "Top Dog" in rhinestones across the back, and his owner's attire complemented his with her faux leather vest and skirt embroidered with a rhinestone Chihuahua. The fashion parade stopped with her shoes: fluffy purple bedroom slippers that scuffed as she walked into the kitchen.

Do they dress up for me, or is this their normal routine? I wondered.

"My precious baby is doing so wonderfully," she gushed with enthusiasm. "His little tutu is perfect now."

I interpreted tutu to mean Chihuahua butt.

"That's fantastic." I quickly slid Little Man around by his jacket and looked at his rear. Luckily the tiny dog carried his tail high in the air, giving me a great view of the old tutu. Little Man emitted a low, half-hearted growl, just to keep up his tough-guy reputation.

"Is he bothering it at all, Mrs. Davidsen?" The abscess site had healed up so well, you could only tell where it had been from the shave marks.

"Of course not, he's a perfect little gentleman." She threw a butterfly kiss at the dog with her fingertips. "Of course, I kept his pants on at all times just to make sure."

"Did you say his pants?" I asked.

"Yes, his little pj's. I figured they'd be nice and soft around his tutu. Oh, and please call me Daffy." Astonished, and not wanting to be rude, I wisely said nothing. "My name is Daphne," she explained, "but everyone calls me Daffy."

I nodded. I bet they do.

I glanced around the room wondering if I was in an alternative universe. Or on the old "Candid Camera" program. Or even "Punk'd." Then I relaxed. If you can't beat 'em, join 'em.

"You know, I would love to see those pajama bottoms," I told her.

Daffy smiled, her eyes widening. "Sure. Can you hold him? I'll be right back."

It was just Little Man and me. I bet he had a tiny motorcycle cap somewhere in the house that matched his coat. The look on his face said it all. Yeah, I know I'm dressed up like Marlon

Brando in a fifties motorcycle movie, but it could be worse, a lot worse.

"I'm with you, Little Man, and I have to say you're looking good, real good."

He almost smiled at me.

By the time Daffy came out with the tiny felt pajamas and other pieces of clothing, I was kind of into the whole dressing-up-your-toy-dog-in-doggy-clothes thing. As it turned out, the pants were soft and ingeniously made, with appropriate openings for bodily functions.

"You know," I said, holding the pants up and checking the seams, "these could be very helpful after surgery."

"Really?"

"Yes. I've put t-shirts on dogs to stop them from licking at a wound or pulling out their sutures, but your clothes are much better made." I handed the tiny pants back to her. "You could probably sell these on the Internet."

"Really?" she repeated.

"How long does it take you to sew something like this?" I asked.

"Not long, maybe an hour. I do my sewing while I watch television."

Little Guy stood up on his hind legs and put his front two feet on her chest. I couldn't help but notice his nail polish today was black in keeping with the punk look.

"Tell you what," I began, picking up my medical case, "I'll have Sandy give you a call to talk about what we might need at the clinic."

She picked up the Chihuahua and straightened out his coat as he licked her hand.

"Dr. Kate, you've made my day."

We walked through the living room, dollies and knickknacks all in place just like the first visit, but this time I saw a frustrated creative talent in everything. Maybe her love of animals and over-the-top interest in dressing them could help some of my recovering patients.

"Thanks, Dr. Kate. We both can't thank you enough." She waved Little Man's paw at me.

"It's been my pleasure."

As I opened the screen door, she stopped me with a hand on my arm.

"I think you're prettier than Meryl Streep." She lowered her voice and looked around, as if Meryl were listening in on us.

"Thanks," I replied in kind.

Little Man growled in agreement.

"Oh, I meant to tell you something, but I got sidetracked." Her mouth scrunched up in concentration. "My neighbor works in the police station as a part-time dispatcher, and she heard that a drug showed up in the Langthornes' toxicology report."

What drug, I wondered. Blood pressure pills? Cardiac medications? Alcohol? I knew the elderly couple liked their liquor at night. Vivian mentioned that after they put the dogs in each evening, they would have a couple of nightcaps together. I suspected they had "daycaps" too.

"It was…now let me get this right." Daffy thought for a moment. "You should know it, Dr. Kate."

Why should I know what medication was in their toxicology report?

"Now I remember. It was ketamine."

"Ketamine?" I felt like someone had punched me in the chest. Ketamine hydrochloride was a powerful veterinary dissociative anesthetic drug. I probably used it several times a week. Our hospital had multiple glass vials stored in our controlled-substances safe at this moment.

And I had a key.

Chapter Thirteen

The next day the toxicology report broke in the local newspapers. Not on the front page, but buried in the middle, just before the recipes and classified ads. A short paragraph stated that both Thomas and Vivian Langthorne's bodies contained alcohol and ketamine at the time of death. Their deaths were now classified as suspicious.

In a panic I called Gramps.

Strangely enough, he didn't react the same way I did.

"Special K is everywhere these days," Gramps told me, his breathing under control. "They could have had it in their house for years, lifted it from a vet or gotten it at one of those dog shows. Kids in high school sell the stuff."

I stroked Buddy on the head. We sat in one of the few private places outside the hospital, near the back entrance and parking lot where there was a small concrete patio with a grill. The second day I stayed there, I had bought a cheap outdoor bistro set for myself. A pot of geraniums completed my Martha Stewart moment.

"You don't think it points directly to me?" I asked him.

"No honey. It's a street drug. But it is an odd choice, I grant you."

"Why do you say that?" The sun felt good on my face. I noticed Buddy's hair had begun to grow back in a patchy, slightly darker pattern.

"Most of the murder-suicides in older couples I saw in the fire department fell into two categories: spontaneous and planned." He stopped to catch his breath then continued. "If it was spontaneous, there usually had been a fight with defensive wounds, breakage, and lots of yelling. Just because you've been married for thirty years doesn't mean you don't hate each other's guts."

"I didn't see anything like that." I thought back to that day. "There was a tea set and sandwiches on the coffee table, with milk, sugar, lemons, and scones. They both had been drinking tea before they died. Nothing seemed out of place except for the dogs running around. Everything else appeared to be normal." Even as I told my grandfather, a tiny place in my mind disagreed. There was something…

Gramps continued speaking, his breathing increasingly raspy. "The planned ones are easy. Lengthy notes, keys where relatives can find them. If they can, they clean the house and have the clothes they want to be buried in hung out with instructions." Again he stopped for a short breather. "One couple I remember apologized to the police for causing any problems."

Buddy saw a lizard crawl across the patio and got up to sniff it. I thought I understood what my grandfather was saying.

"So the Langthornes don't fit into these patterns," I said. "No planning and no big fight." I shook my head trying to figure it out. "If Thomas had ketamine in his system, he risked not being able to pull the trigger. I could see him giving it to Vivian so she would pass out, but why would he take it?"

"Good question." For once Gramps didn't have an answer.

Unless, someone gave it to him, to facilitate a murder.

So why haven't the police announced anything?

Ketamine pointed directly to me. Still paranoid despite what Gramps said, I decided it was time to check out a local lawyer, just in case. My previous experience with lawyers consisted of a few students on my dorm floor in college majoring in pre-law and several seasons of *Law and Order*.

Next to the diner I'd seen a freestanding building belonging to a law firm, so I drove out there first. I parked behind a pressure-treated log that separated the parking lot from a prefab building. The sign read Aronson and Aronson, Attorneys-at-Law. I wiped my feet on the mat and opened the door.

"Yes?" A middle-aged receptionist frowned looking up at me through her bifocals. "Do you have an appointment?" From her attitude you would think the waiting room was jammed with clients instead of being completely empty.

"No." Ignoring her seeming displeasure, I continued, "I'm Dr. Turner, and I was hoping to speak to Mr. Aronson, ah, or Mr. Aronson, about a little problem I have." Yes, I knew I had started to babble, but couldn't stop myself. "That is, if he or they, the two of them, have a moment—although I only need to speak to one of them, at a time."

To her credit she didn't seem to be fazed by my request. "I'll see what I can do. Won't you please have a seat?" She lifted the receiver, then changed her mind and stood up. Her polyester blue pantsuit included a jacket that rode midway over her flat rear end. Purposefully picking up her purse, as if I couldn't be trusted to be alone in the same room with it, she strode to the back of the office.

I glanced around the spare reception area. Everything looked cheap. Worn plastic chairs, worn industrial carpet in a gray-brown color that hid any dirt. Two dog-eared magazines, several months old, and a chipped fake-wood coffee table were the only amenities. Several diplomas or licenses framed in thin black frames hung behind the receptionist's desk, but I couldn't read them.

Somewhere a door opened, followed by heavy footsteps coming toward me, shaking the floor.

"Can I help you?"

The flushed-faced speaker stood at least six-foot-two and weighed a good three hundred pounds. I made a wild guess. "Mr. Aronson?"

"Why don't we step into my office for a moment, little Miss?"

Had this guy been hiding in a cave for the last forty years? If there is anything that makes me mad, it's being called a "little

Miss" in a business setting by some old fart. At five-foot-ten I am not little, and I worked hard to add that Doctor to my name.

I stopped dead in my tracks like a stubborn mule. "Ah, I think you have me confused with someone else. I'm Doctor Turner."

The red face became redder. He stuck out his lower lip and gave it a chew.

"I know who you are. You're pretty famous around here, especially for being a newcomer. I believe you discovered the bodies of Thomas and Vivian Langthorne? You were also involved in the Guzzman shooting?" He acted like it was a question, but it sounded like an accusation.

I looked into his little piggy eyes. "Yes. Actually that's why I'm here. I'm not sure if I need a lawyer or not."

"Everybody needs a lawyer. My retainer is $5,000, plus expenses."

So much for the warm and fuzzy approach.

"Why would I need a lawyer if the police say I'm not a suspect?"

He gave me a knowing look. "Because they've told you you're not a suspect, that's very suspicious behavior on their part."

Thoroughly confused, I followed him into his office, also cheaply furnished, and sat down opposite him. The only luxurious thing in the office turned out to be Aronson's office chair, which doubled as a massage chair.

I waited for him to continue his explanation. He waited for me to continue. I caved first.

"Let me assure you that I had nothing to do with the Langthornes' deaths or the shooting of Maybelle Guzzman. And I certainly never gave ketamine to anyone except my patients."

He held up his manicured hand. "I don't need to know that to defend you."

"Well, don't you want to know if I'm innocent?"

His red face had begun to return to normal now that he had sat down. "Not in particular. My job is to give you the best representation I can."

I clenched my jaw in frustration. "So you think I should hire a lawyer?"

"Of course, everyone needs a lawyer," he repeated.

"What would you do on my behalf?" I really needed to understand the benefits of legal representation at this stage.

"We'd make inquiries, of course. That would be additional, by the way."

I started to hear the ring of a cash register, with my money flying out the window. "Is it wise to do that now, or should we wait until I'm charged with something?"

He frowned and put his big hands on the desk, fingers splayed. "It's best to always be on the attack."

"Attack against what?"

"You never know. Also, don't you dare talk to the police unless I am present." He pursed his lips then drew his index finger across them. "Keep it muzzled."

The imaginary picture of me in a muzzle wasn't pretty.

Would you like to give me your retainer now, little Miss? I take cash or credit cards," Aronson smiled for the first time, "but no personal checks."

Chapter Fourteen

The following day, since no one showed up to arrest me, I went off to work.

My first appointment took me to the opposite side of town. Twenty-two Fairview Lane turned out to be anything but. Did someone with a maniacal sense of humor name the street across from the town dump Fairview, or was there once a beautiful vista here?

The broken front window with a duct tape repair didn't improve the curb appeal of the old farmhouse that had seen better days. Faded white paint peeled and blistered on the railings of the wraparound porch with fancy scrollwork on the corners. At one time someone had taken pride in this place, but now junk filled the front yard. The house oozed sadness and neglect.

The doorbell felt loose, broken. Stepping closer to a side window, I squinted to catch a glimpse inside, but couldn't make out much. I knocked on the door as hard as I could, then stepped back and waited.

"Yeah," grunted the six-foot-two huge guy who cautiously opened the door. Both bulging arms sported tattoos from wrist to shoulders. He wore a tight wife-beater and jeans with a Harley belt buckle. A thin green snake curled around his neck. I had to look twice to realize it was a tattoo, meticulously inked, to show hundreds of scales and a delicate forked tongue.

"Someone call for a vet?" It occurred to me that I was carrying syringes and veterinary drugs that would fetch a good price on the open market. I also was entering a stranger's house alone. My self-preservation instincts kicked in so I pulled out my phone and dialed the office.

"Hey Sandy, I'm here at twenty-two Fairview for that emergency with the owner…excuse me, what's your name?"

"Henry James." He opened the door wider.

"Like the author?"

"Like the nineteenth century author, although he isn't my cup of tea. His prose is too flowery."

It was as if my dog had suddenly recited the balcony scene from *Romeo and Juliet*.

"Anyway," I continued, "I'll call as soon as I'm finished."

"Do you want me to check on you in fifteen minutes?" Sandy asked.

"Good idea," I responded. Now I knew why Gramps had insisted on those self-defense classes. I took a deep breath and said to Henry James, "Can I see the patient?"

"Sure, if we can catch him."

"What do you mean 'if we can catch him'? What kind of animal are we talking about?" For a moment I imagined a house full of snakes slithering around like the inked one around his neck.

"His name is Dante. He's a cat, a really big one, and he's pretty pissed at the moment." Henry eyed me skeptically, as though implying there was no way I could get near his pet.

"Well, let's take a look," I said.

"It's your funeral. Don't you have some big gloves or a pole or something?" He glanced hopefully at the truck, then turned and lumbered down the hallway, his shoulders almost touching the walls. He walked with that stiff, bodybuilder walk, arms sticking out as we moved along the hall.

"I trapped him in here," Henry announced proudly. He stopped in front of a door with a radioactive hazard warning that said Keep Out.

"Okay. Do you have a cat carrier?"

"Yeah, but I was hiding it from him. He goes nuts when he sees it."

"I'll take that chance." From the smell in the hallway, someone who lived here smoked cigars.

He shook his head like it truly was my funeral, took a few steps down the hall, then opened another door and slid a large plastic carrier decorated with Harley decals out into the open. A familiar pungent aroma wafted out from it.

"Just a wild guess here, but I bet Dante isn't altered, right?"

A horrified look told me all I needed to know. "I couldn't do that to the big guy."

I nodded. "Did he get into a fight?"

This time Henry averted his eyes. "I think so. Normally he kicks ass, but this time…" His voice trailed off and slid to a halt. "There's this gunk coming out of the bites."

Enough said. "Do you want to come in with me and help?"

"Uh, can I stay out here? It, uh, the, you know, kinda makes me sick."

I smiled in spite of myself. "Okay, but stay close to the door in case I need you."

He nodded his head reluctantly.

With my left hand I twisted the doorknob using the cat carrier to barricade the open door in case Dante tried to make a dash for it. Quickly I slid into the room and closed the door behind me—so far so good.

This was definitely someone's bedroom, painted black, with dayglow pictures and Grateful Dead posters taped to the walls. A large unmade bed took up one corner, covered with a green comforter all bunched into lumps, any of which could be a cat. I gloved up and started my search. "Hey Dante," I called. "I'm here to help you out. Where the heck are you hiding?"

I gently checked out the bed lumps. No cat. Next I made a survey of the rest of the room, looking behind the dresser drawers and under the table used as a desk. I pushed the trash bin aside with my foot in case he had scrunched himself behind it. Luckily the closet door was solid wood and shut tight. Of course

I knew where he was, but I wanted to let him get used to me in the room. Dante was where all cats head when they are trying to get away from you.

He was under the bed.

Now, I've seen cats climb indoor Christmas trees, and one hide inside a hole in an old piece of upholstered furniture, so I was prepared for anything. I lay down on the floor and looked under the bed, past the old underwear, dust bunnies, and stuff I didn't even want to know about. In the farthest corner a big male cat glared at me. I squinted at him to make sure I was seeing right. Dante was a huge flame-pointed Siamese who'd been in a lot of fights, and it showed. One ear tip appeared chewed off and the other seemed thickened from an old hematoma. Scars crisscrossed his nose, forehead, and jowls. Even his whiskers looked broken.

But there was no mistaking the look in those crystal blue eyes—royally pissed off. A low growl echoed in the enclosed space as soon as I moved.

Growling doesn't work on me.

"One of us is getting into this carrier and it sure isn't going to be me," I informed him. Then I flattened myself as much as I could and began to scoot under the bed. Dante didn't budge. I don't know if he was so astonished that I kept coming in after him that he just froze, or what, but finally I could almost touch him.

In my cat voice I told him how handsome he was and what a good guy I expected him to be. I explained I was here to help him. I softly breathed on him so he could get my scent, then calmly put my hand on his scruff which was tight to his skin, then slid him across the wooden floor and out from under the bed.

Deep bite wounds covered his back and tail. This time Dante had run from a fight, but it hadn't helped. A large abscess near his spinal column would need to be taken care of surgically, under anesthesia.

"Come on, handsome." I held onto his back feet and popped all twenty-plus pounds of him into the carrier. Now my gloved hands smelled pretty ripe. I stripped them off, put them in a plastic bag and opened the door. Henry stared at me, probably surprised I wasn't covered with blood and scratches.

"Did you find Dante?" He peered over my shoulder as though expecting an attack.

"He's in the carrier. Where can I wash up?"

"Uh, bathroom is over there." He gestured to the right down the hall, then looked from me to the cat carrier and back again. Growls and hisses were rocking the plastic box holding the cat. "How'd you do that?" he asked with wonder in his voice.

"Magic," I called over my shoulder, "veterinary magic."

After I got back from trying to scrub the cat odor off me, I sat Henry James down for a little talk. When he rested his arms on the small glass table, it tilted.

"Listen, I know you don't want to neuter Dante, but he's going to keep getting into these fights unless you do. And he's losing to younger males. Each time he fights, he's at risk for catching feline leukemia and FIV, the feline form of HIV."

"What about prostate problems, like some guys have?" Henry shifted uncomfortably in his seat.

"Cats have very small prostate glands."

"Man, are they lucky," he commented, shifting in the other direction. The glass table tilted again.

"Neutering will take care of that, too."

His eyes shifted away from mine, perhaps from embarrassment?

We sat for a moment. I noticed someone had hung frilly white curtains in the bay window of the kitchen that looked out on the backyard. A motorcycle helmet painted to look like a skull sat on top of a stack of cookbooks. Did someone else live in the house? No warm cooking smells beckoned, only the odor of ripe garbage and stale pizza.

"So, I'd like permission to neuter him while he is under anesthesia for the bite wounds— provided he's negative for those cat viruses I mentioned. Do you want to bring him in to the clinic, or would you like me to take him with me today?"

"You go ahead and take him."

"I'll have you sign a consent form and speak to Sandy about an estimate."

He stood up and reached into his pocket. "I don't like owing people." Before I could say anything, he unfolded a wad of money and counted out eight one-hundred-dollar bills on the table. "Is this enough?"

Surprised I answered, "It should be. I'll run his blood tests first. After we get the results I'll have my receptionist call you with a treatment plan." I didn't want to speculate where all that money came from. After taking a consent form from my medical bag, I had him sign it, then I wrote a separate receipt for the cash deposit. He didn't offer to help carry his pet to the truck. With folded arms he stood in the doorway and watched me drive away. I thought I saw tears in his eyes.

◇◇◇

Dante was a big hit at the hospital. First of all, he was the largest flame-point Siamese anyone had ever seen, with deep orange paws, tail, ears and nose. Instead of a long sleek frame like most Siamese cats, bulky muscles bunched up his shoulders and hips. He looked like a kitty sumo wrestler. But underneath that rough exterior he was a doll, sweet as could be. Luckily, despite his misadventures, his blood tests all turned out okay.

Putting a needle with his antibiotics through that tough tomcat skin was a challenge. It even had Mari shaking her head.

"We don't see many of these guys anymore." She checked the injection site.

"No. With the shelters neutering before adoption, and the way male tomcat urine stinks, you're right."

Cindy came in from reception. "Spoke to the owner and he's good to go."

"Okay, put him on the surgery schedule, Mari."

"I wonder if he's the one? Too bad Sandy isn't here today." Cindy looked at Dante in a thoughtful way.

"What do you mean?"

"Doc and Sandy and I have commented over the years about the number of flame-point-mix kittens we see in this town. It seems like every other litter has some Siamese look-alike in it."

Dante gazed at us. His unusually light blue eyes gave nothing away.

"Maybe he's the Genghis Khan of cats here in our town," Mari chimed in. "In biology class I learned that scientists did a Y chromosome analysis of men living in what was once the Mongolian Empire, and eight percent of them were related to Genghis Khan. They think that one out of every two hundred men in the world have that same marker. Cool huh?"

Everyone's eyes swung back to Dante.

"So he could have fathered lots of litters and left his flame-point Siamese marker behind."

"Well, his contribution to the gene pool is about to end." I started preparing for the day's treatments.

"Does cat and dog, uh, sperm, you know, uh, look alike?" Nick, our part-time tech, asked. Currently enrolled in community college, he usually had a million questions. His query prompted some laughs.

"That's a legitimate question, guys," I said. "They are two different species. Why don't you take some samples and we'll look under the microscope."

"Maybe I can use this for my biology research paper. So, what do I do? "

"Okay. We've got the cat, what about the dog? Is there an intact male somewhere?"

Everyone's eyes glanced around the hospital. We had a young female Dobie mix recovering from a run-in with a metal fence, a senior pug with a cyst, and a happy golden named Sally with a lacerated pad in a pink vet-wrap bandage.

"What about your dog?" Cindy asked. "You haven't neutered him yet, have you?"

"Buddy? No, I was waiting for his last few skin lesions to clear up. Sure, he can be your doggie volunteer."

◇◇◇

The rest of the day had its ups and downs. Our Dobie's surgery proved more complicated than I first thought since some of her injuries were punctures and some were flap wounds. Punctures don't get stitched up, but are allowed to heal by themselves after we clean them. If you sew up a puncture, you can trap bacteria in the wound since they tend to be deep. A flap wound is a different ball game because a piece of skin has lifted off the underlying tissue. Sometimes it will heal well when put back in place, and sometimes there is too much trauma. Oftentimes you can't determine how it will go until you are in the middle of surgery.

Our elderly pug sounded like he had breathing problems just walking across the hospital floor. With their squished-in faces and short, thick necks, pugs are an anesthesia nightmare. Modern veterinary anesthesia is much safer now for guys like this, but I doubled up on my surgical team and had two techs monitoring the patient for me. The longstanding cyst near his shoulder blades had grown to the size of a small kiwi. After quickly removing it, I was thankful this was a pug since he had rolls of extra skin to cover the surgical site. A wide excision and skin tuck, and he was good to go. However, none of us relaxed until Pugsley the pug gave up his endotracheal tube and offered up a hoarse bark.

With Mari watching everyone post-op, I made my way into the empty waiting room to speak to Cindy.

"So, have you been talking to your police chief brother-in-law recently?" I tried to sound casual about my question.

"What about?" She briefly glanced up at me then went back to her computer screen.

"The Langthorne deaths, of course. Are they still considered suspicious?"

She stopped what she was doing, a frown on her usually sunny face. "My sister says Bobby thinks it was murder, but he hasn't got any proof yet. The mayor is on his back to solve the case. It's hurting the real-estate market."

"Did they find the source of the ketamine?" Some drugs are specific to different manufacturers, and street drugs are usually cut with something to increase their profit.

"That I do know," she boasted. "It's from the same manufacturer that we get ours from."

I didn't know what to say. "I guess that's bad for me."

"It certainly isn't good."

For the first time I read a look of doubt on her face. If no one knew much about Pippi, the same thing could be said for me. Did anyone in town know the real Kate Turner?

Back in Doc's office I put my feet up and made my call backs. It had slowly started to feel like home over the last four months. I'd cleared an overhead shelf and stacked my textbooks and vet magazines on it. My pencil holder from college stood to the right of the computer. After passing our finals, two of my classmates and I went to one of those paint-the-pottery stores and made "We Survived Organic Chemistry" mugs with our names and date forever glazed on the side.

Looking back, we all thought our lives would be smooth sailing after we graduated. Boy, were we ever wrong. School was the smooth sailing part of our lives. We just didn't know it.

At home I hunkered down in front of my computer with a mug of jasmine-infused green tea. The aroma soothed me as I plugged in different search engines and began to work. I wanted to learn as much as I could about Pippi and her family. Public records probably would be the best place to start. I would have to backtrack from Pippi to her parents to her grandparents, which shouldn't be hard if they all were born in New York State. Otherwise I'd have to jump from database to database.

I started off with Pippi Langthorne's birth certificate and immediately saw something unusual. According to these records, Pippi was born here in the Hudson Valley, and the Langthornes—Vivian and Thomas—were listed as the parents, with a Manhattan address. Why come to upstate New York to have a baby, especially in the wintertime? Maybe she was premature, and they happened to be here visiting. I looked at the birth weight: six pounds, five ounces. Not a preemie.

Thomas had been five years younger than his wife, although by the time I met them you wouldn't have guessed that. There wasn't much difference between eighty and eighty-five, and both had been fit for their ages. Maybe Vivian had had some plastic surgery done, like so many ladies of her social class. Then I saw something that made me take out my calculator. I double-checked myself and then checked again. Vivian, according to the birth certificate, was fifty years old when she had Pippi. Fifty-five before the fertility revolution for a first-time pregnancy was an unheard-of age.

Which means Pippi could have been adopted.

But over thirty years ago, adoption agencies weren't giving babies to couples over forty.

Where did the baby come from? Maybe that was what Cindy was hinting at.

I finished my mug of jasmine green tea and got up to make another cup. Normally I add milk and sugar to my tea, drinking it like the English and Irish do, but this tea I preferred straight. Perhaps I would try a little lemon with this next cup. My hand was on the refrigerator door when it hit me. I knew what was wrong that day I discovered the Langthornes.

Chapter Fifteen

"Lemons?" Chief Garcia almost shouted into the phone. I involuntarily moved the phone away from my ear and sunk back into my office chair. "You think the Langthornes were murdered because they had lemons on their tea table?"

I would bet that the Chief had never sat down to a real English tea. "Thomas and Vivian always had their tea English-style, with milk and sugar. Not lemon. Milk curdles if you add lemon to it. Someone else must have sat down with them that day for tea."

"How do you take your tea, Dr. Turner?" His voice was suspicious.

"I take it the English way, with milk and sugar. Each time I had tea with them it was always the same: sandwiches, scones and butter, milk, and sugar. Vivian had a whole bag of frozen scones. It made it easy for her, she told me, because Thomas loved his scones."

"This isn't evidence," he insisted, becoming more and more annoyed.

I countered, "Then what the heck is it?

"Conjecture."

"Sorry, but it's all I've got at the moment." No way would I tell him about someone swapping look-alike dogs. I needed to preserve some believability. "Can't you go back into their house and check the teacups? Maybe the killer washed his plate and put it back."

"Pippi has closed down the house with most everything being put into storage preparing it for eventual sale. Even if there had been something, it would be compromised by now."

Chief Garcia sounded as frustrated as I felt. Maybe he was more of an ally than he let on.

"Did you read about Pippi getting a million dollars for one of the King Charles spaniels she inherited?"

"Yes." Now he sounded wary.

"That could be a motive for murder."

He cleared his throat. "I checked her alibi a hundred times exactly for that reason. She attended an all-day seminar on investing at the Richmond Hilton on Friday, culminating in a dinner and dance. All ten people at her table vouched for her, as well as her dancing partner, a retired judge, who escorted her to her hotel room at one in the morning after drinks at the bar. Since the coroner put time of death at between five and ten Friday night, Pippi is off the hook."

Since Pippi had a rock solid alibi I was now back to square one. I hung up the phone and got back to work. When I entered the exam room for my next appointment, I got a pleasant surprise. Mama G, owner of the Oak Falls Diner, sat waiting for me in a straight chair, her back to the wall. She wore a black dress with a lace collar. A gold crucifix on a thin gold chain hung around her neck. Her silver hair with streaks of dark gray was pulled into a tight bun. She stared as I entered the room, a frown fixed on her forehead, arms folded across her chest. I was sure she scared her staff half to death. To me she looked like a character from *The Godfather* come to life. A man in his late twenties, dark haired, about six feet tall, stood next to the exam table. Loud yowls came from the cat carrier on the floor. Although I knew Mama G by sight, I'd never formally met her, so I introduced myself.

"Good morning. I'm Dr. Kate Turner."

The man spoke first. "Luke Gianetti, and this is my grandmother."

An elderly Italian voice interrupted him. "Mama G. Call me Mama G. *Luca*, tell her what's wrong."

"Gatto is squatting in his litter box for a long time."

I assumed the cat meowing at full volume was Gatto. "Okay, let's take a look." As always, a list of possible diagnosis started running through my mind. I lifted the cat carrier up to the exam table and unlatched the door. Predictably, the cat that had probably put up a fight getting into his carrier now refused to leave it.

"How are you going to get him out?" Luke asked. "Do you want some help?"

"I'll be fine. It's either Plan A or Plan B."

His dark eyes reflected amusement. He wasn't what I'd call handsome, but something about his face made me smile. From the other side of the room I could feel Mama G's gaze on us.

"Plan A is gravity." I held the cat carrier over the table and slowly began to tilt it toward the ceiling, hopefully forcing the cat to walk out the open door. Maybe fifty percent of the time it worked, but not this time. Even with the carrier at a right angle to the table, Gatto was clinging to it with every paw he had.

"So what is Plan B?" he asked in a deep voice.

"Deconstruction." With the carrier back on the table, I proceeded to take out all the screws and knobs holding the top and metal gate onto the bottom of the carrier. Soon Gatto was revealed, still wedged in his carrier, which now had no top to protect him. He stopped howling and began to look around.

Noting from the look of his face that he was definitely a senior citizen, I began to examine the orange tabby while taking a history from his owner. Some of the answers were in Italian, which Luke translated. With the cat more relaxed, the exam went quickly.

I finished and scratched my patient under his chin, then turned to the humans in the room. "So, let me sum it up. His only symptom is straining in the litter box. Gatto is eleven years old and very healthy. He doesn't go outside anymore and eats cat food plus some people food."

"He likes my Bolognese," Mama G added.

"She's talking about her Bolognese sauce for pasta," explained Luke. "I don't blame him. I love it too."

As if he understood, Gatto licked his chops with a very pink tongue.

Everyone laughed, and Luke reached out to pet the cat. Immediately his kitty rump soared toward the sky and his tail stuck up. Then he turned around in his carrier and head-butted the hand that had just petted him, as if asking for more.

"He's not too sick to appreciate being petted, which is a very good sign," I told the owners. Luke flashed me a sly smile. The warmth in his eyes made my troubles vanish for a moment, a very attractive man.

Obviously worried about her cat, Mama G said, "*Dottore,* what's wrong with my Gatto?" I knew she wanted answers. This woman, who in her seventies actively ran a restaurant, didn't beat around the bush.

"Mama G, I'm not sure yet. He isn't obstructed, meaning his bladder is empty, but he needs to stay with us so I can run some tests and watch him in the litter box. We need a urine and stool sample and possibly an X-ray or ultrasound."

A stream of Italian directed at Luke had me at a loss. At first I thought they were arguing, but then Luke laughed and shook his head. The gold cross around her neck shone as she got up and went over to the cat. With a gentle touch and voice she spoke to Gatto; the cat rubbed against her and purred. Luke caught my eye and gestured toward the door.

"I'll send my technician in to admit him," I told them both. When I started for the exam room door, Luke followed me. Outside, he drew me over to a quiet corner of the waiting room.

"How bad is it?" Concern filled his eyes.

"Honestly, I don't know at this point," I answered, conscious of how close he was. "But there hasn't been any weight loss, his heart and lungs and lymph nodes are all normal, and he doesn't appear to be depressed. It could be a bladder stone, cystitis, or just constipation."

He nodded. "You're doing kidney function tests?"

"Yes, and a CBC—that's a full blood cell count."

"My girlfriend's an ER nurse. I guess I've picked up some of the medical lingo after three years."

Girlfriend was all I heard. I felt guilty even thinking about how neat this guy was. He belonged to someone else.

Annoyed at myself for letting my personal life creep into my work, I got back to practical issues. "Who should I contact with an update, your grandmother?" My concern was explaining medical issues over the phone and being understood.

He shook his head. "No. Mama G wants me talk to you. That's why she brought me along."

"Okay. Give the receptionist all your information and I'll call you as soon as I know something. She'll go over the treatment plan and estimate too. I expect Gatto will be here for at least one or two days."

Luke nodded, began to walk away, then abruptly stopped. "Thanks for all your help, Dr. Turner. Let me go back and explain everything to my grandmother."

I watched his broad back disappear into the exam room before I could say "Kate; please call me Kate."

For the next half hour I sat at the computer in the treatment area, updating my charts and making sure all the lab test results were entered into my patient records. Preliminary tests on Gatto indicated he might be suffering from constipation, probably from a combination of age, diet, and spinal arthritis. However, we still needed to get a urine sample from him to check for problems in the urinary tract. Our patient happily munched down on some high-fiber canned food after giving us a huge stool sample that was much harder than normal.

"How is Mama G's cat?" my technician Mari asked.

"So far, everything looks good. I'll know more by tomorrow." I finished loading in my notes and I logged out. "Her grandson seems like a nice guy."

Still cleaning and putting away things on the shelves where they belonged, Mari didn't answer right away. Since she normally chatted like crazy about everyone, I wondered if Luke had some terrible secret I was about to hear.

"You're right. He's a very nice guy, too nice for that girlfriend of his."

Who could let a statement like that stand without demanding some kind of answer? Certainly not me. In a casual tone I asked, "What do you mean by that?"

She checked the door to make sure we were alone. With a shake of her dark curls she started in. "Luke has been going out with the same girl since high school. Her name is Dina Chassen, former cheerleader, queen of the senior prom, voted most popular in the yearbook. You get the picture. My sister was in their class and, boy, the stories she told me about Princess Dina would surprise you. Her dad is an Episcopalian minister, but you wouldn't know it from some of the wild things she did. Behind that pretty face is a mean little liar."

"So why is he still with her?" Even as I asked I knew the answer. Love. Like my Gramps always said, there are only two motives in life: love and money. Everything else is a variation on a theme.

Mari confirmed my answer. "He loves her, I guess. Also, he feels some kind of obligation to her. Luke went away to college, and for the next three years they were on and off. His senior year, when he came back for Christmas break, they went to some party and had a big fight. People said they broke up that night. Anyway, he drove her home, skidded on some ice, and the car ended up in a ditch. He only had minor injuries, but she broke a whole bunch of bones plus had to have her spleen removed. From what my sister said, she almost died. Luke quit college so he could be with her and took a job with the Oak Falls Police Department. That was five years ago. They've been together ever since."

"Engaged?"

"Yes, for the last year. No date set, though. You know the weird part? She fractured her nose and facial bones in the accident. When they put her back together, the plastic surgeons made her prettier than ever. With my luck I'd have ended up like Quasimodo."

I thought about my long nose. My friends said it gave my face character. I wasn't so sure.

"Why all the questions? Are you finally interested in something besides work, Kate?"

I heard Gatto digging furiously in his litter box filled with a special nonabsorbent material. It broke the chain of conversation for a moment while we watched him give us a urine sample. As Mari opened the cage, I answered her question in a rather indignant voice.

"I don't mind being alone for now. It's working for me."

Mari shot me a disbelieving look. Even Gatto the cat looked at me as though not convinced.

That made three of us.

Chapter Sixteen

It turned out that Gatto only needed a dietary change since his lab tests all came back normal. The big orange tabby would be on a higher-fiber diet and a supplement to help him maintain regular bowel habits. He did, however, continue to meow at us big-time while here in the hospital. Cindy called Mama G to pick him up, who in turn said she'd send Luke.

Instead of coming at five p.m., he made special arrangements to pick up the cat at eight-thirty, when he got out of class. Because we knew he had a grueling schedule, between the police force and attending college, we were happy to accommodate him. Mari offered to stay, but since I was already babysitting a pregnant Persian cat, I told her I'd release Gatto. Living in the same building as the hospital made my commute pretty easy.

Just past eight-forty-five the doorbell to the hospital rang. Buddy started to bark and stayed close to my heels as I glanced out the front window to see Luke waving at me, a flat takeout box from the Oak Falls Diner in his hand.

"Thanks for letting me come by so late," he said as he came up the stairs. "I was at class."

He was dressed in a dark suit and tie. I quieted Buddy with a stand down command and closed the door after him. "I brought some pie for your staff."

"Thanks. Right now you're looking at the staff." Still dressed in the scrubs I put on this morning at seven, I definitely felt a little grubby. Since I now was acting as a midwife for an anxious cat, I certainly wasn't about to change clothes.

Luke followed me into the break room and put the takeout box on the table. Before we had a chance to talk, a low, weird yowl echoed throughout the treatment area. "Sounds like we have kittens coming," I told him over my shoulder as I walked over to the white Persian's cage. Sure enough, a kitten was trying to come into the world, feet first.

We'd set up a low cardboard birthing box in the cage so I could keep track of her labor.

"I might need some help," I told Luke, as I gloved up and lubricated my finger. This was the first kitten, and first kittens usually took the longest. Once the mom delivered a kitten, then the others could pop out pretty fast. Persians' big heads and flat noses didn't always make for easy deliveries.

Drawing up some oxytocin to stimulate contractions if we needed it, I examined Snowflake. She was too busy to pay any attention. Every few seconds she twisted and turned, meowed and growled, at the same time biting at the pillowcase as her labor continued.

I pulled up a rolling stainless steel table with another cardboard box on it and flipped on a portable surgical light for warmth. Nearby I'd assembled a crash cart, along with several small towels, some hemostats, and suture material.

"In the health care area, I've delivered a few babies," he volunteered, looking around calmly.

I had planned on doing it all myself but welcomed some help. "Can you glove up?"

He was staring into the cage. "I've got a surgical gown here you can put over your suit."

Without any prodding he slipped it on over his clothes and began pulling on the exam gloves. He finished just in time because Snowflake cried and out popped a kitten still in the umbilical sack. She stared at it like she had no idea what it was. It wasn't moving. Quickly I opened the sac, cleared the tiny kitten's mouth and began rubbing its chest and face with a terrycloth towel. The roughness, like the mother's tongue, would help to stimulate respiration. I clamped the umbilical cord with a hemostat, tied a hand suture below it, then cut above the tie. The baby opened its mouth as though yawning. Holding it almost upside down, I continued to compress the chest gently and saw fluid bubbles come out of its nose. Finally we were rewarded with a loud mewing sound.

"We've got another," Luke told me.

"Here you go." I handed off the kitten and went for the next one. "Put it under the light to keep it warm and check the umbilical cord for bleeding." The next one didn't need as much help. After hearing her kittens meowing, new mom Snowflake sprang into action. Before you knew it we had four little kittens screaming their heads off. After I examined them all, I gently put them back in with their mom who immediately began washing them off while they searched for their first meal in her long fur.

"That was fun. What now?" Luke stripped off the gloves like a professional and threw them into the medical waste garbage. I did the same. He had a big grin on his face. Some guys would be uncomfortable with a cat in labor, but Mama G's grandson managed to make it look easy.

"I've got to wait here for a while and make sure she's okay with the kittens. We X-rayed her yesterday so I know there were only four, but I'd like to make sure they're all nursing and purring away."

"Well, then I'll bring the party to you." Without another word he disappeared into the break room, coming back out a few minutes later with one of the small round folding tables and two chairs. He set it up next to the cage, then disappeared again, and returned with the takeout box, a handful of forks, and a fistful of napkins.

I clapped my hands. "If this is pie, then I'm officially in heaven."

"Well, open the pearly gates and walk right in. Today's special and my personal favorite: blueberry pie."

We washed our hands in the treatment table sink before we stuffed ourselves with pie. I fetched some milk from my refrigerator, poured it into two wineglasses, and toasted my surgical assistant. Before I noticed, we'd talked for over an hour. By then Snowflake had proven herself a good mom, snuggling her sleepy milky-mouthed kittens.

"I almost forgot. Isn't your grandmother going to worry about you?" My watch said ten-thirty.

"She's asleep by eight o'clock. Do you believe that even at her age she still gets up at four a.m. and starts baking? I'm supposed to put Gatto on his special chair in the living room."

I looked at my watch again, feeling bad I'd kept him here so long. He must have noticed because he said, "I should go now." But he didn't move.

With an effort I stood up and went to get Gatto's carrier. Mari had left all his medications and instructions in a white paper bag with the clinic's name on it. The bill had already been paid by Mama G earlier in the day. After I loaded a reluctant Gatto into the carrier, I turned to Luke.

"Thanks for staying. You were a great help."

"Do you know how much nicer this is than arresting people?"

We laughed and I started toward the front door where his car was parked. A thought occurred to me. "You know, I meant to ask you. What class did you come from?"

"My pre-law class. We had mock trials scheduled tonight." With his left hand he touched his tie. I noticed an Irish claddagh ring on his fourth finger, the heart pointing toward his wrist. It signified that his heart was taken.

He caught me looking at it. "I'm engaged."

"Congratulations," I answered with more enthusiasm than I felt.

I remembered the story Mari had told me about the automobile accident and his decision to drop out of school and stay with his girlfriend, Dina. Not for the first time this evening I felt she was a lucky girl.

"I better get going. Thanks for all your help with Gatto. My grandmother really loves this cat." Lifting up the carrier he continued toward the door. This time I tagged behind.

"Good night," I said. "Make sure you let me know if there are any problems with the kitty."

"Of course I will." He stood at the door, a funny look on his face.

"This was fun," I repeated, somewhat at a loss for words. "I don't know a lot of people outside work."

"Well, next time Dina and I have a party, I'll be sure to include you. That way you can meet the cream of Oak Falls and surrounding hamlets." The corners of his eyes folded into crinkles as he smiled.

Uncomfortable tightness squeezed my chest. My hand had a death grip on the door. "Thanks again for helping out. Good night. Give my best to Mama G."

"Good night, Kate," he called over his shoulder on his way down the steps.

I watched him walk away and get into his car.

I stayed at the door, my gaze fixed, until his taillights faded into the distance.

Chapter Seventeen

On the following Tuesday I finally met Oak Falls' most famous citizen, or rather, his cat. Without the truck's GPS I would never have found his place, set far off the road and unmarked except for an iron gate. After several seemingly random bends in the road, the electronic voice cautioned me in a British accent that my turn was coming up. Even with that guidance I almost missed the turnoff, barely pulling up in time. Twelve-foot-tall stone walls circled the property with what looked like shards of glass embedded in concrete along the top.

Someone didn't want company.

As instructed, I entered a code that opened the gate. Once I was inside, the vague air of menace disappeared. Instead I found a bucolic scene that could have been part of the English countryside. The rolling hills studded with huge oak trees and pastures beckoned me to take off my shoes and run in the bright green grass. Slowing the truck, I lowered my window and smelled damp earth and the sharp tang of pine. I continued past a small herd of horned West Highland cattle busy grazing on hay, their long coats still shaggy from the winter. To the right, a curious sorrel gelding broke away from his pasture buddies and whinnied me a welcome.

Further down the road on a small rise, a weathered barn sat back from the main building— a two-story stone home with a large wraparound porch. A figure walked down the steps and waved to me, accompanied by two black-and-white border collies who danced around at the base of the stairs barking and wagging their tails.

This wasn't the famous Hollywood movie director, Joel Denny. Instead, a small girl, about eleven or twelve years old, a worried look on her face, waited for me. Very pale, with light blue eyes and translucent complexion, she resembled a character in a fairy tale, without the wings.

"It's okay. Stand down," she told the dogs. Obviously well trained, they went off guard but kept an eye on me. "Are you the veterinarian?"

"Yes. I'm Dr. Kate Turner." I bent down to pet the now-relaxed border collies, their intelligent brown eyes smiling at me.

"I wanted you to look at my cat because I'm worried there might be something wrong." Her face scrunched up in concentration while she pushed her flaxen hair behind her ears. "My dad doesn't think so. But I do," she stated in a determined voice.

After one last shake of the collies' paws I said, "Well, let's find out."

"I'm Miranda." She opened the front door, giving the dogs a hand signal to stay. "And our cat's name is Jimmy."

Two abstract paintings hung in splendid isolation, the only color on the bright white walls of the wide hallway. What had looked like an old farmhouse on the outside looked completely modern on the inside. A soaring two-story living space on the left was punctuated by a massive stone fireplace rising in the middle of the room, open on both sides. Off to the side, the dining room gave a glimpse into a gleaming kitchen.

"We can take the elevator if you prefer," she advised me, her speech pattern somewhat formal. I wondered how many kids she hung out with on a daily basis.

"Stairs are fine." I followed Miranda up the graceful staircase to the second floor.

"He's in my bedroom." She carefully opened it a crack, checking to make sure her kitty wasn't behind the door waiting to escape. We walked into a room filled with bookcases. On the four-poster bed staring at us with big green eyes lay a striped tabby cat.

"Miranda," I said as I sat down in an armchair near the window seat, letting the cat get used to my presence, "tell me why you think Jimmy is sick."

"Well…" She sat down on the bed and gave him a pet. "He's always hungry, and I feed him all the time, but he isn't getting fat. I think he's lost weight. Also, he's waking me up at night, and he never used to do that."

I watched the thin cat relax as she stroked his dry fur. He head-butted her and then stared at me from the safety of her arms.

"How old is Jimmy?"

"We're not sure. Jimmy showed up here the day I was born, my dad said. I tell people about it all the time." She smiled telling the familiar story. "I was born in January, during a snowstorm. Jimmy showed up at the door meowing right after Daddy got home from the hospital. It was an omen, he said."

I smiled too. "So, then, how old are you?"

"I'm almost thirteen."

That brought another smile to my face. Here it was June, but she couldn't wait to be a year older. Those were the days.

"So if Jimmy was an adult when your dad found him, he is at least thirteen, maybe older."

"That's right."

I stood up and felt for my stethoscope. "I think it's time I meet Jimmy." The cat looked up at me as I sat down on the bed. After letting him sniff me, I began to examine him.

Without blood tests I couldn't be sure, but I had a pretty good idea what could be wrong. As I held the cat in my lap with one hand, I slid the other down his head and neck, gently petting and palpating for abnormalities. Under his coat he felt bony, and I quickly discovered a small nodule on the side of his thyroid gland located in the middle of his neck. Even though Jimmy seemed calm, my stethoscope picked up a heart rate of over two hundred and twenty beats per minute. Much higher than it should be. Using both hands to steady the cat, I continued to palpate along his spine, briefly checking his kidneys, then concentrating on his abdomen. I'd do a more complete exam later, but for now this would do.

"Well, Miranda, you're right. Something is wrong with Jimmy, but I think it's something that we can treat."

"What is it?" She hugged him close to her chest, her pale face stricken.

"I think his thyroid is making too much thyroid hormone. It's located here," I pointed to my own neck, "and helps control his metabolism. I felt a bump on it. Do you understand?"

"Yes," she nodded her head. "Our cook, Sylvia, takes pills for her thyroid. She says it's why she is plump, but I think it's because she eats a lot."

"She probably has just the opposite problem. Her body doesn't have enough thyroid hormone. Too much thyroid hormone is why Jimmy has lost weight."

I looked around Miranda's room, wondering if she had a cat carrier. If not, I had a spare one in the truck. But I had a more pressing problem than that.

"Is your father or mother around? I need their permission to take Jimmy to the animal hospital for tests."

"Mom's on location in Budapest, but I can text Dad." She pulled out an iPhone and proceeded to text her father at lightning speed. Within seconds her phone rang.

"Dad, the vet needs to talk to you." She thrust the iPhone at me.

At first it felt awkward speaking to the famous Joel Denny and advising him of the need to admit Jimmy for testing. But, like his daughter, his only concern was for the cat. In fact, I found him both calm and intelligent on the phone, not the eccentric recluse the tabloids made him out to be. After getting his permission, I handed Miranda back her phone.

"Can I visit Jimmy?"

"Sure you can, but I don't expect him to have to stay more than one day. I'll have most of my lab results tonight and the rest by tomorrow morning." Because of the advances in veterinary laboratory equipment and in-house tests, I would be able to rule out diabetes and primary kidney disease and confirm my diagnosis of hyperthyroidism in a few hours. If all went as planned, I could start him on his medications tonight, and release him in the morning after we discussed the several treatment options available to them.

"What does Jimmy like to eat, Miranda?" I asked.

"He munches his dry food all day and mostly tuna at night. Should I take out his carrier?" Her voice still sounded worried.

"Sure. Tell you what. When I get to the hospital I'll take a picture of Jimmy and send it to your phone. Will that make you feel better?"

Her face beamed. "Could you? He always sleeps with me at night. I'm going to miss him."

"And he'll miss you." I leaned over and looked at her. "You did the right thing calling me, Miranda. Jimmy is lucky to have you taking care of him." With that I gave her a high-five and we loaded the cat into his carrier for the trip to the hospital.

As I drove away from the house, a loudly meowing Jimmy in his carrier belted in on the passenger side, I felt happy. Left untreated, hyperthyroidism could have been a death sentence, but now my diagnosis and treatment would be a lifesaver for this dearly loved pet. With everything going on, the mysteries surrounding the Langthornes and the dog show shooting and my attempts to uncover the truth, it felt good to be practicing medicine. I became a vet because I loved animals and wanted to help them. It was just that simple.

Until I got back to the clinic and *simple* hit the fan.

The first thing that tipped me off were the two police cars parked in front of the entrance and Sandy arguing with one of the cops on the front steps. From the size and shape of him, it looked like Police Chief Garcia had struck again.

In the few months I'd been here, I'd had more contact with the law than in my previous twenty-eight years. Strangely enough,

I was getting used to it, like I was stuck in an endless episode of *The Practice.*

Cat carrier in hand, I got out of the truck and walked into the discussion. Nobody stopped long enough to take a breath or say hello to me.

"A search warrant is in the works," I heard Chief Garcia say.

"Bobby, I can't believe you are even thinking about going through Doc's files." She shook the broom she had in her hand for emphasis.

I learned something at that moment. From Sandy's attitude I figured she must know him very well. They both were red-faced and having one of those standoffs you knew couldn't end well. I glanced at the good-looking officer with dark curly hair leaning against the squad car taking everything in. It was Luke. He was laughing, his arms crossed over his chest. Then he waved at me.

"Time-out, guys." I walked up the stairs past both of them. "Sandy, we need to draw some blood, stat." I opened the clinic door and headed back to the treatment room. In a moment the door opened again, ringing the chimes, and I heard footsteps following me down the hall.

"This is getting worse and worse," Sandy muttered as she rumbled along past me. "Search warrant, my ass. He has some nerve."

I gave her a moment to calm down. "Did they leave?"

She mumbled, "Yes."

"Both of them?"

"Yes."

So Luke had gone. I felt disappointed. I'd half-expected them to follow us inside. On the other hand, I didn't want Chief Garcia to mention my lemon idea in front of Sandy. I'd never hear the end of it.

"Okay. What do you need?" Besides being the office manager, Sandy had been Doc's vet tech for over twenty years.

"A full blood profile, thyroid panel, FelV, FIV, urine analysis, fecal, and let's get a weight on him. Where is everybody?"

"I sent them home. We're all caught up with the hospital patients but I had paperwork to do so I decided to wait for you to get back. But Bobby showed up instead, the little know-it-all."

"He's just doing his duty, I guess."

"Sure. Who is this?" Her voice was particularly cranky as she organized the lab forms and test tubes.

I popped open the cat carrier and lifted the cat out. "Meet Jimmy Denny." The cat looked at us with those big green eyes, a stoic expression on his face as if this was just another trial in his nine lives. He didn't even complain when we drew his blood and repeated his exam.

The preliminary diagnostics taken care of, I told Sandy, "I'll set up the cage while you get the labs started."

I lifted Jimmy into my arms then labeled and put away his cat carrier. He would be staying in a double cat condo with sleeping shelves and communicating door to a separate space with his litter box. After I put a blanket, food, water, and the t-shirt Miranda put into his carrier on the sleeping side, I took a picture of the tabby cat and sent it to her phone. Then I set up the other side with a non-absorbable litter in his box which made collecting urine and feces a breeze. Gently I closed the cage, double-checking to make sure the lock had set. Finally, I slid a metal ring through the cage door eyelets, securing it from exploring cat paws that might try to slip open the cage. Jimmy looked like he could be a kitty Houdini.

Office hours being over, I waited on the back patio with Buddy while the tests were running. Sandy joined me, lit up a cigarette and cracked open a box of Cheez-Its. The preliminary thyroid hormone test confirmed hyperthyroidism in Jimmy so we started him up on the medication. Now we needed to find out if the disease had damaged any of his other organs. While we sipped our Diet Cokes the conversation came around to murder.

"Why do you think they want Doc's medical records?" I gazed up at a jet passing overhead.

"Because they don't have anything else to do," Sandy snapped back, clearly annoyed at the whole thing. "Those records are confidential and without Doc here there is no way anyone else is getting a look at them."

"That might not be possible," I began, trying to get a word in.

"Besides, Doc wrote all kinds of things in those records. He had codes like PIA or SAS for different clients that I don't think he'd want the world to know about.

"Okay, I get the PIA for Pain in the Ass, but what is a SAS?"

"He made it up. It stands for Stupid as a Stump."

That tickled me. I'd have to remember it.

Sandy took a drag from her cigarette. "One time the Langthornes had a litter of their King Charles spaniels that became sick with parvo virus. Those puppies were all show prospects and he shaved both front legs on each dog."

"So I wasn't the only one." I tossed a Cheez-It in the air but when it came down it missed my mouth and conked me on the nose. Buddy scooped it off the bluestone floor.

Sandy took another pull on her cigarette and continued. "Then he put a dab of nail polish on their heads, each with a different color, so we could quickly tell them apart. You should have heard the cuss words that came out of those old folks."

"They yelled at Doc?"

"They went ballistic. But Doc stood up and yelled right back at them…how he had saved their dogs lives and that this was a hospital not a damn doggy beauty parlor. He topped that off with a threat to write a letter to the AKC and Westminster expressing doubts on the validity of their stud records."

"Holy mackerel!"

"Needless to say they immediately calmed down and even apologized to Doc." Sandy reached into the box and took a fistful of crackers.

Something she said bothered me. "Do you think Doc was bluffing about the stud records? Those are super important for a breeder."

"I'm pretty sure he was. However we noticed as Thomas and Vivian got older their record-keeping started getting very sloppy. Sometimes they confused one dog for another. But for the most part I think they are accurate." Sandy took a sip of Diet Coke then tossed more crackers in her mouth. "We did see more mixed breed King Charles spaniels in the last few years. Your dog looks like one of them. Periodically one of their females in heat would escape from the backyard kennels and who knows what happened while they were gone."

We both looked at Buddy sleeping peacefully at my feet. With his now short tail and scars he did look like some kind of mix. Only his beautiful head showed his breeding.

I sat for a moment, thinking. What if Doc wasn't bluffing; what if he knew something?

Or what if someone paid a lot of money for a dog with the wrong bloodline? After getting acquainted with some of the dog show breeders I wouldn't put anything past them. Including murder.

Sandy continued her questions. "What am I supposed to do if they come back with that search warrant? Doc put me in charge while he was gone. I can't remember half the stuff he wrote in the Langthorne file."

"Why?"

She flipped a Cheez-It in the air and caught it in her mouth. "For one thing, his handwriting is difficult to read and of course, he's got his private shorthand remarks."

"I bet they got classified as PIA."

"No. They were CFH."

"CFH? What does that stand for?"

Sandy lowered her voice even though there was no one around. "That's his shorthand for the worst kind of client."

I frowned. "CFH?"

"Client from Hell."

By ten that night Sandy and I had read through all of the records Doc had on the Langthornes. There were hundreds of pages over the last ten years. We'd even pulled the dead records to be extra thorough. My eyes burned from trying to translate Doc's chicken-scrawl handwriting. Thank goodness he switched to computerized records three years ago.

Most of the calls were pre- or post-whelping visits. One thing you had to say about Doc's medical records, he was meticulous in jotting down all the details on number of pups, sizes, health of the bitch, and any distinguishing features or problems.

"I need to cross-reference some of these, so we can draw up a breeding chart," I told my office manager, who looked as tired as I felt.

"I'll help you tomorrow. My bed is calling," she said, standing up and stretching. "I've got some big sheets of paper we can tack up on the wall. It should make things go faster," the last part of the sentence muffled by a yawn. "I don't know what you expect to find, though."

"If we're lucky, maybe some kind of clue to their murders. Maybe the old couple's pattern of threatening to sue people backfired on them big-time."

"What do you mean by that?"

"It's hard to file a lawsuit when you're dead."

We walked to the reception area door. No one else was around, which was good, or bad, depending on your outlook. Normally the parking lot looks inviting with all the mature trees providing lots of shade and the long driveway setting us back from the road. Tonight it seemed sinister.

"See you tomorrow," I called out before she slammed the car door shut.

After I locked the front door I wiggled the handle to make sure the deadbolt had been thrown, then set the alarm. Doc had sensors on all the windows and doors, but no motion sensor inside the building because the animals were always setting it off.

Jimmy meowed at me as I passed his cage. I gave him a pat through the bars and made sure he had everything he needed for his overnight stay. We had texted Miranda to call us in the morning and arrange a time to pick him up and go over his lab work. It was Sunday, but I knew a little girl who would be very happy to get her furry friend back.

What was I achieving by looking at Doc's breeding records? I wasn't sure, but since someone obviously switched the Langthornes' champion dog I wanted to know why. Was the key hidden somewhere in their records? I certainly couldn't figure out a motive. I'd missed an opportunity to discuss the murders with Luke the other night. For some reason talking about the deaths with him had slipped my mind.

While getting ready for bed I analyzed why living in the hospital apartment suddenly had made me feel uneasy. No neighbors, no streetlights. What would happen if someone cut the electricity, bypassing the alarm, in the middle of the night like they did in the murder mystery I just finished reading? Buddy lay sound asleep in his bed. So far he hadn't exhibited many signs of being a watchdog. With that happy thought I pulled the covers up to my ears and turned off the light. My hand checked the nightstand for my cell phone.

It was right next to my Christmas gift from Gramps: a dainty container of pepper spray.

Chapter Eighteen

Jimmy the cat went home early Sunday morning awash in a flood of happy tears from Miranda, who arrived with a chauffeur and her father's Swedish personal assistant, Astrid. As if ordered up from Hollywood, the sky shone a brilliant blue with a few plump cumulus clouds scattered like puffs of whipped cream. Joel Denny, Miranda's father, busy working on a new film starring Ryan Gosling, would keep up-to-date via texts and email. In the next few days the entire entourage was scheduled to fly back to their home in Beverly Hills on a private jet. Jimmy included.

Packed into the crowded exam room together, Astrid, who turned out to be both beautiful and efficient, took notes for her boss on an iPad and asked me several intelligent questions about the surgical and radioactive iodine options available to treat the cat. Being pro-active, she had Googled hyperthyroidism in cats.

I couldn't figure out if Astrid had started out as Miranda's nanny but now handled general staff duties as well. Their reality seemed like something from the old TV program "Lifestyles of the Rich and Famous." However, when Astrid kissed Jimmy on the head and began talking to him in Swedish I warmed up to her, because, realistically, she couldn't help being effortlessly gorgeous.

Miranda's face had lost its pinched look and she insisted on learning how to give Jimmy his pill. Convincing Jimmy to get into his carrier was another story but finally we all walked down the front steps to their black Mercedes sedan. Stuffed into his carrier along with several toys and his favorite blanket, Jimmy ended up securely belted in the backseat next to Miranda.

I waved as they pulled out of the hospital parking lot and disappeared down the road. The air smelled fresh with a light breeze blowing from the west, a beautiful day. Maybe I could squeeze in a short hike this afternoon. After a final look around I went back inside and locked the clinic door, shutting inside the flickering florescent lights and slight medicinal smell that created an artificial landscape of its own.

I settled into the familiar therapeutic environment of my office, sipping the dregs of my coffee, and returning to work on the breeding chart. It was slow-going at the start. Each time Doc noted a birth in his notes I wrote down the sire's and dam's names, the number of pups whelped, and their AKC whelping number. After an hour of extrapolating, things started to shape up. It became obvious that the Langthornes used a breeding technique called line breeding, in which the bitch was bred back to a relative other than her father and brothers. The male used had to have an ancestor in common with the female. Their favorite participant, over and over, was Charles Too. In fact, most of their younger dogs had Charles Too as an ancestor on one or both sides, which explained why their dogs all looked so much alike. Unfortunately, although this technique standardized the look of the dogs it could increase any genetic problems.

The front door chimed.

Someone had come into the clinic. Where was a pit bull when you needed it?

"Hello. Are you here, Kate?"

Sandy's familiar raspy voice made me realize how jumpy I felt recently being alone in the building.

"I'm in the office," I yelled, then turned to refill my coffee from the Mr. Coffee machine.

"Look who I found wandering around outside."

"I've been wondering where Mr. Katt was hiding out." The hospital cat had a habit of sneaking out the back door and sitting under the bird feeder. "We've got to find a better way of keeping him out of trouble."

"That's what they all say." Not Sandy's voice that time, and definitely not the cat talking.

I swung the desk chair around so fast it felt like a Tilt-A-Whirl ride. A wave of coffee slipped over the cup rim and sloshed onto my shirt.

My former boss/boyfriend leaned against the door jamb, arms crossed, with that easy elegance he had in spades. Brooks Brothers shirt, leather jacket, perfectly cut jeans, and well-worn Frye boots. Country sophisticated rat.

"Hey, Jason." I tried to keep my voice casual. Damn he looked good. "What brings you up here? Need to see the country folk at play?"

My lame attempt at sophisticated banter hung between us like wet laundry on the line.

"I've missed you, Kate." He gave me that familiar crooked smile.

I put the coffee down and looked around for some water. Maybe I could get the stain out if I worked fast. "Did you bring Tiffany with you?"

A deep sigh slid out followed by a pursing of his lips. "We've had a fight."

In my mind I jumped up and fist-pounded the air. *Yes!* A movie scenario leapt inside my head starring Jason and me in a happily-ever-after film, the evil girlfriend vanquished. In the real world however I simply dabbed at the spots on my blouse and said, "That's too bad. What did you fight about?"

"Oh, the usual, you know." He walked over and sat down in the extra chair in front of the desk. "She's so young," he added, as if it had only now occurred to him.

Way too young for you! I yelled in my private film which was becoming Academy Award material.

"Want some coffee?" My mind raced ahead with lightning speed. Is he here to tell me he dumped the girlfriend? Before

I knew it my crazy fantasy included a wedding on Martha's Vineyard and two kids.

"Sure."

"Do you still take it black?" I smiled an inane smile as though I had remembered the secret to life.

He nodded. I handed him some coffee. Real life didn't hold a candle to how I imagined this script would go.

"So, how's work going? Seems kind of slow."

"It's Sunday. We're closed."

"How's your surgical load up here?"

"Well, more animals go outside so I see a good amount of trauma cases."

"It's always something," he agreed.

I noticed that we were having a dull work-related conversation. With reluctance I closed down the romantic movie set in my head and fired the director.

Now it was my turn to nod, like a tennis game.

"This is great. Just like old times," he took a sip from his mug, "even the bad coffee."

"I should have let Sandy make it. You've introduced yourselves, right?"

He leaned back and looked around Doc Anderson's office. "A little long in the tooth for the job, don't you think?" Not bothering to lower his voice he kept at it. "She should retire. A pretty face at the front desk would do wonders for this place."

His remark annoyed me. That's why he hired Tiffany and look where it got him. Now I remembered how obliviously he scattered hurtful remarks wherever he went and how I always found an excuse for it. This might not be my veterinary practice but I felt loyal to it and to Sandy just the same. "Our clinic may be older but we do just fine. I think I've seen more interesting cases here in the last four months than in the two years I worked for you."

"Really?" He raised his right eyebrow in disbelief.

"Yes, really." I tried to match his expression but only succeeded in squinting at him.

Sandy poked her head in, breaking the impasse. "I've finished up. Everyone is doing fine. Kate, Smokey's owners are picking up in the morning."

"Okay, thanks," I told her. "Enjoy the rest of the weekend."

"Nice to see you again, Doctor." Her eyes went back and forth between us. "Why don't you two go out and enjoy the rest of the day? Go ahead," she swooshed us out with her fingers. "Take her out of here. She works too much."

"Good-bye, Sandy." I said forcefully, hoping she would leave before saying anything else.

"That's a good idea." Jason rose from the chair and held out his hand. "Come on, let's take a walk."

We walked down the side road perpendicular to the clinic, about three or four feet apart. The trees grew so thickly along this stretch that most of the sunlight ended up blocked by the top untrimmed branches. Even though the afternoon was warm the constant shade chilled the air. I pulled my coat closer and stuck my hands in my pockets.

"It's beautiful here." Jason picked up the pace, briskly walking a few feet ahead of me. "No wonder you like it so much."

"I've been too busy to notice," I replied, truthfully. "So much has happened, especially with the murders." My fingers searched for gum to get rid of the coffee breath.

"Oh, right. I forgot about that," he kicked a stone off to the side of the road. "How's that going?"

"Okay, I guess." Let's see. I remembered how he took his coffee but he forgot I'd discovered two bodies? Not to mention witnessed a shooting. Massive ego anyone? Why exactly have I been mooning over him?

"You know, I told you Tiff and I had a fight." He kicked another stone to the side of the road.

"Yeah, you mentioned that." I tried to kick a stone in my way but almost tripped on it.

"So, I was thinking…" He paused, as though I should be able to finish the sentence. "Some kind of trip would be a great idea. Get away from work and all the stress."

Was he asking me to go away with him?

He stopped dead in the road and turned to me. "So we can concentrate on the baby and the wedding."

"The wedding?" My feet refused to move, stunned by the news. They're getting married? Then what did he want me to do? Be their flipping travel agent? The skin on my face started to feel tight and hot.

"Anyway," he began to walk again. "I wanted to ask you to come back for a month and take over the practice. Tiff has never been to Europe. I figure that Venice would be fantastic this time of the year."

I stood in the middle of the road, still unable to move.

"It could be your wedding present to us, to me."

If heads could explode, mine would have shot into outer space.

"I, uh. I've got a contract here," I babbled, surprised I could even talk.

Jason laughed and it echoed down the asphalt. "Contracts are made to be broken. Besides, you're wasted at this place. I'll even start you with a five percent raise."

I choked back a laugh. He knew that was a pay cut from what I was making now.

"Hey," he continued, "I know it's a surprise. You don't have to answer right now. Why don't you come join Tiffany and me for lunch? She's shopping in the village."

Tiffany is here? I stared at him. For once a cat had gotten my tongue.

"I gave her twenty bucks to spend," he laughed and checked his watch. "She's probably blown through it by now."

"Jason," I shook my head in amazement. "You always were a cheap bastard."

"What?"

The cute little grin I used to like so much had vanished, replaced by a petulant look. Someone wasn't getting his way. I stood opposite him face-to-face and let him have it. "I won't break my contract with Doc Anderson so you can go on a

vacation with the Tiffster. You'll have to hire someone else."
I could almost hear the leaves of the trees applauding, "Great
catching up, on your news. Now excuse me, I've got work to
do." Anger flooded my system right down to my toes. I turned
and began to walk back toward the clinic.

"Kate?"

I picked up speed as I began to jog down the road. The sun
broke through an opening in the trees and dappled the ground
in front of me. That and my fury warmed me right up.

It hurts to peel a one-hundred-eighty-five-pound ex-boy-
friend off your back. The memories, the hopes…hell, all the
unresolved emotions. Not to mention what I spent on makeup,
clothes, and shoes. But now that it was finally over, it felt good.

Really good.

Chapter Nineteen

"So, you'll come to our party tomorrow?" My friends Tim and Tina called Friday night, after I'd spent the week seesawing from being happy I'd finally let go of Jason to feeling immensely sorry for myself.

"It's extremely spontaneous, but we just heard Maybelle has been released from the hospital. Everything Tina said sounded like it came with an exclamation point. Despite my mood, it was contagious.

"Sounds like fun. Are tails optional?"

My joke was rewarded with more peals of laughter. In the background I heard Tina repeat it to Tim.

"What a great idea! I'll shoot you an email with all the details and directions to the house. Bring someone if you want. Ciao."

She hung up before I asked if my special someone could have four legs.

Tim told me he marked the entrance to their driveway with balloons and streamers. By the time I got there it was almost two o'clock and cars were parked all along the stacked-stone walls that flanked the long driveway. After maneuvering past a grove of tall maples the road turned up a slight rise to reveal a circular cobblestone driveway with a spectacular fountain in the middle. Whoever installed the Greco-Roman statuary must have admired Bernini's work since I counted at least three cherubs, a lady whose dress seemed to be slipping off while getting water, and a naked guy with a spear. I had no idea Tim and Tina lived in a marble mansion. Set on a promontory surrounded by manicured lawns, the main house looked down on the Hudson River sparkling in the distance. It reminded me of a museum or an extravagant bed and breakfast, not a private home. I stopped counting Grecian-inspired columns which held up the wraparound porch. Off to the side the glitter of multi-paned windows on an old-fashioned greenhouse caught my eye. A pair of formal topiary Italian Cyprus flanked the carved mahogany front door. When I pressed the doorbell chime it rang one somber note. For a moment I felt like I had stepped back in time hundreds of years.

That lasted only for a brief moment.

"Party time!" My hosts flung open the door and greeted me exuberantly, tall drinks in one hand and something fluffy in the other. "Saw you in the driveway. Come on in."

"This place is gorgeous, just, unbelievable," I stammered.

"Inherited it from my Uncle Theodore," Tina explained as she thrust a lavishly garnished drink into my hand and escorted me inside through a granite foyer. "He was the black sheep of the family and a confirmed bachelor. Showed papillons, which is how I got interested in dog shows. I think I was the only member of the family he talked to. Thank God he left a trust fund to take care of the place."

As I followed I noticed each of my hosts had a tail attached to their pants.

About fifty people milled around in the largest living room I'd ever seen. Tina let go of my arm and clapped her hands. "Hey everyone, we'd like you to meet our good friend Kate Turner. Now be nice. She hasn't lived here long enough to know the dirt about all of you!" She punctuated her announcement with a contagious giggle.

"Okay, Kate. Let's put your tail on." Tim twirled me around and quickly tied a fluffy German Shepherd-like tail to my rear, looping the ties through my belt loops. I pleaded no to the pointed dog ears.

Then I realized everyone in the room was wearing a dog tail. Some had complemented their tails with dog ears and masks. Others had their faces made up. I felt like Alice tumbling down the tunnel.

I needed that drink in my hand.

Tim watched as I took a sip. "Hope you like it. We call it Hair of the Dog."

The amount of vodka in the Bloody Mary made my hair stand on end. With a burning throat I swallowed the first sip.

"So, what's new, Kate?"

The burn was followed by a blast of horseradish mixed into the tomato juice that cleared out my sinuses. I gave myself a moment to recover. "Nothing much, but I'm anxious to talk to Maybelle, to see how she's doing. Do you know where she is?"

"Our guest of honor is holding court over by the bay window." He gestured like Vanna White toward the front of the room. A cluster of people stood in front of a large purple sofa and chairs nestled in the circular space, windows rising up at least twenty feet behind them. You could clearly see the circular driveway and clusters of parked cars. As I watched, a familiar-looking blue truck with a double grid on the front bumper drove up, braked, then, quickly backed down the driveway. Somebody must have made a wrong turn. For a moment I thought it might be Sandy's truck, but why would she take off like that?

It was almost a half an hour before I got a chance to speak to Maybelle. Someone noticed me on the outskirts of her group and pushed me to the front, regaling everyone about how I saved her life on the day she was shot. Of course, that got me a big hug. I could smell baby powder on her neck, a lingering medicinal odor, and what looked like a fresh surgical scar tucked behind her ear.

"So glad to finally meet you and say thanks," she said, a slight tremor in her voice. "I'm afraid I don't have much memory of that day."

"Oh, I've got enough memory for both of us. It replays in my brain over and over." I took a sip of my drink. Maybelle slugged down half of hers. Even from that tiny sip my lips stung from the combination of hot sauce and vodka, but the rest of the guests seemed to have no problem chugging them down.

A hand plucked at my sleeve. Maybelle gestured me toward an iron bistro table overlooking the side garden. "I'd love to listen to what you saw, if you don't mind. I still have no idea why I was shot. The police haven't been able to help me much."

"If you think it won't upset you," I said, truthfully.

"My therapist insists it will help." Maybelle's eyes unfocused for a second then refocused on my face. She took my hand. Hers were cold and damp. "Go ahead." Both her palms squeezed mine. Part of me wanted to run away as fast as I could.

I pulled my hand away and pretended to look at my phone.

"Ah, let's see…" I stalled wondering why her touch made my skin crawl. "I was coming back from going to the…restroom, but I walked into the wrong side of the tent. You were in the show ring and the rest of the dogs were moving in a large circle around the judge."

She nodded, licked her lips expectantly.

"Then I heard two shots behind me and saw you clutch your chest. I climbed over the seats in front of me and ran to your side. My friend Tim yelled for someone to call 9-1-1, then he took off his sweater and used that as a pressure bandage. The Fire Department EMTs got to you in three or four minutes. Luckily they were assigned to provide emergency services to the show. We stepped aside while they worked on you. You were in shock, you never said anything to us."

"That's it?" She seemed annoyed.

Puzzled by her response I thought for a moment. "Well, yes. It happened so quickly. None of us saw the shooter. He must have been in the back of the tent."

"You didn't listen to my heart or give me any medication?" Her smile had turned into a scowl.

"No. The EMTs did all that."

"Damn." Maybelle stood up and smoothed out her skirt. "Well, thanks for nothing. By the way, didn't you find Thomas and Vivian Langthorne? After some of the things they pulled on me, I can't say I'm surprised at their deaths." With that cryptic remark she lost interest with me, then, added over her shoulder, "You've been a very busy girl."

That's weird, I thought, tempted to take another hit of my volcanic drink. What did she think I saw? Everything I remembered I told to the investigative team. Did she expect to learn new details from me or was something else on her mind? Why wasn't she surprised that Thomas and Vivian had been found dead in their house?

A roar of laughter exploded from a group of party guests clustered in front of a big-screen television in the living room. The screen showed a sweet-faced golden retriever sitting next to a torn-up sofa cushion. The dog was trying to look innocent as the owners asked him if he did something bad.

I laughed too.

Then I wondered if one of the suspects I'd talked to played innocent like that.

The buffet lunch had a doggy theme. After stuffing myself with gourmet hot dogs, mushroom canapés that looked like small piles of dog poop on a cracker, and dog-shaped pasta salad, I decided to head home. Maybelle studiously ignored me while periodically shooting a nasty stare at me. What I had done to piss her off was a mystery to me. I was sorry there wasn't more drama to my story. At the time it seemed dramatic enough. Perhaps she had post-traumatic stress disorder and somehow my presence ended up being part of it.

"Going so soon, Katie?" Tim slightly slurred his words. After watching him down a couple of those killer cocktails I was surprised he was still standing.

I gave him a hug. "Thanks for inviting me. It was fun."

"Did you get to mingle? I saw you with Maybelle. Did she thank you for saving her life?"

With the television acting as a background noise I lowered my voice and answered. "She wasn't too pleased with me and I don't know why."

He pulled me into the kitchen. Obviously not original to the house, it had been remodeled, stainless gleaming everywhere, even on the kitchen island which looked a little too much like a surgery table for my taste.

"Yep, she pulled that on me too. I just found out. She wanted to sue both of us for practicing medicine without a license."

"What?" That came out way louder than I expected it to. The sound bounced off the glass door cabinets and boomeranged back to us.

That echo struck him as insanely funny but his laugh ended up in a coughing spell. Finally he spit it all out. "Someone told her she could sue both of us because as veterinarians we aren't supposed to be practicing medicine on people. Can you believe it? After my wife and I are throwing this party for her." The irony of it made him laugh again.

I wished I could laugh along with him. My forehead wrinkled in a frown.

Tim continued. "Don't worry. We're covered by the Good Samaritan Act. Luckily all I did was press down on the wound with my sweater. Everything is on that video those Goth kids told you about. Seems all the teenagers there whipped out their phones so they could post it on YouTube."

"Thank goodness for technology," I said.

"No date with you today? What's up with that?" He gave me a big squishy hug. "You don't still have a thing for Dr. Perfect, do you?"

A quick denial almost escaped my mouth. "By Dr. Perfect I assume you mean Jason."

He reached behind me and pulled some paper towels off the roll then proceeded to clean up a spill from someone's cocktail glass. I thought he had decided to change the subject but I was wrong.

"Yes, I mean Jason. I remember him always reminding everyone about his perfect hospital, his perfect house, his perfect car, and his last perfect vacation—and now his perfect little fiancée. What is she? Nineteen?" With a flick of his wrist he threw the tomato juice-stained towel in the trash. It looked like blood. "Tell me you're ready to move on?"

I had a smart ass remark all ready. How I'd already called the movers and packed up my emotional baggage. How he tried to get me to quit my job and take over his practice while he went on his honeymoon. How I had a list of inconsiderate things he's said and done.

Instead I looked at my friend and told him the simple truth. "I think so."

◇◇◇

I drove over the Kingston-Rhinecliff Bridge toward home and took the turnoff to the animal hospital thinking about my conversation with Tim. Being three hours away from my past life in New York City gave me unaccustomed privacy. I lowered the window and smelled the fresh air. The truth was I had begun to recover from Jason. Why emotionally hold on to someone who is engaged and about to be a father? Did I think he would come to his senses and suddenly want me? The argument we'd just had sealed the deal. I'd begun to build a life away from him. I vowed not to make the same mistake with Luke. No more guys with strings attached. Lots of other things held my attention now. Maybe I would take time off to travel like Doc. Visions of a more popular, sophisticated me with better clothes played in my head until I rounded the corner and saw my old boss and former flame Jason standing next to his Porsche waiting for me in the hospital parking lot.

"What the hell are you doing here?" It wasn't much of a greeting but it felt pretty good to say it.

Jason's puppy dog eyes looked at me, hurt and disappointed, like I'd taken his bone away. And I was the bone.

"Don't be mad at me Kate. I'm sorry we argued last weekend. I had to get away from everything for a while."

By everything did he mean his extremely successful veterinary practice or his hugely pregnant teenaged girlfriend/fiance/ whatever? I didn't want to know.

"Do you want to go get a cup of coffee in the village?" After a quick chat I'd make up some excuse to dump him like he'd dumped me. Make him understand the days of dropping in on me are over.

He whipped out his cell phone. "That sounds good. How about that Judy's Place? She had great soup and sandwiches if I remember."

"Okay. I'll meet you there in a few." Before he could suggest going in one car I leapt into the truck and made my getaway, leaving him with yet another puppy dog face.

My face turned anything but kittenish when I strolled into Judy's Place twenty minutes later to find Jason and Tiffany in a corner table kissing over identical bowls of chili. I'd assumed wrongly again that he came to see me, that he'd come to realize he'd made a mistake and wanted me back. In my imaginary scenario I would break his heart by turning him down.

Instead he probably gave more thought to his lunch order than to me.

"So, what brings the two of you up here again?" I settled into the only empty seat at their table.

"Didn't Pookie tell you?"

I looked around for someone else, then realized who Pookie was.

Tiffany turned to me, her seven months' pregnant belly barely sliding under the table. "We're looking at wedding venues here and over in Rhinebeck. Like the Clintons."

"No, *Pookie* definitely left that out of our conversation." I gestured to the waitress for a cup of coffee.

"We were wondering if you knew any of the people we are working with. Maybe you could get us a discount?" she added hopefully.

"Oh." I tried to keep a smile on my face. Don't hold your breath, Tiff. Or better yet, why don't you and Pookie-face hold your breaths together for, say, a million years.

"Gee, I'd love to help," I lied, "but I don't know very many people in town."

She pushed a folder across the table to me, her manicured nails sporting pictures of daisies. "Here, we have a list."

I bet you do. Keeping my snarky comments to myself was getting harder to do. Luckily the waitress came by to refill my coffee. She caught sight of the folder on the table marked "Wedding Plans" and her face crinkled into a broad smile.

"When are you two getting married?" she asked as she topped off my cup.

I half listened to Tiff and Pookie chatting about venues and flowers and caterers, but mostly I looked at them. Really looked at them. Noticed how he clutched her hand, how she beamed up at him, how excited they seemed.

And I accepted that I'd lost this game of love. I was being a sore loser, hoping the ref would somehow intervene and award me the trophy. Standing alone in the stadium when I should have moved on.

"Hey," I interrupted, "a toast to the happy couple. Best wishes for a healthy baby, beautiful wedding, and a wonderful life." We lifted our cups and clinked glasses.

"Okay," I said, "let me see that list."

Chapter Twenty

"It's nice to get back to normal," Sandy commented as she ran through my list of appointments the next day.

"What do you mean?" I reached for my coffee and took a bite of my breakfast bagel.

She looked up from her paperwork. "You know. All the Langthorne stuff, you seeing suspects and conspiracies everywhere. If you ask me, you were starting to get obsessed with it."

"Obsessed?"

"That's right. Obsessed. We were all beginning to worry about you." I caught our tech, Mari, looking at me. She shrugged her shoulders and took a sip from her own coffee mug.

They both watched for my reaction. Time to put my amateur snooping on the down low, I thought. Can't have the people you work with thinking you've become a nut job.

"Well, now I'm back to my normal boring life here at Oak Falls Animal Hospital. So let's start the day before one of my patients tries to murder me."

I remembered those words as the sleepy gelding Lucero started to lean against his stall trapping me like the filling in an Oreo cookie. Not ready to be squished between a fifteen hundred-pound horse and a wall, I pushed back with my hands flat against his shoulder and he gracefully stepped to the side. Rita, the nervous owner of this backyard animal, hadn't even noticed, being too busy cooing and fretting over her big quarter horse.

Luckily, Lucero had a sweet gentle nature unaffected by his nervous caregiver. Normally I leave the horses to the equine practitioners, but after trimming an ingrown dewclaw on her elderly Shepherd mix, Rita asked me to take a look at her horse and the terrible cut she had just discovered on his rump.

"It's not really a cut," I explained to his worried owner. "It's an abrasion that has already started to heal. Has he been wormed recently?"

"Yes. Does it need stitches?" she asked with tears in her eyes.

I gave the big horse a pat as he nudged me with his nose looking for a treat. "No. But I'm going to leave some saline for you to clean it with three times a day and some salve. It should be fine in about a week, but please call your horse vet and let them check it out. Meanwhile, I'll forward their office a picture and a copy of my exam."

"Did someone do this to him?"

"No," I laughed. "He did it to himself."

"What do you mean?"

I pulled an apple wafer out of my pocket and let Lucero enjoy his snack. "He was itchy, so he rubbed his butt on this post in the stall." I leaned over and pulled some long tail hairs off the rough surface. "Increase his grooming and have someone smooth that rough spot out for you. If he keeps doing it, you might have to replace the post. There are some scratching devices for horses you can order through the feed store."

She smiled then and let herself relax a bit. "He does have a pretty big horse butt."

"That he does. You definitely don't want him to gain any more weight."

"It's because he isn't being ridden as much, now that the kids are gone."

"How long have you been taking care of him?" I'd noticed the stalls were clean and tidy, with fresh feed and clean water. His stallmate next to him, an American Paint, was placidly chewing on a flake of timothy hay.

"Not that long, probably three months. My daughters are the riders but they're both off at college. They used to take care of the horses." She stroked the gelding's long nose as he nuzzled her hand. "I guess you can tell."

"Honestly, I think you are doing a great job. You just need more experience. Why don't you contact a trainer and have them work with you so you get more confidence? And when your farrier is here to shoe the horses, have them show you how to lift up the hoof and pick it clean. It's not that hard to do. Brushing your horses will make all of you feel better and it's a great way to build trust." The more bonded Rita felt to her horses the less likely they would end up as another unwanted horse statistic. "You also can check around and see if any riding students would like to exercise them for you."

"Thanks for the suggestions. It was great meeting you, Dr. Kate." Rita walked along with me to my truck, her boots kicking up puffs of dirt. "How do you like working at Doc's place?"

"I'm enjoying it," I said, truthfully, "although it was pretty rocky recently."

"Vivian and Thomas Langthorne. That was such a shock." She took out her wallet as I entered the charges into the office laptop. "My parents played bridge with them for about fifteen years or more."

"Really? Did you know them too?"

"Only a little. My mom said that the dogs were their lives. That's why they moved up here permanently from Manhattan." She took a look at the bill I printed up and flipped the wallet open to her checkbook, then balanced against the truck to write the check. "I guess they were disappointed in their daughter and turned to the dogs for comfort."

I tried not to sound like I was prying. "How so?"

"My parents weren't very specific, but Pippi started getting into trouble as soon as she hit her teens. They sent her away to boarding school and then to finishing school in Switzerland, but nothing seemed to help."

I dawdled as much as I could printing up her receipt.

"After she stole some checks and took over $20,000 from them, they cut her out of their lives."

All this was news to me. "How old was she?"

Rita took the receipt, folded it and stuck it into her front jeans pocket. "She must have been about eighteen or nineteen. I remember Vivian sitting in our parlor crying and my mother telling me to go to my room."

"They didn't prosecute?"

A look of horror replaced the smile on her face. "Prosecute? Then everyone would have been dragged out in public and they would be mortified. People didn't talk about their private lives. That's how they thought back then. My mother agreed."

"Do you know if they reconciled?"

She thought for a moment. "I'm not sure. It's possible. Vivian was way more forgiving than Thomas. But if so, they kept it to themselves. Not for nothing but every family up here has their own secrets."

"Like what?"

Rita handed me the check and smiled a weak smile, half her mouth trying to appear carefree. "What's that thing they say all the time? If I told you I'd have to kill you?"

Chapter Twenty-one

I took a towel and wrapped my next house-call patient up in it, burrito style.

Captain Hook, the yellow-headed Amazon parrot, didn't like having his nails and wings trimmed and who could blame him. However, it was the only way to keep him safe, since he moved about freely in his owner's home. Every month or so he suffered the indignity of being restrained in a towel for his own good. He wasn't convinced.

Trimming bird wings is a minor art form. There are several different styles but I was using the one recommended by the American Association of Avian Veterinarians. Ideally you want to cut the flight feathers so you can't see them when the wings are in their normal position. The angle of the cut is critical to how it looks and feels to the bird. Gently I slid his right wing out and Mari held it in the middle and extended it so we could trim it.

In the background we heard his owner, Destiny, muttering. "I'm so sorry Hookie, but this is for your own good. Mommy loves you. Be a good baby."

I wasn't sure who was more traumatized, the bird or the owner.

"We're almost finished," I called over to her, only the nails left to do. Thankfully we hadn't encountered any unexpected bleeding from the trimming. The growing feathers, called blood feathers, have small veins in them and bleed instantly if nicked. Since a small parrot doesn't have a lot of blood to begin with, every drop lost is critical, which is why I kept my crash kit with

Kwik Stop styptic powder close by. Better to take your time and check every feather before you cut.

"Okay, Mari. Let's let him up." Gingerly my technician began to peel back the layers of towel until she uncovered the bird. Out popped Captain Hook onto the kitchen island looking for a fight. His brown eyes bored into us as he flapped his now shortened wings at us. His vivid yellow head contrasted well with his sleek green plumage.

"Pretty bird," I told him. He wasn't buying it.

"Destiny, he's all yours," Mari called out, stepping back from the pet bird who was busy squawking loudly what he'd like to do to us.

This was the third time I'd been to Destiny's double-wide trailer to tend to Captain Hook. For a trailer it was very comfortable inside. The kitchen had new wood cabinets and an island that we had used as our surgical table. There was a flat-screen TV and a micro suede sofa and chair set in the living room along with an elaborate bird perch and expensive cage hung with bird toys.

"Where is Mommy's big boy?" Destiny cooed and held out her finger. Captain Hook hopped right on and began to walk up her arm, talking all the way. Once propped on her shoulder he snuck his head under her hair and began to nibble at her ear. Definitely all male, he had been sexed at a young age with a DNA test.

Both had a look of contentment on their faces.

"Did you save his feathers?"

Mari and I said yes at the same time. We'd trimmed Captain Hook's wings and nails before and we knew the drill. Destiny saved all his feathers. Why? I didn't ask and probably didn't want to know.

As I gathered my equipment I watched the two interact. Most people don't realize how intelligent parrots are and how intensely they bond to their owners. Destiny was a well-groomed blond in her mid thirties who worked as our accountant. By her appearance you would never think her life companion was a parrot. We saw these two often since every month she stopped by the hospital to straighten out the receipts and balance the checkbook for Doc Anderson. Sometimes she brought Captain Hook.

Even though Doc's software program kept track of things, it was only as good as the data entered. We always had piles of invoices for special diet foods, prescription drugs, fluids and medications, some on back-order that had to be justified in the checkbook. Since I'd been there the books had balanced out, which was a big improvement over the last practice I worked at where discrepancies had popped up at least once a week because a staff member either forgot to enter a charge or entered it wrong.

As Destiny approached us, Captain Hook started to screech, preparing for round two. With her index finger she stroked the bird on his forehead and between his eyes. Immediately he quieted down, lids drooping in bird ecstasy.

"Wow. I'm so glad that's over." Dressed in spotless black slacks and a linen blouse even in her own house our accountant looked professional. At home I wore sweats covered in dog hair and an old pair of flip-flops.

Can I get you guys a soda or some coffee? " she offered.

My tech immediately said, "I'm dying for a coffee. Black, please."

"Make that two. By the way, Destiny, I've been meaning to ask you. I never see any," I tried to find a nice way to say it but didn't succeed, "ah, bird poop in your house. How do you do that?" Most bird owners walk around with cloths on their shoulders, like baby spit-up rags, to keep down the mess to their clothes.

"Oh, my baby is potty trained. If he's somewhere new he tells me when he has to go."

Mari looked astonished but nothing surprised me anymore.

"Does he use the toilet?" A bizarre picture of Captain Hook falling into the bowl and splashing around flashed into my brain.

Our hostess stared at me like I'd lost my mind. "That's too dangerous. No, there are two sinks in the master bedroom. Hookie has one for his own use."

It made sense in a weird way.

I watched our hostess walk into the kitchen with her feathered passenger riding on her shoulder. A twenty-first birthday present from a boyfriend now long gone, Hookie was hers since he was a fledgling baby bird and it was obvious the two had bonded big time. With a life-expectancy of fifty years or more for Captain Hook, this relationship might end up being the longest one in her life, and possibly the most rewarding.

"Thanks again, guys," she told us when she walked back with two steaming mugs and a plate of chocolate chip cookies. The rich coffee aroma spiked my appetite and I reached for a cookie.

We sat down in her living room and enjoyed a well deserved moment of rest.

"Oh. You have to see Hookie's latest trick." She took the bird off her shoulder and placed him on her sofa cushion. "Get mommy's keys from her purse."

Captain Hook cocked his head to the side for a moment and stared at her. After a moment he waddled across the sofa, hopped down with wings outspread and used his beak to unzip her purse sitting on the floor. His bright head disappeared into its depths for a moment then emerged with a big wad of keys in his beak.

I watched fascinated as he tossed the keys onto the sofa then climbed up after them, using his claws and beak. When he reached the sofa cushion he picked the keys up and placed them in Destiny's hand.

Mari and I burst out in applause and laughter. Captain Hook preened with pleasure.

"Did you notice how he threw the keys up onto the cushions? I didn't teach him that. He figured it out for himself," she said with pride, lifting the bird up and giving him a kiss.

"That's very impressive," I told her. Slowly I put my hand next to hers and after a moment the Captain hopped onto my finger. "Pretty bird," I cooed. You are a very intelligent boy."

Captain Hook glared at me before hopping back to his mom.

"He's forgiven you," she told me.

"Good. I don't want him mad at me. He's too smart." Shifting in the chair to check my phone for any texts from the office I asked, "So, how's everything going with you?"

"Great. I'm doing the books for Randy down at the Tube Depot now, as well as Mama G's diner, which I hear is your favorite place. Pretty soon I'll be balancing the books for the whole town."

Mari interrupted our small talk. "Can I use your bathroom before we go?"

"Sure. It's right down the hall on the left," she pointed out. Captain Hook rolled with the movement, keeping his balance with ease. "That reminds me. Have you seen the new addition?"

I glanced around the trailer. Destiny had inherited it from her mother she'd told me on my last visit. It looked the same to me.

"Oh, you've added to the trailer?" I asked, politely.

She laughed and Captain Hook danced up and down. "No." They both bobbed their heads in a strange symmetry as if to punctuate the point. "I'm talking about Randy's store. He added a high end coffee shop with espresso and sandwiches and expanded the store along the Main Street side. It came out nice."

"Business must be good," I commented while scrolling through my emails.

"Luckily he didn't have to move. That would have been a disaster."

Did Thomas Langthorne really intend to close him down? Maybe Destiny could verify if it was a rumor or the truth.

The hall bathroom door opened and Mari came out.

"Would you put this in the truck and let Sandy know we're finished?" I asked her, handing the medical kit box to her. "I'll be there in a minute."

"Sure. Good-bye, Destiny. Good-bye, Captain Hook."

The bird bobbed his head when he heard his name. I suspected he was glad to see us getting ready to go. Well, he would have to wait. I bent over and tightened the shoelace of my leather work boot.

"Why was Randy thinking of moving?"

"Oh, I guess you don't know. Mr. Langthorne planned to rent the store to another tube company from Fleishmanns for a lot more money when his lease was up. They fought terribly about it. Randy built the business up for the past ten years and would have lost everything. The bend has the only public access to the river in town and it's grandfathered in."

Still curious, I asked, "How did they resolve it?"

"They didn't. The day after Mr. Langthorne died, Randy made a deal to buy the building and land from Pippi for cash. Now, I understand, he's making a killing."

Captain Hook cawed in agreement.

My brain ticked off a list of suspects as Mari chatted about training for a marathon coming up in two weeks. Pippi had the best motive for murder—money. But according to Chief Garcia she also had an airtight alibi. Maybelle harbored some kind of resentment with the Langthornes. Did she hire someone to kill them, then fall victim herself to the killer? What about Randy, the new owner of the Tube Depot, whose whole lifestyle depended on his business? Then there was Mama G and her family, trying to renew the lease on their very successful diner.

Now that the deaths had been ruled suspicious by the police, any of those scenarios could be true. How would I ever find out?

Or was there someone lurking in the shadows somewhere with a different motive for murder?

Chapter Twenty-two

The sun still shone brightly by the time I finished my last appointment the following Saturday. Since I had some free time, I decided to check out the Tube Depot and perhaps talk to the owner, Randy Molinari. With any luck I wouldn't freeze my ass off if I ended up floating down the river in one of their giant tubes. I hurried home, changed into my bathing suit, pulled an old pair of jeans shorts over it and grabbed a complete change of clothes.

My plan consisted of some inconspicuous snooping around a little, then heading over to the diner for an early dinner.

To say it didn't turn out that way is an understatement.

Right away I noticed the improvements Destiny had mentioned. The parking lot glowed with new asphalt. A large addition bumped the store out along Main Street and on the second floor an all-weather screened-in porch with tables and chairs wrapped around the building giving diners a great view of the river. Waitresses flitted in and out with drinks and food.

After parking the truck I headed toward the entrance, noticing recent landscaping and fresh paint. A big Harley was parked outside, every piece of chrome shining. In the parking space next to it, a classic cherry red Corvette with vanity license plates gleamed back. Things were looking up for the little town of Oak Falls. Big wooden doors led right into the store which gave off a spruced up, hip yet country vibe. It was stocked with interesting items from all over the world, displayed in cool ways designed to separate you from your money. A new yoga and meditation area sold statues of Buddha, garden globes, yoga mats in rainbow colors, and environmentally friendly clothing. Along the walls hung framed museum-quality prints. A tower of sports shoes beckoned on the opposite wall while games, gadgets, camping gear, and the latest electronic trends all had their own areas.

Displays of specialty products flanked the restaurant entrance, as well as plates, cups, and pots for sale. A row of coffee mugs sported the Tube Depot logo, the black-and-white silhouette of a person in a tube floating on a blue green river.

I decided to put off the tubing and go for the snack first. A ponytailed hostess seated me on the deck overlooking the river. Glancing down I noticed a new addition to the tube experience. Several people got on what looked like a cross between a raft and several tubes. It allowed you to enjoy the experience of floating down the river, tubes acting as bumpers, without getting wet.

Whoever thought of that was a promotional genius. It extended the tubing season, letting people enjoy the river experience even if the water remained fairly cold. The party of four who drifted past me in the super-sized raft waved as they floated past.

"Have you had a chance to look at the menu?" someone said behind me.

A waitress smartly dressed in black pants, white shirt, and a black tuxedo-cut vest stood waiting politely for my answer.

I turned back to the menu and asked her what the specials of the day were.

"Let's see. The soup is beef barley, then we have a spinach salad with grilled chicken or shrimp.

Suddenly I felt starved. "I'll have the soup and the pie, plus a coffee."

"House roast, hazelnut, Columbian, or Mountain blend?

"House roast."

"Do you need cream or milk?"

"No. Black is fine." I closed the menu and noticed another one of the giant rafts getting ready to leave the dock. "What are those things?" I asked her, pointing to the boat.

She laughed. "Strange aren't they? But they're really popular. They're old white-water rafts modified for tubing."

I had to admit it was a great idea. "Who came up with that?"

"Randy. Now that he bought the place, there are so many new plans. We even had a crew from the Travel Channel filming us a few days ago." She beamed with pride, "I might be in it."

"That's cool."

"Totally cool. One minute he's telling us we may lose our jobs, then the next day we're going to expand instead. Ying and Yang, I guess." She shrugged her shoulders.

After she left to put in my order I glanced toward the river below. Another big raft loaded with six people bobbed in the water below me, much slower than the first, probably due to the increased weight.

Someone glanced up at me and waved. I waved back.

That's when I noticed two men arguing. I recognized Randy, who faced my direction, a scowl on his face. Opposite him, a big man with a shaved head held a hand up and pointed his finger in an angry gesture. Fragments of their conversation drifted up to me.

"…not what you promised." Randy lowered his head, glanced quickly to the right and left, mindful of the paying customers passing by them on their way to the dock.

The big guy moved closer and lowered his voice but the sound carried up to where I sat. "Don't…threatening you…" before a group of tubers cheered after their raft dropped into the water.

I couldn't hear anything else after that because Randy turned away and stalked back into the store, leaving the big man standing alone. Because of the angle I strained to make out any features other than his shiny dome.

I was about to give up and start on my soup when my luck changed. Shiny Head decided to walk toward the dock. There he waited for a moment, lit up a cigar, and stared at the island created by the bend in the river. He wore heavy motorcycle chaps and thick leather boots.

A vague twinge of recognition hit me. Something about his walk and the shape of his shoulders and neck.

Then I knew, knew before he turned around.

Shiny Dome was Dante the cat's owner, Henry James.

While I ate I wondered about the angry exchange I'd witnessed between the two men. The biker versus the sports entrepreneur. They didn't seem as though they would have much in common. Like cats and dogs.

After paying the check and giving my waitress a good tip, curiosity got the better of me. Pretending to be interested in a pair of spandex shorts, I surveyed the room searching for Randy and Henry. A glance out the window showed no Harleys parked outside, which meant Henry James had left the building.

Moving along to another display, I reached for a shirt only to find more spandex. I guess people who wear this stuff are in such good shape they welcome the embrace of stretchy manufactured fabric. Me, I gravitate to cotton t-shirts and pants with lots of pockets. For a moment I forgot about my real motive, distracted by a pair of black cargo pants. As I searched for my size I heard Randy speaking to a customer a few rows away from me. Quickly I pulled a pair in my size off the rack and pretended to look for the fitting room. I headed in the direction of his voice and almost ran him down turning a corner.

"Oh. Hi," I said, eloquent as usual.

"It's Kate," he smiled in recognition. "How's everything at Doc Anderson's place?"

The pants hung over my arm like a bar towel. "Fine, everything's fine." To look at him you would never guess he'd been in an argument a few minutes ago. He seemed way more relaxed than me.

"What brings you here?" He leaned against the wall, his smile as white as the plaster.

For a moment I panicked. What was I doing here? Trying to find out what you and Henry James were arguing about?

"Destiny told me about your addition, so I decided to come take a look. By the way the food in the café is great." I smiled back at him but now held the pants up like a wall between us.

He reached over and looked at the tag. "Doing some shopping I see. Those are one of our most popular items."

"I love pockets." Where did that come from?

Obviously he thought I was making a fashion statement. "Yes, cargo pants are still popular even after all these years."

Time to stop the chitchat. "Didn't I see you talking to Henry James a moment ago?"

A certain rigidity crept into his face. "You know him?"

"Yes. He's a client of mine. Such a nice guy," I babbled on. "And he loves his cat."

"I wouldn't know." Randy jerked the phone off his belt and stared at the screen.

"What were you two arguing about?"

His stony gaze turned to granite. I thought for a moment he would walk away or tell me to mind my own business.

"A deal fell through, nothing much." With an effort he continued to smile at me. "Let me get someone to help you with that." Before I could say anything he stalked off in the direction of the main cash register station. A few moments later a young salesperson popped up, her curly blond hair tight with ringlets.

"Can I help you?" she asked in a cheerful tone.

Randy disappeared into his office. "Yes. I was looking for a shirt to go with these pants," I lied, slowly moving away from the shoppers around us.

"Oh, I just love these pants," she said, focusing on the rack in front of her, "Casual or dressy?"

"Ah. A little of both," I replied.

"Very smart, double duty," she nodded vigorously.

I started to look at some homespun cotton blouses. "I'm so glad Randy sent you over to help. Too many choices overwhelm me."

"How about this one?" In her hands she held a bright red silk blouse.

"Uh, that's nice." Perfect if I was on my way to a bullfight.

"There are lots of colors, see?" She flipped through a rainbow of colors each more intense than the next.

"You've got some great things for sale here." I picked up a knitted vest. "Who does the ordering?"

"Karin and Randy work with different suppliers to get the latest things."

"What does Henry James do here?" I questioned her casually. "He left before I could say hi."

"You mean the biker dude? I don't know. Maybe leather goods from the look of him. He's only come around recently." She held up an embroidered shirt.

"How recently do you mean?"

"Just before we expanded. I remember he came in while Randy was telling us about maybe losing our jobs."

"Are you sure?"

"Positive. I felt like crying so I deliberately didn't look at the boss. That's why I noticed the dude leaning against the wall chewing a toothpick. He wore the same silver belt buckle, the one with the Harley on it. I always notice people's clothes." With that she took in my ripped jeans and old t-shirt.

I ignored her scrutiny. "That's interesting. I guess he heard everything."

"I'm sure he did. Then the next day we found out we had our jobs. It was the day the old couple was found dead, because I didn't know if I should be happy or sad."

"A little of both, I guess. Can you go ahead and ring these up?" I handed her the pants and followed along to the register, my mind racing. So, the Langthornes' deaths were not only lucrative but suspiciously convenient for Randy. Two elderly people who stood in the way of everything he wanted. I thought back to the day I met Dante and Henry James. His wallet was stuffed with cash and unlike everyone else in Oak Falls, he never asked me anything about finding Vivian and Thomas dead in their home.

Maybe he didn't have to.

Maybe he already knew.

Chapter Twenty-three

My new cargo pants were a hit at work until an Irish setter lifted his leg and peed on me. His aim ended up being pretty good. He got my pants, my sock, and one shoe all at the same time. Back I went to my place and changed into a new pair of scrubs and fresh sneakers. One good thing about living at the hospital, I didn't have a long commute.

Rather than dumping them in the dirty clothes hamper, I decided to soak them in the slop sink in the hospital laundry room.

As the sink filled up I waited and thought about the tangled investigation of the Langthorne deaths. My list of suspects kept growing every day and most had the same motive, money. But there was a huge difference between wanting someone dead and pulling the trigger.

The door swung open and Mari stood there, a laundry bin in her hands.

"I'll just be a sec," I told her, checking the water level and adding some liquid detergent.

"No problem." She deposited the green plastic bin on top of the dryer. "Are you soaking your pants?"

"Definitely. Hopefully they'll be all right. I'll wash them in the machine sometime tonight."

"They should be okay." With that she opened the old top-loader and started emptying the bin.

"If you need the sink, go ahead and take the pants out and hang them over the tub."

"Okay. By the way, I told Sandy to tell her cousin what her dog did. I thought they'd get a kick out of it."

"The Irish setter with the infected nail belongs to her cousin?"

"Yes. I was joking with them, actually, about getting an Irish setter."

"What was so funny?" I spot treated my pants then lowered them into the soapy water.

Mari laughed again. "They all match. Everyone has red hair, even the dog."

"Okay." On a scale of one to ten that only merits a two on my funny network.

We both left the laundry room, Mari behind me humming a tune. I started for the office, then, thought about my release orders for the setter. Instead of using the office phone, I wandered out to reception to check the printed copy.

To my surprise the Stevens family was there in the reception lobby picking up their excited Irish setter who was busy licking the kids on their faces with a long pink tongue.

Another surprise, I recognized them. I'd seen them not long ago at the diner. The little girl with the pale red hair who looked like Pippi Langthorne stood in front of me again.

"Hi there," I said to them all. "I'm Dr. Kate Turner. Are there any questions about his home care? Do you feel comfortable with the bandage changes?"

"Honestly, I'm going to let her do it." Mrs. Stevens waved at Sandy who stood behind the counter watching.

The setter jumped up on one of the boys almost knocking him to the ground. "We're planning on doing some training sessions along with those bandage changes." Our receptionist's tone gave no room for discussion. The way she eyeballed the three kids I wouldn't be surprised if they weren't included in the doggie discipline class.

"Yes," I agreed. "He doesn't mean to, but he could hurt someone jumping up or pulling at the leash. If Sandy doesn't have time I would recommend the puppy classes held by our local chapter of the American Kennel Club."

"Thanks. I'll do that. Come on kids," she called clutching the paper bag of bandage materials and the dog's antibiotics. In his excitement the Irish setter made a complete circle around his owner, effectively tying her up with the leash. To her credit she simply twirled in the other direction and continued out the door. I watched as the little girl skipped her way to the car while her brothers gave each other noogies on their noggins.

"Chaos."

"What did you say Sandy?" I turned away from the window. The room felt like it still vibrated with their energy.

"I said *chaos*. Terri has a very permissive parenting style and that goes for her dog too."

"Well, I can't comment on the kids but definitely the dog. In fact, I'm going to note that in her record and email her some training info."

"Good." She turned back to the file folders. Our conversion of old paper records to computerized files was ongoing since Doc refused to let anyone but his own staff look at his medical records. Part of the reason, I thought, might be that no one but his longtime staff could read anything he wrote. More often than not I needed a translation from Sandy or Mari. I sat down at one of the reception computers and made a note in the Irish setter's file. Then a thought struck me.

"Is your family related to the Langthornes?" I asked Sandy.

With her back to me she answered, "Not that I know."

"The reason I asked is your cousin's little girl looks a lot like Pippi Langthorne."

"You think so? I don't see it." File in hand she crossed over to the other side and put the folder away.

"Come on, same hair color. Same shape of the face. Their eyes are that funny light greenish color too."

"I still don't see the resemblance. Melody looks like her dad. We've got lots of redheads in upstate New York from all the English and Irish who settled here."

I almost told her my suspicions that Pippi was adopted but the office phone rang. Leaving Sandy to do her job I went into the back to get a cup of coffee and finish my paperwork. Just as well not to spread gossip about something you can't prove. The locals can talk about each other, but I hadn't earned the privilege.

"See what I mean?" Mari asked while I took a mug from the shelf.

For a moment I didn't get it. "Oh, you mean the redheads."

"That's how Frankie got arrested," she laughed pouring a cup of her own.

"You lost me," I chided her as I watched three teaspoons of sugar plunk into her coffee.

"The father of those kids. He's in Shawangunk Correctional Facility, not too far from here, serving time for murder and armed robbery."

Bewildered I stared at her.

"It was his hair. When he robbed the bank he wore sunglasses and a baseball cap on his head, but his hair stuck out from under the hat. Witnesses saw his red hair and that led to his capture."

"So Sandy's cousin is married to a felon?" I don't know why but the news shocked me.

"No." Mari took a sip of her sweet drink then winked at me. "Sandy's cousin isn't married to a felon."

"I don't understand."

"Sandy's cousin Frankie is the felon."

Why did the revelation that Sandy's cousin committed violent crimes disturb me so much? Every family had its secrets, as both Rita and Cindy kept telling me. What possible connection could there be between someone in prison and the Langthornes?

I wondered if Freddie grew up around here, maybe went to the local high school. What if someone he knew visited him in prison? Maybe asked for a favor. Felons know other felons. What if the Langthorne deaths were a contract hit?

One thing I knew for certain.

Whoever hired the killer would make sure they had a perfect alibi.

Chapter Twenty-four

"She wants to see you today and she is very upset with you."

That's how my Wednesday started. No "good morning, how are you?" just Sandy's stern greeting before my first cup of coffee. I felt like turning around, getting back into bed, and pulling the covers over my head.

"What?" Until my mind functioned more clearly, that was my best response.

At eight a.m. the morning cleaning and treatments were in full swing. The dogs needed to be walked, kennels and cages scrubbed, treatments done, any bloods or lab tests drawn, and everyone, except surgery patients, fed and watered. Technically I didn't have to start until eight-thirty but since I lived next to the hospital I always came over for my pre-breakfast big cup of coffee. I'd stopped calculating the amount of coffee I was drinking now.

After checking on a dog being picked up by its owner later in the day and petting Mr. Katt, our resident tabby, I retreated to Doc's office.

Sandy followed me in.

"You told me to call her this morning so I did and she is still upset." Her folded arms and grumpy stare indicated that the client wasn't the only one still annoyed.

After another sip of coffee the cobwebs began to clear. "Wait a minute. Are we talking about Precious the beagle's owner?"

"Of course, who else would it be?"

Since I still felt half asleep, in theory it could be any of my patients. I thought about making a joke but one look at the receptionist's face killed that idea.

"I know she's mad I suggested that Precious go on a diet. Maybe I wasn't as politically correct as I could have been. Go ahead and squeeze her into my schedule somewhere."

Still not content she fired off her parting shot at me. "We need to keep all of Doc's clients happy, just remember that. I've got bills to pay, staff paychecks, and a million other expenses, not to mention your salary."

I used Doc's old butterfly net to try and close the door without getting up from the desk. Not successfully, since it still gaped open an inch or two. Light streamed in from the window behind me as the sun rose in the sky. The desk chair, now protected from animal gunk with an old towel, felt more and more like my own every day. Putting the problem of Precious and her owner away I continued my morning routine—quick scan of the headlines then on to my email. This morning, in addition, I planned to check out Doc's travels on Facebook. Several of his clients asked me where he was, and this way I could keep track of his itinerary.

Doc's page showed places I had only dreamed about. Lots of friends posted questions and wished him luck. Most of the pictures included his sunburned sister, also with a broad smile on her face. The latest photos showed a beautiful beach with palms and expanses of glistening white sand. Doc faced the camera, a streak of zinc oxide over his nose wearing a battered Indian Jones-type hat. Over thirty years as a single practitioner, working every day like so many vets he made himself available to his clients twenty-four-seven before the rise of emergency clinics. Younger practitioners like me owed them a debt of gratitude. Doc stood tall like the legendary small town doctors who work until they drop. He deserved the best vacation in the world and I didn't want to be the one to mess it up.

"Dr. Kate, you've got to see this," Cindy interrupted and pushed the door open wide. I didn't mind. Everyone knew the open door meant I was available. The only time I closed it was when I had call backs to make or an important consultation.

I glanced up from the computer and she slid something from behind her back. It was a kitten. Light blue eyes looked calmly at me from a flame-point face. She handed it to me.

"Where did this little guy come from?" I asked her while I did a quick exam on him.

"From our parking lot. He was in a box at the front door. Someone rang the bell and took off. They left a note asking us to find him a home."

"He's not completely feral. Obviously is used to people." I stroked his soft fur and immediately was rewarded with a purr like a buzz saw.

The little kitten curled up in my hand and began grooming himself. I figured he was about six or seven weeks old. "You know, this kitten looks a lot like Dante, that big tomcat in the treatment area. I'm betting this is one of his sons or grandsons."

Cindy shut the door with her foot.

Surprised, I gave her a quizzical look.

"My brother-in-law Bobby is still looking for clues on the Langthorne murders. I thought you should know."

"I wish they would call it murder in the newspapers."

"Well, that's kind of what suspicious circumstances means, doesn't it?" she joked. "I know you're frustrated with our small-town justice that's as slow as a snail, but I think you're brave to try and figure it out. I'd be too frightened to do anything."

"Thanks, Cindy." I appreciated her vote of confidence. At least one member of the staff didn't think I was a crazy.

Casually, she continued on her way out. "So, what do you want to do with him?"

"Let's make sure he's healthy. I'll tell Mari to check for worms, ear mites, and do a FeLV and FIV test." Walking across the clinic put the little guy on high alert. His blue eyes widened and fur began to stand up along his spine when he heard one of the dogs bark.

I searched for a free cage to put the kitten in and realized there was one right next to big Dante, who was back for his recheck. What a contrast, one starting his life with soft fur and a pink nose and the other beaten up by life, scratch marks across his face, chewed-up ear, and healing bite wounds.

"I'm calling you Junior D," I told the kitten who meowed and stuck his paw out through the bars of the cat condo cage.

Looking at them side by side gave me an idea. Henry James promised to keep Dante in from now on. Maybe it would be easier on the older cat if he had a little companion.

I settled the kitten in and gave him some canned and dry cat food to see which he'd eat. No worries about his appetite. He dove in, put his front foot into the canned food and then began to gobble the dry. After I entered his exam results into the computer I asked Cindy to contact Henry James and see if he wanted to adopt Junior D on a trial basis. Although the big male Dante had a sweet personality, the introduction of a kitten could go both ways. He might love him or hate him. My last glance at Junior D noted he had discovered the cat food on his foot and was deliciously cleaning himself.

By the time I drank half of my second up of coffee, Mari knocked on the door.

"We're just about ready, Kate."

"Okay. Pull up the schedule on the treatment room computer and let's read through it together before we go. I'll be right out." I finished my coffee in one last gulp, grabbed a yogurt and a bag of granola mix from the fridge then logged out. The hospital smelled fresh and clean. After checking my hospitalized patients, I cleared both Dante and my gastritis dog to go home. Mari stood next to the lab computer waiting for me.

"You've got quite a few appointments but most are rechecks." With a smile she scooted over so I could view the screen. I saw the beagle lady, Mrs. Frankle, scheduled for noon.

"Let's make sure we have plenty of client information hand-outs on board today, especially the latest on obesity and diet food options."

Mari jotted it down.

"Are Jimmy's blood tests from California in?"

"Yes. I wanted you to look at them before I posted them into his record."

"Thanks." Surprisingly, Doc's computer system and record-keeping were more modern than many clinics in rural areas. We kept an almost paperless office and all the staff felt comfortable in the veterinary software program he used. It certainly made life easier for me and the staff since data retrieval and storage was at our fingertips. The bloods drawn by their California vet on Jimmy the cat looked good. I sent a note to reception to thank the feline practitioner who forwarded their lab tests to us. In addition I wanted the staff to send the owners a link to information on a new diet for hyperthyroidism.

"Are we done?" My question to Mari hung in the air for a moment.

She glanced down at her notes, took a quick look around the room then gave me a big thumbs-up.

Just in case of a messy client, I took an extra scrub top and jacket from the hall closet and trailed Mari out into reception. "We're off."

Sandy looked up from scanning bills into the computer. "Good luck with Mrs. Frankle."

"No problem. We'll have Precious ready for her bikini in no time."

Her laugh followed us out the door.

The truth is, a sixty-pound beagle is not a pretty sight.

Beagles are medium-sized hunting dogs that usually range from twenty-two to twenty-eight pounds. Poor Precious weighed over twice as much as she should. I'd ruled out hypothyroidism and run a full diagnostic panel on her. Although healthy at only two years old, if she didn't lose weight, the future could include arthritis, knee problems, diabetes, and heart failure.

Her sweet brown eyes looked up at me and her tail wagged side to side like a pendulum. But between the eyes and tail her body resembled a bratwurst with legs.

We all sat together in Mrs. Frankle's cozy sitting room in four red velvet armchairs placed around an ornate metal-and-glass coffee table, Mari and I on one side, Mrs. Frankle and Precious arranged on the other side.

"How long has Precious been using the stairs to get to her chair?" I pointed at the portable carpeted stairs next to the dog.

"Oh, only a couple of months now. I got them on eBay," she offered the information with a smile. "It's amazing what you can get on the Internet these days."

Brenda Frankle's face betrayed no sense of worry. Gone was the anguish and anger I heard in her voice the previous day. We might as well be gathering here for tea and cookies.

"I'm so sorry to make you come back today, Dr. Kate, but yesterday I was so upset.

"Well, I think with increased exercise and a veterinary reducing diet—"

"We don't need that now," she interrupted. "Precious is going on a blue-green algae supplement with extra vitamins and things to help her burn fat and lose weight. It's all natural."

Lots of things are all natural, but that doesn't mean they're good for you. Most people never researched their all natural products. Exotic berries from Hawaii, secret plants of the Australian aborigines, pink salt from the Himalayas, it never stopped. There was always something new on the horizon. Now, I do believe in using complementary medicine when appropriate, but was pretty sure without cutting calories blue-green algae alone wasn't going to do the trick.

I was about to launch into a lecture on unregulated supplements, possible contamination with heavy metals and who knows what else, but stopped myself. Really, Brenda wanted what everyone in America wants, instant results in a pill.

"I know how hard it is for us to eat right and exercise, but it's just as important for our pets," I began. "I'm as guilty as everyone else; too much fast food for lunch, too many pieces of pie at the diner, and not enough veggies. Most nights after work I flop down on the couch and break out the chips."

Mari spoke up. "I can vouch for that."

"But our pets have it easier—because they can't open the refrigerator and help themselves to food anytime of the day or night."

"What?" Brenda acted bewildered.

"Feeding Precious from the table and giving her snacks in addition to her regular food is only going to make her life harder. I know you don't want that."

Out the sitting room window I saw a neighbor walk slowly by with an overweight pug. "Once she is on a reducing diet see if you can get some of the other pet owners in your neighborhood involved in a group walk. Socializing would be good for everyone."

Mari chimed in. "We have some other dogs on special diets. You could share your experiences on the Internet. Set up a blog."

"We'll help you set some realistic goals for her."

"I'm willing to try." Brenda smiled at her dog who thumped her tail in response. "I don't want to blame myself for making her fat."

"The most important thing is you won't be alone. If you want we can check in with you every week."

"I'd like that."

"Precious is a beautiful happy girl because you've taken such good care of her, Brenda.

Now we need to make sure she gets healthy too."

Brenda got a little teary-eyed. "I've been feeling guilty. That's why I got so mad at you."

"Group hug," Mari yelled out.

With another crisis averted everyone began to laugh.

"Why don't you and Mari go over some canine weight loss strategies while I check on our next appointment?" I left them busy talking canned versus dry food.

I walked out to the truck. The hazy morning still hung in there, clouds obscuring any chance of sun. A damp smell promised rain sometime soon. After glancing at my watch I opened my cell phone and dialed the animal hospital back line.

"Is there anything doing?" I asked Cindy when she answered.

"No, things are fine. Do you need to talk to Sandy? She's right here."

Before I could answer, the office manager's raspy voice came on the line.

"Hope Brenda isn't crying again, it's bad for business. We can't afford to lose any more clients, you know." That was Sandy, right to the point.

"Actually, she's smiling and working out a diet plan with Mari right now. Can you make a note to schedule Precious for weekly weigh-ins? And can you both put your heads together and come up with some other clients whose pets need to lose weight?"

"I guess I can cross-reference it in the computer base. Maybe Cindy can help. She remembers stuff like that. Oh, your last appointment had to reschedule so you might be finished a little early today."

"Cool. We're leaving here now."

By the time I got back, the two of them had figured out a game plan. On the way out I mentioned to my tech that Sandy seemed worried we were losing clients.

"Are you kidding?" she said. "Cindy told me our numbers are all up, number of transactions, new clients, average client transactions, and daily receipts. You're doing great."

"That's good to know." I'd been so busy I hadn't bothered to check any stats.

Mari continued, "I think Sandy feels some pressure running the office without Doc. Everyone thinks she needs to chill."

With that pronouncement we headed to our next appointment. The change in my schedule was a welcome surprise. That meant I had the late afternoon open. And I knew exactly what I would do with the free time.

Snoop.

But how to go about it? I'd found most of my clues by accident from talking to people, but you can't walk up to a stranger and start asking questions about murder and motive. I'd have to think of a better way.

◇◇◇

It turned out there was a dog show that night at the Saugerties armory, only a half hour's drive away. I arrived early so I could walk among the contestants before the show. Like the previous show near Rhinebeck, organized chaos ruled behind the scenes. The noisy symphony of barking dogs reverberated in the high-ceilinged hall. Clusters of dogs and people with their kennel signs and crates worked in assigned spaces. Near the door silky haired Afghan hounds, their fur in large sponge rollers, gazed across the room at the other dogs. Bred to hunt, these elegant sight hounds were more at home in the field than the beauty parlor. Searching for the Cavalier King Charles spaniels, I passed the bichon frise, whose white coats were being teased out with special combs into curly perfection. A frustrated owner trying to flatten down a cowlick on an Old English sheepdog stood next to the massive dog, tears streaming down her face. No one offered her any hair gel or pomade to solve the problem. Ruthless behavior was the norm in the dog-eat-dog show ring.

Across the room in the far left corner I spotted the spaniels. None of the handlers looked familiar. Most of them were rapidly brushing the feathers, those long silky hairs on the legs and chest, making sure no knots or tangles marred their dogs' beauty. One dog in particular caught my eye, a pretty young female who looked vaguely familiar. I walked over to the grooming table and stood for a while before saying anything.

"How do you keep her coat so shiny?" I asked after the young woman grooming her had finished.

She put the dog in a large kennel then answered. "My mom and I mix two different conditioners with a vitamin E capsule in the final rinse. It works great. I even use it on my hair." As if to prove her point she flipped her dark brown hair with her hand. Darned, if it wasn't just as shiny as the dogs.

"You dog is so pretty. What can you tell me about her?"

Like many young girls she was more than eager to tell me everything about her favorite dog. "Well," she began, "my mom heard that all the Cavaliers in a kennel were being sold because of a death, I think. She contacted someone named Pippi Long-stocking and she sold us Stratford's Lady Jane. Her nickname is Janie. We've only had her for a couple of weeks now and she's already on her way to a championship."

No wonder the dog looked familiar. I was pretty sure I'd examined her when she'd belonged to Thomas and Vivian Langthorne.

"Was Pippi sad to see her go?"

The girl began to clean up her station, pulling long strands of hair from her brush. "When my mom and I got to her place she only had Janie left. Mom wanted to give her a business check but she only took cash and warned us there were no returns. She acted like she was selling a piece of furniture or something on Craigslist."

I thought Pippi had only sold dogs to Maybelle. "Did your mom get a receipt?"

"You bet. She insisted on it and made Pippi write down the date and all Janie's breeding information too."

Good for you, I silently told that diligent mom. "Well, best of luck. I'll come back and say hi to your mom after the show."

"We'll be here." She turned her attention back to Janie, who looked show ready.

Waving good-bye I entered the auditorium and sat down in the bleachers. I wondered what Thomas and Vivian Langthorne would have thought about having their dogs sold off. That big manila envelope labeled "Last Will and Testament" I saw on Thomas Langthorne's desk. I wondered if there were any specific instructions pertaining to their dogs.

Chapter Twenty-five

No wonder some people can't wait to leave their small towns and head for the city. Everyone knows everything about everybody and they never forget.

I jolted awake in the middle of a dream about a red-haired killer with no face, waving a will, who chased me on a motorcycle with a sidecar loaded with Chihuahuas. It was Saturday morning and this was my half day. I'd glanced at the schedule last night and it looked full. Maybe if we could leave a little early I would have time to find out who sold the Tube Depot to Randy. I was betting Pippi was Thomas and Vivian's sole beneficiary.

After taking a quick check of the animals in the hospital I poured a coffee and reviewed the appointments. If I thought I might need an usual medication or instrument I'd add it to our inventory in the truck.

Mari walked in as I was checking the last record.

"You're here early."

"Well, if we start early we might finish before noon."

"That's wishful thinking. I stocked the truck last night before I left so we should be good to go. We aren't seeing anything weird today, are we?"

In my profession that could mean a pissed off llama to a mouse with a tumor.

"Not that I know."

Another beautiful day rolled out in front of us, upstate New York at its finest. The trees so green and lush they looked like they were growing right in front of you. Flashes of color from rhododendron and azaleas could be seen even in the forests that we zoomed past.

As we drove to our last appointment I realized we were close to Fairview Lane and Henry James.

"Mari. I'm going to check in on Dante, you know, the cat with the bite wounds. See if that area on his spine healed up or if he needs a refill on the antibiotics. I also want to make sure everything is working out with Junior D, the kitten he adopted.

"Okay. Do you need me?"

"No, I should be fine. Why don't you go to the gas station, fill up, and call the office? By the time you get back I'll be done."

"That works. We're ahead of schedule anyway. Can I get you anything?"

"No thanks."

She dropped me off at the old farmhouse. Henry's Harley stood parked in the driveway and I saw a corner of the front curtain lift when we pulled in.

"Go ahead. I'm pretty sure he's here." With a wave I turned and strode toward the house with more bravura than I felt. Before I got to it, the front door opened. Henry stood there, a glass of milk in his big hand.

I guess my surprise showed in my face because he said "stomach problems," then invited me in.

"How's Dante?" I questioned him as we walked into the kitchen.

"Take a look yourself," Henry answered and pointed to the table. Curled up in the sun watching birds, perfectly at ease was the big guy himself. I noticed his tail occasionally twitching when he looked out the window. Good. Fine movement of his tail indicated that he was not suffering any motor damage to those nerves. Nearby lay the kitten, Junior D.

I sat down and gave the cat a pet on his head. He swung around, stared at me, then decided to ask for more by slipping his forehead under my hand. There were subtle changes to his jowls already as his testosterone levels dropped, identifying him as a neutered male. My hands slid along the shaved section of his spine, his fur growing back a little darker than before. The surgical site had healed better than I'd hoped it would and showed no evidence of infection.

"Are there any problems? No litter box issues?"

"Nope, he goes like a champion, regular as clockwork."

"Great."

"How are the two of them getting along?" I already knew the answer because big Dante was grooming the little one who had wrapped his paw around his neck.

"Fantastic. They keep each other company. I think he gets a kick out of watching the kitten run around the house."

We watched the two look-alikes for a moment, then a bird caught their attention.

Henry surprised me again. "Want a piece of zucchini bread? It's homemade."

"Absolutely, but make it a small piece. I'm cutting back on my sweets."

He walked over to the countertop and picked up a knife.

Seeing him with a knife in his hand made me uneasy. To break the silence I said, "I didn't know you cooked."

"I don't. But I enrolled in a class at the community college to reduce my stress level. Baking is good for the soul I've been told. Instead I'm gaining weight." He ruefully touched his stomach. "So zucchini bread instead of chocolate cake."

As Henry moved around the kitchen I tried to think of a way to question him about his argument with Randy at the Tube Depot. Turned out I didn't have to.

Henry put a thin slice of the greenish speckled bread in front of me, followed by a fork and paper napkin. I noticed the kitchen had been cleaned up. A bag of flour and some vanilla extract sat on the counter next to some baking dishes.

"You know I saw you yesterday," he confessed, "over at Randy's place, but I was too mad to say hello. That A-hole." He sank back into his chair that creaked a little under his weight.

"Oh." My fork hovered in front of me.

"I'll say it again. That Randy is an A-hole."

My mouth full of zucchini bread, I could only nod in agreement.

His gorilla arms bulging in yet another sleeveless t-shirt, this one honoring the late singer Amy Winehouse, banged down on the table. My plate slid an inch across the glass from their impact. "You're probably wondering what it was all about, arguing like that in public."

I nodded again and kept my thoughts to myself. Did Randy hire you to kill the Langthornes? If so, then what was I doing having zucchini bread with a killer?

Henry became visibly upset. "Well, our argument was private."

I was about to tell him that was okay but he continued.

"He owes my baby sister some money, the creep."

Wiping my mouth I interjected, "Could I have a glass of milk, please?"

"Sure." He got up and went to the refrigerator. With his head behind the door he continued, voice muffled.

"He runs around stringing half the girls in town along with his promises."

I didn't need to ask who he referred to.

Coming back with milk in hand he repeated "I don't want to talk about it."

Respecting his privacy I took a sip of milk to wash down the bread.

"What kind of guy takes money from women?" he asked, voice anguished.

I would have told him but he already knew the answer.

"Pretty fortunate for Randy that Thomas and Vivian Langthorne died when they did." I took another delicious forkful. If he was the killer maybe he could bake in the prison kitchen.

He looked me straight in the face, as though calculating something, his brown eyes a muddy color, mustache newly waxed. "That did occur to me."

"I still wonder about that day."

"Death is like that."

"For a while I think the police thought I did it." I finished half of the slice on my plate, then drained the last bit of milk, and waited for his reaction.

"You?" he laughed. It came out like a growl.

The honk of the truck's horn jolted me. I got up and hoisted my backpack on. I could see Mari out the kitchen window. "Okay, well, then I'll be going. Thanks for the zucchini bread, it tasted great. Feel free to call me if you have any problems with the cats."

Together we walked to the front door, but unexpectedly he put his arm up in front of the screen door stopping my exit. The bicep twitched making his Chinese character tattoo do a little dance. I could smell a musky scent coming off him. A prickle of fear raised the hair on my neck.

"No one could suspect you of murder, Doc." Then he whispered, "You're a pussycat."

It didn't sound like a compliment.

"Randy is another story altogether." The snake around his neck moved while he lowered his head toward me. The tail disappeared in a fold of skin.

I lifted my backpack between us, than pushed past him. My departure felt like an escape.

Mari leaned against the truck, eating an apple. Once she saw me she opened the passenger door as I walked around the vehicle and slid into the driver's seat.

"So, how did it go?" Not waiting for an answer she ate down to the apple core, then stuffed it into a paper bag and shoved it between the seats.

"Okay." My heart pounded so loud I was surprised she didn't hear it.

"Sorry I didn't save you anything. I was starved."

"No problem. I ate some zucchini bread."

"Cool."

Checking my rearview mirror I quickly shifted into reverse and backed the truck up. Once the road cleared I zipped out into the street. Mari must have programmed our next stop in because the GPS told me, in his British accent, to turn right in one point two miles.

"Yes. Dante is fine, Junior D the kitten is fine, and Henry James is fine. Everything is fine," I repeated, more to myself than anyone else.

Sunlight dappled the leaves of trees as we drove to our next appointment. Our morning was almost over, no major problems and in front of us a beautiful weekend to look forward to. So why did I have a nagging suspicion that something was amiss?

Like I'd been played.

Everything wasn't fine.

Not fine at all.

Chapter Twenty-six

I half listened to Mari chatter away as we drove to our next appointment. Randy's reputation plus his military background made him a prime suspect in my mind. Losing your business and livelihood was one heck of a motive for murder. Despite his denial maybe Henry James was involved. It didn't take much imagination to cast him as a killer. How thoroughly had the local police department investigated? I wondered. The town paper now described the Langthorne deaths as suspicious, but named no suspects and no motive. If anyone asked me I could come up with bunches of suspects and the compelling motive of money.

The GPS instructed us in an English accent to turn left.

"I love the way that sounds," Mari commented, "Mine sounds like it's from outer space."

Shifting gears, I concentrated on driving.

"How many different accents are available on these things? Could you imagine a sexy French voice or a Russian yelling at you?" she mused.

My mind wandered imagining Scotty from Star Trek giving us directions, when I began to recognize the scenery. Silver Hollow Road. We were headed to filmmaker Joel Denny's home.

"Who is our next appointment, Mari?' Maybe we were going to one of his neighbors. When I looked at our appointment sheet this morning I hadn't seen his name.

She refreshed the screen and double checked our list. "It's Joel Denny. They asked to be squeezed in today, so Sandy added them in at the last moment. They just got back from California."

"I hope Jimmy the cat is doing all right."

"It says a recheck. Oh, I meant to ask you. Do they do vasectomies on dogs?"

"Not usually. Why?"

"We couldn't find any live spermatozoa from your dog, Buddy."

That didn't surprise me. "His malnutrition could account for that. Remind me later to repeat his blood tests and run a urine sample on him." When we stopped at a traffic light I noticed Mari adjusting her knee brace. "By the way, how was the latest MRI on your knee?"

"Perfect. I consider myself very lucky. No pain and almost full mobility back."

Up ahead I saw the turnoff to the Denny farm at the same time the GPS dinged to signal to turn. Miranda Denny, Joel's daughter, had been one of my most rewarding clients. I remembered her, their cat Jimmy, and the Swedish nanny/personal assistant very clearly. The approach to the house was as impressive the second time as the first time I saw it. Once again I appreciated the towering elms and oaks lining the long driveway. Mari rolled down the window to look closer at the sheep grazing on rich grass in the pasture on the left, lambs mixed in with the adults. Their white wool dotted the grass like walking cotton balls.

As we continued up the road a sorrel gelding trotted along the fence, pacing himself with the truck, just as he had done before. This probably was his biggest form of recreation. Before we rounded the curve and lost him from sight I glanced back in the rearview mirror. He'd stopped to watch us, red coat glowing in the sunshine, then trotted away as if to say "catch you next time."

Miranda waved to us from the front step, their border collies again standing guard next to her. They immediately began to bark at us, setting off a flurry of activity running up and down the steps, hackles up.

I rolled down the window. "Hi, Miranda, is Jimmy okay?"

She quieted the dogs down with a hand signal. Well trained, they immediately stood down and returned to being the friendly and intelligent creatures that they are.

"Oh, he's fine. I thought he should be checked out by you, though. We just got back from California and with the time difference I think his medication timing got wacky."

I laughed and opened the driver's side door. "Wacky we can deal with." Mari jumped down and began gathering my small animal kit. "Can you make sure we have some TB syringes and a butterfly in there in case we need them? We may repeat his thyroid profile and kidney function," I told her.

"Sure thing, Kate."

"Are you ready?" Miranda looked up at me with solemn blue eyes, so mature for a girl of eleven.

"Ready," I replied. We climbed up the steps, the border collies swirling around our feet. Miranda opened the heavy wooden door of their modernized farmhouse and we entered the foyer. Once again the dramatic two-story ceilings and massive wooden beams reminded me of homes you see in magazines. This time I looked around more, past the fieldstone fireplace and open kitchen gleaming with glass and stainless steel. I noticed the piles of books and papers on the coffee table next to the fireplace. A teddy bear patiently waited on the loveseat next to a chess game in progress on a gaming table by the window.

No question it was luxurious, but it also was a home.

When I glanced up I caught Miranda watching me from the stairs. "You live in a beautiful house filled with lovely things."

"It is pretty, isn't it? The house I mean," she answered.

"Very pretty. You and your family are lucky to live here."

"Gustof Andrews was the architect. I want to be an architect."

I noticed she didn't say when I grow up. Miranda probably thought of herself as a grown up.

"That sounds like a great career choice for you."

"Thank you." Again the solemn eyes caught mine.

She turned and continued up the stairs, sliding her hand along the polished railing. I followed behind her, then, paused when she gestured for me to lean down.

"I locked him in my bedroom again. Just like before. Is that okay?" she whispered.

"That's fine," I whispered back.

"It's not going to hurt, is it? The needle you use?" Her eyes were solemn no more. They were anxious little girl eyes.

"Don't worry," I assured her. "We use tiny needles that our cat patients don't mind too much."

With a nod she carefully opened her bedroom door. Curled up on a fluffy pink blanket lay Miranda's cat, Jimmy. The cat I expected. I didn't expect to see Joel Denny sitting next to him checking messages on his iPhone. With all the Apple products in this family he should buy some stock.

Denny stood up when we came into the room. I'd seen pictures of him but they missed the sensitive face and stillness of the man.

"Hello, Doctor." His voice, low and quiet, fitted the size of the small bedroom. Miranda ran up to her father and grasped his hand.

"Hello." I returned the greeting. "Miranda says Jimmy has been doing well."

"Thanks to you." They both smiled at me. You could see the resemblance in that smile.

Mari poked her head in through the open door. "Do you need me?"

"Yes. I'm just about to start my exam. Mari, come over and meet Miranda's father, Joel Denny, and of course you remember Jimmy."

The old cat heard his name, raised his head, and then stretched. I leaned down and listened to his heart with my stethoscope before he could begin to purr. Nice solid heartbeat and a normal 180 beats per minute.

"Miranda, when did he last get his medicine?"

She looked up at her dad then answered. "He gets it at breakfast and dinner, so around seven a.m. then again at seven p.m. But in California it's three hours earlier."

"Do you like math?"

She nodded her head enthusiastically. "I love math."

"Let's adjust his pill time one half hour each day for six days, and in a week you'll be adjusted to the new time zone."

"One half hour each day for four days when we aren't in daylight savings time."

Joel kissed his daughter on the top of her head.

"Exactly."

The rest of the exam went smoothly. We drew blood and Jimmy didn't even wince. My impression was he'd put on weight, a good sign with hyperthyroid cats. When Mari checked our records she confirmed it, almost three quarters of a pound.

After making sure they had medication refills in place and would continue his regular dosage until we checked the new blood test results, Joel escorted me down the stairs while Miranda stayed in her bedroom reading with Jimmy now sleeping on her lap.

Joel briskly trotted down the stairs without holding onto the banister. Every movement seemed fast and purposeful. I realized he'd been still to keep the cat calm. "You know," his voice trailed back to me, "sometimes I think my daughter loves that cat more than she loves me."

"Sometimes she probably does," I answered, making my way more slowly down the stairs.

"What?" He stopped mid-step, a bemused expression on his face. "Are you agreeing with me?' Obviously he had expected a politically correct answer.

"It's my personal experience that children sometimes prefer their pets to their parents. I know I did when I was Miranda's age. Then you grow up and redefine the loves in your life."

"A scientist and a philosopher, impressive."

"I saw your documentary on the international seed bank project. Also impressive."

"Thank you." He strolled into the living room and I followed.

The fieldstone fireplace, on closer look, had silvery lichen growing on some of the stones. A caramel-colored leather sofa and chairs were arranged around it, soft but weathered at the same time. The furniture cost more than my truck.

"Mari will be here in a minute with your invoice," I said. "Do you have any questions?"

"Yes, but not about Jimmy." He hesitated for a moment. "I understand you discovered the bodies of Viv and Tom Langthorne?" For some reason the question sounded very formal.

"I did." We sounded like two characters in one of his movies.

"I was fond of old Tom."

That shocked me. He spoke kindly about the deceased, the only one who had.

"We got to know each other through the Rotary Club. He helped us train the collies."

"I didn't know he also trained dogs." Many times breeders left training to their handlers.

"Dogs were his life. Unlike a lot of the dog show people around here, he didn't just turn them over to the hired help." Joel picked up a polished wooden box from the coffee table and ran his fingers along the edges.

Father and daughter shared the same tapered fingers.

"I had no idea, but then I only met him a few times. Usually Vivian handled all the veterinary issues. "

Gently he opened the box as if something was going to pop out of it.

"Would you like to see him in action?" he asked, getting up before I could answer.

"Sure."

Joel beckoned me to follow then briskly walked down the hall, disappearing into a room on the left. I don't know what I expected but not a small movie theater. The walls glowed, painted a silvery metallic color, with the carpet and chairs a darker tone of charcoal gray and blue. Very sophisticated. Rows of roomy armchairs stood in place of bolted metal seats.

"It will be up in a minute," he said, head bent over a flat-screen monitor. "You wouldn't believe the amount of stuff I have in my files. Go ahead and sit down."

I took a seat in the first row.

The lights dimmed and the screen lit up with what obviously was a home video. Standing at a podium, a Rotary Club banner behind him stood Thomas Langthorne. By his side on a leash sat a Cavalier King Charles spaniel. Was that Charles Too? I leaned in closer.

His voice surprised me, the same slightly nasal accented speech as royalty.

"A native-born Englishman?" I asked Joel.

"British mother, American father," he said as he slipped into the seat next to me.

Langthorne smiled into the camera and began a history of the Cavalier King Charles. How they were bred in an attempt to recapture the original look of the breed seen in paintings of the 1700s. Then he talked about early domestication of canines as pictures of fox and wolves and coyotes flashed by on the screen behind him. It felt odd to experience a picture within a picture.

Then he walked from behind the podium and began showing simple commands, with voice and hand, explaining how to begin a training session. The dog watched him for signals. They worked as a team and it was beautiful to see. I noticed he signaled with his right hand and when he petted the dogs head and gave him a treat, again he used his right hand.

When the camera zoomed in to the dog heeling I noticed something else, a slight weakness in his left hand and arm.

"When did he have his stroke?" I leaned over and asked Joel.

"About two years ago. It didn't slow him down at all but he had a little problem with his left side. Physical therapy was taking care of it, though."

Another piece of the puzzle confirmed. I'd spoken maybe two sentences to Thomas Langthorne, but had seen him on the phone at his desk the first time I went to their home. Like many veterinarians I remember in snapshots, very helpful when seeing patients. In my mind's eye I saw him, headset on, left arm flat on the desk, taking notes with his right hand. Did his left hand have enough strength to fire a gun?

And why didn't Chief of Police Garcia know all about this?

◇◇◇

I sat straight in that armchair in Joel Denny's home theater barely paying attention to what was happening on the screen. What should I do? Bother Chief Garcia with information he probably already knew? My bet was the motive still boiled down to money. But money for who?

The screen went black and the lights began to come up.

"Nice to see the old boy in happier times," Joel said. He stood up and went over to the electronics bank at the back of the theater.

Maybe I should confide in Joel, I thought. He liked the victim and he's a documentary filmmaker. He's used to righting wrongs, pointing out cover-ups. I made my way to the exit and waited for him. If I was going to say something it should be now. He beat me to it.

"I'm glad the police ruled out murder," he said, still at his keyboard.

"What did you say?" I asked. Just having arrived from California he probably didn't know their deaths were now considered suspicious.

He turned and smiled. "I said I'm glad the cops ruled out murder. I'd probably be their main suspect. The old fool was suing me for ten million dollars. Defamation of character, loss of income, you name it, they threw it at me, all because I filmed their kennel and used some of it in my exposé of the life of show dogs. They never signed a release. A complete oversight by my legal team." With a deft touch the cabinet doors closed. Still smiling he began walking toward me. I noticed his eyeteeth were pointed like a wolf.

"Bitch of it is my lawyer thought they were going to win."

I nodded and opened the door. "Weren't you in California at the time of their deaths?"

"A little secret," he raised his finger to his lips. "My cameraman and I hitched a ride on a friend's plane. We needed some background shots ASAP. After two days we hopped back on the plane and returned to LA."

I wished he hadn't told me.

"Old Tom was a feisty guy." The filmmaker smiled, remembering his friend. "He even took on the Police Chief Bobby Garcia."

"What?" I swiveled my head so fast my neck hurt.

"The Langthornes spearheaded a campaign to oust the chief of police. Said he was incompetent and a danger to public safety. Boy was Bobby pissed at them. I doubt he cares much how they died."

Suspects and motives everywhere I turned. A town full of people who wanted them dead.

Even the chief of police could be a suspect.

Maybe I should let sleeping show dogs lie.

Chapter Twenty-seven

My cell phone rang at five-thirty the next morning, startling me awake. I reached for it on my nightstand and managed to knock it onto the floor. No one calls me so early. The county veterinary emergency hospital took all our calls until seven when the staff came in. All I could think of was Gramps. I lunged for the phone still ringing on the floor, slid out of the bed, and banged my elbow.

"Hello," I croaked into the phone. The rug burn on my arm stung.

"Hello there, Maybelle here."

"Who?" My position on the floor felt mighty uncomfortable. I wished the floor had room service.

"Maybelle here," she repeated like a demented parrot. "It's Maybelle Guzzman. This isn't too early for you, is it?"

My reply at this point would have been X-rated. Instead I managed a grunt as I stood up.

"Every vet I ever met started their day at five." Her perky voice oozed enthusiasm that I definitely did not feel. I wondered who gave her my personal number.

Not waiting for an answer, and with limited input on my part, she kept going. "I wanted to thank you personally for all you did for me. We didn't get a chance to talk at the party so I'd like to invite you to lunch tomorrow, if you're free."

We didn't get a chance to talk because you walked away from

me, I thought. Not to mention wanting to sue me for rendering first aid. Did I want to see this woman? It was a toss-up.

"It's nothing fancy. Just a little place we girls go before playing golf."

She kept on talking while I climbed back into bed and pulled the covers up around me. Another hour of sleep beckoned. "Okay," I murmured, "Where?"

"Bennity Country Club, eleven-thirty tomorrow, in the snack bar."

"Mmmm."

"See you there."

By the time she hung up I'd fallen back to sleep.

I didn't remember our date until eleven o'clock the following day when Sandy phoned to remind me.

"Maybelle called to say she was running a little late. You have a date for lunch?"

"Oh shoot. I totally forgot."

"Why are you meeting her?" The tone in her voice said it all.

"She called me." I didn't feel like explaining myself.

"Next time you schedule something during office hours, please let me know." Sandy acted quite miffed considering I never have lunch dates.

Since we were on speakerphone Mari figured out the situation and came to my rescue.

"No problem, Sandy. Our next appointment isn't until two. Kate should be able to eat lunch and come back in plenty of time."

Only static greeted her statement.

"Okay, see you later." I disconnected and breathed a sigh of relief. No power play confrontation between our office manager and myself. A nice sit-down lunch was a novelty for me. It might be fun, and this time Maybelle couldn't walk away from my questions.

Mari dropped me off at the Country Club at eleven thirty-five. The snack bar sounded about my speed since I only had my cargo pants and scrub top on. I started thinking about questions for one of Vivian Langthorne's best friends as I opened the glass and wood main door. Never having been in a country club before I didn't know what to expect. Not this entryway as expansive as a fine hotel with killer views of the golf course.

Classic elegance shone in the blue-and-white Chinese lamps, large bouquets of fresh flowers set on polished wood, and casual clusters of chairs and sofas, about half occupied. Most of the members wore designer sportswear although many of the women obviously weren't there to play golf. Sitting in the middle of a cluster of ladies all groomed to perfection, Maybelle looked up then waved at me. I almost didn't recognize her. Usually she swathed herself in various knitted garments, layering them like cabbage leaves around herself. Today she looked smooth and sleek in a toffee-colored linen dress, a turquoise scarf casually tied around her neck.

In comparison, I looked like a busboy.

"Hello. Over here, Dr. Kate," she trilled across the room when our eyes met. To make sure I didn't miss her, she stood up and began waving at me as if I were a taxi.

Obediently I moved over to the cluster of women with her. Blend in, I did not. These ladies reminded me of exotic birds with a shimmer of green here, a flash of scarlet there, and lots of curved sharp nails. They all had bleached blond hair, bleached white teeth, and bleached who-knows-what else. Maybelle was effusive in her introduction. You would think we were best friends forever.

They proceeded to greet me warmly and immediately began telling me about their pets' problems, starting with pooping on the carpet. It didn't bother me. As soon as anyone finds out I'm a veterinarian that's all they want to talk about. I often wondered if proctologists have to listen to details of everyone's colonoscopy at cocktail parties. Of course I can't diagnose without seeing a patient, but I can give pet owners general information. In the middle of discussing the merits of one cat litter over another, I felt a tug on my arm.

"We have to get going, girls. You know the snack bar. They get annoyed if you're late for your reservation." She laughed and skillfully moved me along while waving to the other ladies. In a flurry of good-byes, nice to meet you's, and general goodwill, I turned and tagged along behind Maybelle who moved at a fast clip. The snack bar turned out to be a gorgeous formal dining room patterned after an English men's club with lots of mahogany furniture and hunting prints on the wall.

Maybelle immediately ordered a dry martini as we settled into our booth. She was astonished I didn't order a drink even though I had to go back to work. As she sipped her cocktail and cast a sharp eye around the room I formulated some of the questions I needed to ask her.

The server deftly went through the lunch specials then took our orders. As soon as he was out of sight Maybelle began. "I have so many questions I'd like to ask you."

"Me too," I told her. I figured after we discussed the shooting I could work my way around to her relationship with Thomas and Vivian, find out if they were in financial or emotional trouble when they died.

She drained the rest of her martini then carelessly set it down on the white tablecloth. It teetered back and forth for a moment then came to a stop. Maybelle focused all her attention on me. Her stare became uncomfortable.

"I didn't know the last time I saw you."

Not surprisingly, I had no idea what she was talking about.

Seeing the surprise on my face she backtracked. "I didn't know there was anything fishy about the deaths of Thomas and Viv until after Tim and Tina's party. No one told me while I was in the hospital. They didn't want to upset me."

"Oh. I'm so sorry." I wondered what else she didn't know while she was recuperating.

"Who do you think killed them?" she whispered in an urgent tone. "Who murdered my friends?"

Her question surprised me so much I said the first thing that came into my head. "I thought you did, over the competition in the dog show. Your dogs weren't getting the ribbons," I answered truthfully, after I got over the shock of her question.

"Get real." Her tone said it all, sarcastic and to the point. "I loved those two. Well, sometimes I hated them, but I loved them despite everything. We went through a lot together, the three of us. Good and bad, but we always worked it out." Strangely enough, I understood what she meant. Did I believe it? Despite the sincerity in her voice, her eyes stayed bulging and cold.

Our server arrived with lunch so we stopped talking. I pretended to be interested in the silverware, then, filled up more time by drinking my water. She ordered another martini, this time a double.

"Is someone picking you up?" While I spoke her fingers drummed on the table.

"My husband is. Anyway, three is my limit at lunch." As if summoned on command another drink arrived, the iced vodka frosting the sides of the glass. Eagerly she held it up to her lips. "Did you see anything weird at their house? There's so much gossip going around I decided to ask you directly. So, tell me everything." She slurred the last few words and so far hadn't touched her Caesar salad.

It was my turn to take charge of this conversation. "No. You tell me everything. Why are you suspicious about the circumstances of their deaths? What is it that you know but aren't telling the police?"

The last bit of vodka slid down her throat followed by the daintily nibbled olive on a toothpick before she answered me. "Thomas hated guns, almost fainted at the sight of blood, but he kept all that well hidden. He wanted to be a man's man, which is why he walked around like an English gentleman. Vivian had to take care of any emergencies with the dogs because her husband would pass out if he saw blood." She punctuated the sentence with a hiccup.

Thinking back, every time I came over to their place Thomas would greet me, then, disappear into his office to conduct some business. He conveniently finished as soon as I was done.

"Maybelle." Her head slowly swiveled toward me, eyes slightly unfocused. "I thought he couldn't do it because he was right-handed."

Her face remained a blank.

"You know. He was shot in the chest and the gun was by his left hand, the one weakened by his stroke."

The bleary eyes slowly came into focus. "The physical therapy for his stroke worked. His arm and hand strength were normal. But it didn't matter so much for him because he was ambidextrous." She waggled a French-manicured finger in my face. "You're reading too much Agatha Christie."

With lunch over, I waited outside for Mari to pick me up. I kept shaking my head in frustration. Every turn presented an obstacle. If you went to the police and said Thomas was afraid of blood, how could you document it? A hundred psychiatrists would testify that in a rage, fear might be forgotten. My belief that they would never have left their dogs without food and sufficient water was only an opinion, again, open to interpretation. Chief Garcia laughed at my lemon theory. My well-meaning search for the truth seemed doomed. Trying to fulfill a promise to find out the truth only led me down a dark path to a dead end.

I could hear the sheriff ordering me to stick to helping animals and leave the detecting to him. Sandy, annoyed as always, telling me over and over again to let it go. Even Gramps, warning me about getting involved. The only other person who thought Thomas and Vivian had been murdered was Maybelle, their eccentric friend with a drinking problem.

Perhaps their deaths were destined to remain suspicious, never solved. Just another cold case.

Two quick beeps of a car horn made me look up. Mari turned the corner and slowed down past the circular fountain to come to a stop in front of me. She hopped out and slowly walked over to greet me. It was obvious she was curious about my meeting.

"Have a good lunch?" She yanked open the passenger door and swung up into the seat.

"Sure."

Sometimes it's best not to tell the truth.

◇◇◇

We drove back to the clinic mostly in silence. I had no idea how to continue my amateur investigations. What can you do with lots of suspects and lots of motives but no hard evidence? I decided to give up. I felt a wave of sorrow that somehow I had failed the elderly couple.

That's when the bombshell hit.

Not a physical bomb but a verbal bomb that would blow this case wide open, and it started with an innocent question from Mari.

"Did Maybelle ask you about her King Charles spaniels?"

Lost in thought, I barely listened to her. "What?"

"I heard from a tech who works in Rhinebeck that she's having breeding problems."

The turnoff from the highway was approaching. Switching lanes to get ready to exit I focused more on the driving than the conversation. "What kind of problems?"

She tilted a water bottle to her lips. It took a while for her to answer back. "She had some kind of fertility issue. Her bitches couldn't get pregnant."

A million reasons for doggy infertility flashed into my head from a simple husbandry problem like poor diet or miscalculating the female cycle to viral or bacterial diseases.

"I'm sure she's getting great advice from the vets over there. They can always refer her up to Cornell if necessary."

Mari twisted in her seat and reached for her purse. After downing some ibuprofen with another swig of water she continued the story.

"Oh, they found out what was wrong. The stud she used was firing blanks."

I almost passed the off ramp, turning at the last moment across two lanes of traffic while hitting the brakes to slow us down.

Mari gave me a look then a laugh. "Miss something?"

"Yeah, I almost missed it." I came to the end of the off ramp and braked at the light.

"But I've got it now."

Chapter Twenty-eight

"Gramps," I said excitedly as I paced around my apartment. "I think I figured out the murder."

I heard some kind of grumble in the phone, probably Gramps trying to ease himself into his green recliner, usually with a beer on one side and the TV remote on the other.

"Listen to this," I continued, still pacing. "The Langthornes had a secret. Some of their dogs contracted a viral infection and ran terribly high fevers. It made the males sterile. One of those dogs was Charles Too."

"What does that matter?"

"The Asian industrialist who bought Charles Too wanted him for a stud dog. Pippi must have heard about the million dollars from her parents and tried to persuade them to go through with it, but substitute his look-alike son for the real Charles Too. When they refused, she had them killed and switched dogs. The only person who knew the dogs really well and could have put two and two together was Maybelle Guzzman. Pippi shot her to keep her out of the way. A million dollars is a great motive for murder."

"I know someone who was killed for twenty bucks," he said in a matter-of-fact tone.

"So, should I tell the police?"

"Do you have any proof? Where is the dog they made the fuss over?"

"He's in Hong Kong."

"Who signed his paperwork to fly out of the country?"

I waited for a moment before I answered. I knew where this was going. "Okay, Gramps. I signed the health certificates."

"So how can you claim now that the dog was switched? Do you see what I mean?"

I conceded the point.

"Then, where was this Pippi at the time of the murders? Does she have an alibi?" His voice sounded like the old days when he would talk with his police buddies about cases, making them sound like exciting mysteries to a young girl listening in when she was supposed to be in bed. "I'm sure someone checked her whereabouts when all the questions started popping up. Believe me the cops wouldn't let that slide."

The logic was irrefutable. I remembered Chief Garcia insisting Pippi's alibi held up under intense scrutiny even involving a late night date with a retired judge.

"So what you are saying is I have no suspect, no motive I can prove, and no physical evidence."

"Bingo," Gramps said. "I'm telling you again to leave it alone. Feelings can be wrong, *are* wrong most of the time. Like eyewitnesses, very unreliable. Please stay out of it, Katie."

"Maybe she had an accomplice?"

"Honey, drop it. Go get one of those pedicure things you like. Take your mind off murder."

I wanted to reassure him but I felt as though I was caught in a whirlpool that kept sucking me back in no matter how hard I tried to climb out.

Chapter Twenty-nine

On the pretext of buying another pair of pants I went back to the Tube Depot, hoping to get more information on the relationship between Henry James and Randy. I'd barely walked through the door when the owner himself confronted me.

"Have you seen much of Oak Falls?" Randy asked, moving slightly closer. He smelled good, a musky-citrus high end cologne.

I leaned back, since I smelled like Windex. He seemed suspiciously friendly.

Thinking I must be shy he continued flirting. "If you're free tonight I'd love to take you to dinner and give you the million-dollar tour." His smile appeared deliciously sincere.

"That sounds perfect. Could we meet here, at six-thirty? I've still got some errands to run." That way I wouldn't have to fend him off at my apartment.

If he was taken aback by my calling the shots he covered it up completely. "All right, I'll see you at six-thirty. Is there any place in particular you'd like to try for dinner?"

Since I'd only been to three places in the last four months, not counting gas station quick stops, I thought I'd leave it to him. "Whatever you'd like is fine with me." I sounded super accommodating, which is what I wanted, the better to pump him for information during dinner.

◇◇◇

Hurrying home I fed and walked Buddy, who tried to catch a squirrel out on the terrace. Then after a quick shower I changed into one of my two all-purpose black dresses. Pulling my hair into a ponytail I dug through a pile of sneakers and work boots to find a pair of heels that matched. After vowing for the thousandth time to organize my clothes I carefully applied a full makeup, rescued from the back of the closet a dressy jeans jacket Gracie had given me, and then headed out the door. After almost tripping several times I recovered my sea legs for high heels and slid into the truck, butt first. At the halfway point to the Tube Depot I realized I'd forgotten my perfume, so I rubbed some sunscreen behind my ears and hoped for the best.

Although the tubing part of the store closed at five, the restaurant was crowded. From the parking lot I could see that most of the creek-side tables were filled. Music filtered down from the bar, conversation and laughter carried along with it. I left my backpack in the car and transferred my keys, wallet, phone, and lipstick into a black Coach purse that belonged to my mother. Feeling suitably sophisticated I slipped on a pair of sunglasses and strolled into the bar.

Not seeing Randy anywhere I continued on to the patio and sat at a small table overlooking Main Street. The sun low in the west cast shadows that emphasized the wooden clapboard and scrollwork in the older properties. Oak Falls could have been a postcard for a typical sleepy New England village. I sipped on a white wine while thinking of questions for my dinner date.

"Here you are." I heard Randy's voice over my right shoulder then he slipped into the chair opposite me. He'd taken the time to change into a fresh shirt and jacket. "You look great," he told me with some surprise.

"Thanks, so do you." With his slightly tousled hair streaked with blond from the sun, he made a perfect advertisement for the outdoor lifestyle he promoted in the store. His white shirt contrasted with his tan and slight five o'clock shadow. The jeans jacket he wore coordinated with mine. I had a pang of regret that I wasn't attracted to him at all, but I figured this would be a novelty for him. I didn't think many girls said no to Randy.

He drank the rest of the drink he brought to the table, then, signaled the waitress for a second. She obviously knew what he drank since it arrived at the table almost immediately.

"Would you care for another white wine?" he asked before the server left.

"No thanks. What are you having?" I wondered what people who ran a bar ended up drinking on their own time.

"Johnny Walker Blue Label. It gets the job done."

What job that was I didn't ask. Getting loaded?

With a flick of his wrist he finished the second drink than said, "Shall we go?"

"Sure." I left my half full drink on the table and stood up.

Randy wasn't subtle as he slowly looked me up and down. I half expected him to ask me to turn around so he could check out my booty. Not used to being treated like meat, my face froze trying to keep a smile going. He took my arm and guided me past the bar and then out through the double doors. I noticed more than one look from his female staff. Randy remained oblivious.

"So, where should I begin?" We started walking down Main Street toward the center of town.

"Well, how about some town history?" I suggested as we passed a store displaying local pottery.

"Good start." He squeezed my arm and pointed across the street. "See the old church with the wooden spire? That's where the original town started back in the Revolutionary War. Most of the important stuff took place by the Hudson River and Rhinebeck, but Oak Falls supplied meat and game to the soldiers and did its part. I did my part too. In high school I used to sneak away and smoke a little weed in the graveyard."

"I'm shocked," I told him with a laugh.

He joined in. "The graveyard and the little island in the river were my high school secret spots. Just above where we launch the tubes there's a narrow point with some big flat rocks you can use as stepping stones. Don't try crossing there if you're stoned. I speak from bitter experience."

This wasn't the sort of history I expected but I liked it. It humanized growing up here.

"Now it's my turn." His voice grew softer, more seductive. I braced myself for Randy suggesting we skip dinner and go to his place.

"Tell me about the day you found Vivian and Thomas Langthorne."

Not exactly romantic talk. The motive for this date was finally revealed. He was pumping me for information. I gazed up at him with my sunglasses still on. Our date promised to be an interesting one. Editing as I went along, I gave him a quick synopsis of discovering the bodies and being interviewed by the police.

"So you didn't see anything, hear anything or find anything that would shed light on their deaths. No murderer hiding in the foyer closet?" His eye was drawn to something across the road.

"No." I searched my memory. Why did he ask me that? Did the foyer even have a closet? All I remember is that it was dark when I entered the house. Could someone have hidden there, then slipped out when I went into the living room? Between the dogs barking and the thunder that day anything was possible. It frightened me to think about it.

The restaurant Randy chose, Casa Toscana, was off Main Street overlooking the river. It would be a short walk back to the Tube Depot. Considering my date drank two more Johnny Walkers with dinner I definitely didn't want him driving. What was it about small towns that made people drink like fish? Or was it me? My only glass of house white wine remained untouched. I didn't want liquor to cloud my goal of learning about his relationship with Henry James.

The only problem I had was keeping him focused and his hands to himself, now that he'd gotten the information he wanted.

"How is your Osso Bucco?" I asked.

"Fantastic. I wish I could get Piero to work for me but he's making too much money here. Did I tell you he started out making pizzas at the diner?"

"Yes, I think you did," at least twice so far. I watched him mop up the sauce with bread and went in for the kill. "What made you decide to expand your place?"

He swallowed the bread and drained his glass of whiskey then explained. "I'm an entrepreneur. Like Donald Trump. People are coming up on weekends and quite a few are moving here permanently. With so many people telecommuting our population base has soared. Most of them go tubing and they all have to eat."

Amazingly he appeared stone sober.

"But you didn't own the property. Weren't you worried about such costly renovations to a place you only leased?"

"Fate intervened." He broke off another piece of bread. "I'm a lucky guy."

"How so?" I pretended to take a sip from my wine.

"I got a shipment from Nepal a few weeks ago. They sent me the wrong order. I was so pissed the distributor told me to keep the stuff and he'd send me the correct order immediately. My floor manager put the clothes out on the floor, real hippie-looking things and they were a huge hit. Now I can't move them fast enough and I'm only one of two stores in the U.S. with this line. Lucky break, huh?"

More lucky, you hired a good store manager.

Finished with his main course he signaled the server to bring the desert menu. "Now, where was I?"

This time he did slur his words and the glazed look in his blue eyes showed the booze had hit. He was hammered.

"Telling me how lucky you were that the Langthornes died when they did."

"Right. I didn't even have to use any muscle to get what I wanted. I should thank whoever knocked them off." He reached over and took my hand.

"At first they thought it was a murder-suicide," I said primly, loosening his hand to grasp my wineglass. "Now it's classified as suspicious."

"Right." Randy lowered his head and voice. "I heard what you told the cops. No suicide note, those dogs running around like crazy. Shooting her in the heart? Thomas couldn't have done that. He was an Old School gentleman. You can't even say he had dementia. We'd just had a huge fight and I will testify there was nothing senile about the old coot."

His sentences became more choppy as he explained.

"Had a conversation once with him. Carbon monoxide poisoning. That's what they decided. A couple of drinks and start the car in the garage. Dogs outside in kennels. Email friends with instructions. Or pills. One of those two." Nodding to himself he looked again at the desert menu.

Maybe they told their plans to someone else who decided to improvise.

"What can you tell me about your relationship with Henry James?"

A hand snaked over the table and caught mine. Randy leaned toward me, his breath stinking of garlic and whiskey. "I could tell you a lot. But I won't." A crazy grin lit up his face.

"Please?" It took all I had to give the creep a sultry look. Unfortunately, it worked too well.

He lowered his voice. "How about skipping dessert and going to my place?"

Date over.

After depositing an unsteady Randy at the Tube Place to sleep it off in his office I walked back to the truck. An elderly couple makes plans to die together once the burden of life is too much. You read about it all the time. That choice was taken from them.

Given tonight's performance at dinner, Randy didn't seem to have the focus or intent of a cold-blooded killer. Hiring someone definitely would be his first choice. Is that what happened? What was the purpose of this dinner date? Did he want to find out what I knew? Or since I didn't constitute a threat did he simply relax and drink his way to happy? Too keyed up to go home I decided to get some dessert after all.

At ten p.m. the parking lot of the Oak Falls Diner was packed. It was the only place open until eleven at night where you could get a reasonably priced quick meal in town, I rarely saw it empty. I slipped out of the truck and, feeling overdressed, went in for something sweet. My worry immediately evaporated when I saw two tables full of prom dresses and tuxedos chomping down on hamburgers, French fries, and gravy.

I tried to get away from the noise and sat at a booth by the wait station. Any of the desserts made by Mama G were fantastic. Unable to see the special board I stared out at the rest of the customers, still thinking about what Randy had told me. How many people sitting here had secrets they wouldn't want anyone to know?

"Hey, Kate, you're here late." Rosie placed a menu in front of me. "Can I get you any coffee?"

"Too late for high test, only decaf please. What are the desert specials? I've got a sweet tooth tonight."

"Well, we're out of pie. There's still some strawberry shortcake or lemon pound cake and chocolate mousse. Those kids beat you to it." She pointed at the prom group who had finished their burgers and had started on their deserts.

"The strawberry shortcake is fine, but make it a half-portion." Feeling sorry for myself was no reason to fall completely off the sugar wagon. My choice made, I handed back the menu.

Rosie stood back and said, "You look very nice tonight. Got a date?"

"Had sort of a date, but not really." My garbled explanation spurted out.

My server nodded wisely. "I had plenty of those myself until I married Joe. Dating is hell." Rosie took off to put in the order.

Suddenly tired I leaned back into the booth and closed my eyes. Mentally I reviewed what I had found out. I knew why Charles Too had been switched but had no proof Pippi was involved in the murder. Perhaps I was looking at this the wrong way. Could the switch be separate from the murders? Maybe Gramps was right and the crime was never going to be solved;

just a bump in the cosmic road. What could an amateur like me hope to accomplish that the police hadn't?

Rosie came back with a modest piece of strawberry shortcake. The sugar rush and the coffee aroma revived my senses.

"If you have a moment, Kate, Mama G wants to talk to you." She sounded as surprised as I was. "Let me know when you're finished and I'll take you to her office."

The luscious desert barely registered as I hurriedly ate and speculated on why she'd summoned me. I'd seen her cat a while ago, maybe she needed some advice? Mama G was the queen of the diner and I gather she ruled with an iron hand. No item got on the menu without her approval. Most of the work staff either was directly, or indirectly related to her. Although seventy-four years old, she still baked pies six days a week.

A few minutes after I finished, Rosie escorted me to the back of the diner and into the addition the Gianetti family added to the original metal structure. We stopped at a door plastered with pictures, some old and yellowed around the edges, most new with smiling faces. I recognized Rosie and her two dogs amid the couples, children, and grandchildren.

After knocking on the door a voice said, "Come." Rosie told me to go in, then abandoned me to go back to the restaurant. I didn't know what to expect.

Mama G sat at her desk. Wire-rimmed reading glasses perched on her nose but her dark eyes sought mine above the glasses. Wrinkles pleated her cheeks. She wore an old-fashioned black dress with a lace collar, a golden crucifix resting in the hollow of her neck. Frances Ford Coppola could have cast her in *The Godfather*. I waited to see what she wanted.

"*Doctore*, sit. Sit." She ordered me, her English still accented with Italian after so many years in America. "My grandson Luke tells me you're a good person."

Taken by surprise I agreed. "I try to be, *Signora*."

"You found my Vivian and Thomas, may God rest their souls." She made the sign of the cross and raised the gold crucifix to her lips.

"Yes, I did. And every day I wish it had been someone else," I told her truthfully.

"*Cosa?*" The Italian for *why* came more easily than the English. Her eyes darkened.

I took a moment to answer. "I am puzzled by their deaths. It's as if they won't lie still."

She clasped her hands and muttered what might have been a prayer. Then she spoke.

"Murder, my friends were murdered, not suicide. We talked about it many times. No guns. Not this way. Thomas, he afraid of blood, needles, anything like that. He passed out. They had pills saved for that. They weren't *Catholica*," she explained. "*Episcopaliana.*"

"Have you told anyone about this?"

"No. I kept it only in my heart. Who would believe an old woman?" she said in a matter-of-fact voice. "But when Luke told me you had many questions, you tell police you think it murder, I had hope."

The room closed around me. I had more validation of my suspicions from someone who knew the elderly couple well.

"So, why you do this, *Katerina?* Why you not be quiet and go back to your life, leave this alone?" Her concern shown in her face.

Good question, I thought, one that I've asked a dozen times at least.

"Mama G," I explained to us both, "it's the right thing to do."

She smiled at me, eyes twinkling, the tension gone. "*Vero.* The truth."

We sat in silence for a moment. What if she helped me and put us both in danger? Would the murderer wait patiently for us to find them, or would they strike first? I was willing to take a risk but I didn't want anything to happen to her.

"You need to talk to my Luke," she said conspiratorially. "I give him a call."

◇◇◇

I hadn't spoken to Luke since the night he picked up his grandmother's cat Gatto, but now his dark brown eyes looked at me as candidly as Mama G's had. Off duty, and dressed down in jeans and a black hoodie, he didn't look too comfortable.

We had scheduled our meeting just before seven, at the McDonald's next to the off ramp of the New York State thruway, one exit north of town. Kids were running and screaming everywhere, but mostly confined to the playground. Tired parents watched their offspring while loading up on soft drinks and fries.

"Sorry about meeting here," he told me, "but the town loves to gossip. We don't need to get folks started talking about this before we're ready."

I thought about what he said while I drank my coffee. My last memory of him was when Police Chief Garcia argued with Sandy. Luke had leaned against the police car and laughed.

"So you aren't speaking to me now in your official capacity as a member of the Oak Falls police department?"

He shook his head. "My grandmother asked me to talk to a friend of hers. What we talk about now is no one's business but our own."

Finally I had someone who wanted to hear what I had to say about the Langthorne murders, someone who could turn it into an official investigation. And I didn't know where to start.

So I started at the beginning.

Our coffee turned cold so we decided to walk for a bit. Dodging children, we went out into the parking lot and paced to the end, the blacktop still warm beneath our feet as the sun went down.

"I had no idea," Luke explained. "I went to visit some college buddies in New Mexico that Friday. By the time I got back the whole thing was wrapped up. Chief Garcia said it was a done deal."

"With a murder-suicide there are no suspects, no trial, no uncomfortable loose ends."

The whine of a siren caught his attention for a moment. You could see the thoughts flying through his brain. His was an intelligent face, more than a handsome one, a face for the long haul. His dark wavy hair had no product, no gel.

He caught me staring at him.

"You have nice hair," I blurted out, then immediately regretted it.

"So do you."

Surprisingly it didn't feel as awkward as I thought.

"You've given me a lot to think about, Kate. I'd like to check a few things before I bring you down to the station for a statement," he said. "I don't know that there is a lot of evidence, but there are sufficient questions to warrant a second look, in my opinion. I'll investigate Pippi's alibi myself. "

"Do you know anything about their wills?"

"It's my understanding everything went to the daughter. That bears checking into too."

"What about Randy and Henry James?"

His face showed contempt. "Randy is a user, always has been. He fools a lot of the people up from the city though, especially women. If it wasn't for Kristin handling the business for him he probably would have run it into the ground."

So Kristin must be the person behind the great products displayed in the store. "I have to confess we had dinner together the other night. He got so loaded I had to drag him back to the Tube Depot. The only new info I got from him was that he didn't think the Langthornes killed themselves."

"As far as Henry James goes, he's the wild card in this thing."

My eyes met his. "I feel as though he could be dangerous."

"That's why it's time to let the professionals handle it. You've uncovered a number of people with motives for murder. I suggest you back off and let me and the department handle it."

"Okay," I agreed. "I hope Chief Garcia isn't the murderer."

Luke laughed at the thought, but then his face became serious.

"Don't do any more investigating on your own," he warned me. "If there is a killer, and I believe now there is, it could be dangerous for you. Go to work, keep to a regular schedule, and call me if you think of anything else."

I promised him I would.

Unfortunately, it didn't work out that way.

Someone had other plans.

Chapter Thirty

Saturday started off fine. Buddy and I went for an early morning walk before I left for work. For the first time in a long while I didn't think about murder. Someone else was taking care of things. I didn't have to do everything anymore.

I threw the ball and watched as my dog shot across the grass and scooped it up. The changes in the last few weeks were amazing. No ribs showed under his short but glossy coat. To my mind there now was a happy smile on his face all the time. He'd started to trust that I wouldn't leave him and it showed in his relaxed demeanor.

We finished up and after a quick shower I pulled on my scrubs and went into the clinic.

"We're slammed today," Mari said as soon as she saw me, "but in a good way, a full schedule with no disasters." My technician liked to keep a positive attitude, which made working with her a pleasure.

"Let me grab some coffee and check the animals and we can be on our way." I walked over to the treatment area and quickly examined the patients that I'd admitted to the hospital. None were critical. There was a cat with diabetes we were monitoring for the owner, a Silky terrier with a bite wound on his lip and nose from a fight with his brother, and an egg-bound cockatiel. After writing up treatments and release instructions and touching base with my other vet tech I poured some coffee and ate a handful of granola.

"See you later," I yelled to Sandy as we headed for the truck.

"Any more lunch dates for you?" Her face looked gray from the reflected light of the computer.

"Yeah, the Queen of England at three for tea."

"Very funny," she replied. There was no humor in her voice or eyes. I figured she got up on the wrong side of the bed today and let it rest. Maybe something else was bothering her that I didn't know about. I'd ask Mari later. She knew everything.

The day zipped by. Our final appointment turned out to be a barrel of fun, a box of eight-week-old kittens with ear mites. The look-alike gray kittens ran around the house, thinking being chased by their owners was a new game. The litter was exceptionally lively and not ready to have their ears cleaned. After letting the owners try to round them up, Mari and I took over. We herded the kittens together, bribing them with food. Then we worked on them one at a time and relocated them to a holding room, also supplied with food; food being the operative word. If you've ever seen kittens eat they will push anyone and anything aside to dive into their cat bowl. At this age nature encourages them to be greedy.

As we worked on each kitten I cleaned their ears and then we applied a topical medication between the shoulder blades which would clear it up for good. The Russian Blues had great personalities and didn't even hold a grudge after all we did to them. The owner explained that the ear mites came in with her new breeding queen and she didn't notice them until the whole litter had become infested. She'd tried to drown the mites with ear drops but got most of it on the floor and walls. I made a note to have the staff send the owner info and links to feline sites dealing with breeding your cat. When I phoned it in to the office Sandy grumbled that we were making more work for her.

In the truck on the way back to the hospital I asked Mari about Sandy. "She seems more uptight than ever," I commented.

"I totally agree. There's talk she wants to retire once Doc gets back."

A dump truck barreling toward us made me move over in our lane in self defense. "I can see that. She's put in a lot of years."

"Unfortunately she refinanced her house a few years ago, so I'm not sure how that will work out," Mari revealed. "But a lot of us are in that same boat."

"One of my cousins did the same thing."

Mari reached into her purse and came out with a pack of gum. After offering me one she took a piece and put the rest back. "She must have straightened it out somehow because she isn't complaining about money anymore."

"That's because she's complaining about everything else."

I was feeling pretty chipper since Officer Luke Gianetti had joined the investigation. I didn't have to question my clients, sneak around town hoping to filter gossip from the truth. Someone else other than Gramps was in my corner. Sure no one knew about it yet, but if he found something and could prove it then the town mystery would be solved whether they liked it or not. Things were beginning to fall into place. I liked my work, ditched my cheating boyfriend, and adopted a dog who adored me. Single and loving it for now.

When I got back home Buddy and I went for a walk. As soon as I was far enough away from the hospital I called Luke to tell him about the fertility issues as a motive for murder. Unfortunately it went to voice mail. "I'm going to check with Sandy on this and then get back to you," I told him. "A million dollars is a good motive for murder. It also explains why Maybelle was shot, so Pippi could get her out of the way during the switch. She was the only one left who might be able to tell the difference between the father and son."

Buddy decided to chase a bird foraging in the grass. He took off after it and seemed astonished when it flew away. Before he could get his paws muddy by the stream I called Luke back. We headed up to the porch when my cell phone rang.

"Luke?" I asked.

"No, but that sounds promising." Destiny, the hospital accountant, said to me. I mentally kicked myself for almost giving the police involvement away. Luckily she didn't pursue it. "Do you think you can trim one of Captain Hook's nails for me? It looks like it split in two."

"Sure. That's pretty easy to do."

"Can I come by now? It would save me a trip next week to get this month's stats and income stream early. I tried calling Sandy but her phone must be dead."

Buddy put his paw on my leg, wanting attention. "Pull up at the back entrance and call me when you get here. I'm in for the night." I knew Destiny always put the info on a thumb drive, worked the numbers at the office, and finished the reports in her home office.

"Thanks, Kate. See you in a few."

About a half hour later Destiny showed up. Sure enough, Captain Hook had somehow split his toenail. A little surgical glue fixed it right up and I made a note in his medical record to file it down a bit at his next wing clipping appointment.

Destiny handed me a small box of Baci di Perugina chocolates. "How did you know those were my favorites?" I asked.

"I didn't. I love them too."

"Well, I hope Hookie splits a toenail more often."

Buddy sat by my feet staring at the parrot. Captain Hook ignored the dog, having eyes only for his mommy. We waited in my apartment while the thumb drive finished loading all the data Destiny needed while we both sampled the chocolates.

"Don't you usually do the books in the middle of the month?" I asked her.

"Yes, but I'm going on a mini vacation to Maine in two weeks and wanted to get a jump on it. I'm doing the same for Randy and a couple of my other large clients. That way payroll won't be interrupted."

Since most of our employees lived paycheck-to-paycheck any disruption would be a disaster.

Destiny jumped up, shoved Captain Hook into the front of her blouse, and went to check on the download. The parrot's head stuck out of her décolleté. I didn't ask why.

Data complete, she gathered up her things and said goodnight. The hospital and apartment became quiet again, almost too quiet.

Buddy and I fell asleep in front of the television.

Luke never called back.

Chapter Thirty-one

It drizzled all Sunday morning on and off, one of those overcast damp days that pop up in late spring or early summer. It didn't bother me. The apartment was way overdue for a cleaning and I couldn't stuff another thing into the laundry basket. With a Harrison Ford festival playing on the television and a pepperoni pizza in the freezer I looked forward to a peaceful day in my sweats.

I'd put the second load of laundry in when the phone rang.

"Kate?" I recognized Destiny's voice.

"Hi, Destiny, what's up?" With my cell phone tucked under my chin I poured the detergent in and started the washing machine.

"I'm sorry, but do you mind if I come over again either tonight or tomorrow morning? I must have screwed up the files last night because my thumb drive is corrupted. None of these numbers make any sense."

I laughed. "My social calendar this weekend is filled with doing my laundry and watching old movies, so it's no problem at all."

Folding laundry while watching Harrison Ford jump off the Hoover Dam to Tommy Lee Jones' horror, I lost track of time. By the time I took Buddy out an hour later I figured Destiny had changed her mind and was going to wait until tomorrow. Settled in bed with my book I still felt a little cold from the damp weather. A hot toddy like Gramps always made sounded good. After I brewed a strong cup of decaf tea and put lemon and honey in it I decided to sneak a small shot of Doc's whiskey. A little bit of whiskey was my grandfather's Irish secret ingredient. Still in my sweats I padded out to Doc's office and poured a little into the cup. Waiting for the tea to cool I turned on the computer and started to play a game of spider solitaire. Halfway through the game I took my first sip.

◇◇◇

A noise startled me and I woke up in darkness. I'd fallen asleep at Doc's desk, face mashed on the computer keyboard, the only light the faint blue from the screensaver. The motion detector had automatically turned the overhead lights off. Gramps' hot toddy had put me right out. The last thing I remembered was starting a new solitaire game.

Another noise echoed in the stillness. Not an animal noise but footsteps, then the schwoosh of the swinging door leading from the treatment room to the reception area. Still groggy, I strained to hear. My watch read ten o'clock. No one should be here at that hour. The alarm hadn't sounded, I didn't hear any hurried movements like I imagined a burglar would make. Maybe one of the staff forgot their purse and came back to get it? That happened just last week.

Something stopped me from yelling out.

Now wide awake I carefully got up from behind the desk and made my way to the treatment area. The dim night lighting revealed no prowler lurking. Everything looked normal and quiet. A sleeping cat raised its head to stare at me for a moment, then stretched and went back to sleep. Did I dream a noise? After looking around I decided to go back to my apartment when I heard a loud grinding sound.

This sound I recognized. It was the safe in the pharmacy, the one that contained the controlled substances. Each time anyone pulled the door open the hinge grated. We joked about the noise all the time. Inside that safe we kept all the controlled substances, anesthesia products like propofol, acepromazine, and ketamine or Special K, the drug found in the Langthorne autopsies. There was no reason for anyone to be in that safe at this hour. No one could access it without knowing the combination.

Was one of our employees either selling or using the hospital drugs?

I took out my phone and debated calling 9-1-1. Maybe there was some explanation? I heard the safe close then someone walked back into the reception area.

The pharmacy has a glass pass-through area right next to the reception desk. If I could get in there I would be able to see who this night visitor was. With all the lights out whoever it was must have figured I was asleep for the night.

Silently I crept over to the pharmacy and lowered myself to the floor. I could hear the computer keyboard clicking. Good. If they were working on the computer their back would be toward me.

I raised my head to counter level and peered through the glass.

Her hair gave her away. The dyed brown strands, streaked with gray, were piled on top of her head, just as they had been every day for the last four months. With the reception lights shining, Sandy stared at the computer, then with her left hand entered numbers into a calculator laying next to the keyboard. With her right hand she kept checking an open notebook.

Relief flooded my body. I hadn't realized how tense I was. Sandy probably decided to catch up on something she forgot to do during regular business hours, although ten at night was a strange time to be doing it. Then I remembered, tomorrow Destiny came in to do the books. Maybe she needed to get every-thing in order. Doing an inventory of the controlled substances was part of her job. That explained why she had checked the safe. Not wanting a late night confrontation with our prickly office manager I was about to sneak back to my apartment when I noticed something strange.

It looked like she deleted an invoice.

Doc's computer software system wasn't the latest one on the market. Since it worked okay for him he left it alone. When you deleted something a screen popped up. There were two choices buttons, one red for delete, one green for cancel. The staff thought it looked like a traffic light.

That's what I saw on her screen. And she kept moving her arrow to the red button.

Nobody was supposed to delete an invoice. Nobody! That had been made clear to me from the first day I began to work at the hospital. You could delete an estimate or save it into the client record, but once payment had been made it was permanent. How else could you know how much money you were making?

Sandy must be stealing from the hospital. She took a chance tonight so the books would be accurate for the accountant. Destiny's message must have prompted it. No wonder the books always came out so perfect.

As if she could sense someone behind her she turned, swiveling the office chair in my direction. I ducked down below the counter and held my breath.

"Kate, is that you?" Her gruff voice sounded perfectly normal.

I stayed put. What would I say if she saw me in here? Crouched under the workspace I was completely hidden from view. She'd have to walk into the room and even then might not notice me in the dim light.

My ears strained to hear anything in the silence. A minute went by with no movement. Finally I heard the chair swivel again followed by the quiet click of the keyboard. My heart beat so loudly I thought it would give me away. I remained in that crouched position, leg muscles complaining for five minutes, then slowly crawled across the floor on my hands and knees aiming for the open doorway. Once through, I straightened up and crept back toward the treatment room and my apartment. Part of me couldn't comprehend what I saw. Sandy had been one of Doc's first employees. She'd worked for him over twenty-five years. He trusted her completely. When I'd spoken to him about the job he'd said if you need anything, ask Sandy. She knows where the bodies are buried.

"Kate. I thought I heard someone."

Startled, I turned around. Sandy stood about five feet away, notebook sticking out of her jacket pocket. Everything about her screamed completely normal.

Everything except the gun in her hand.

"What's that for?" I pointed to the weapon trying to keep my voice calm. "Did you think I was a burglar? You can put that down now before someone gets hurt."

She smiled at me. I tried to smile back, my lips stretched across my teeth, mouth suddenly dry.

"Nice try. I know you were spying on me just now. Did you figure it out?

I relaxed my body, trying to get her to think I didn't see anything. "What are you talking about? When I saw you at the computer I didn't want to disturb you. Frankly, I've had a long day so if you don't mind I'm going to go to sleep. Just put the alarm on before you leave, will you?" My voice sounded normal even to me. I turned my back to her and started toward the apartment.

The press of steel in my back stopped me in my tracks. "I can't take that chance. Sorry, Kate. Why couldn't you leave well enough alone?" My office manager's voice had an edge to it. I turned to face her. The cranky old Sandy was gone. The woman who stared back at me had a steely smile to match her icy glare. "Did you figure it out?" she repeated.

With my hand in my pocket I tried to text 9-1-1 on my cell phone. Working blindly I only hoped it had gone through. Right away she noticed the movement in my pocket and snatched the phone away from my hand.

Sandy glanced at the screen. "It didn't go through, Kate. Don't expect someone to come rushing to your rescue."

"Aren't you overreacting over a case of petty theft?"

The peals of laughter caught me by surprise. "There's a little more to it than that."

"What do you mean?" I genuinely felt the world had slipped to one side. All my theories had been wrong? Concern for myself forgotten, I needed to know the truth.

She leaned up against the door, the gun still focused on my chest. "I've watched Doc get rich over the years while he kept paying me half of what I am worth. So I started taking a little bit of money from the receipts every day. He owed it to me for all the work I did, all those extra hours I put in without ever asking for overtime. And he had no clue I was robbing him blind. The problems started when he hired Destiny to do the books. Then I had to cover my trail. That's why I came back tonight. But you had to see everything." A flicker of something crossed her face. Was it sorrow?

"Don't make things worse," I told her. "If you go now I'll wait until the morning to call the police. That will give you a head start."

Any softness in her resolve disappeared. "Why should I go? I've got everything I need now."

"You won't get away with this," I told her. "How much have you embezzled over the last twenty-five years? Maybe five or ten thousand dollars? If you talked to Doc I'm sure he would understand."

"Try over a hundred thousand, give or take a few," she proudly confessed. "Twenty dollars a day adds up."

We stood there in silence. I had youth, physical strength, and agility on my side. She had a gun.

The doorbell rang.

Sandy stared at me. "Expecting someone?"

I shook my head.

It chimed again. Then my cell phone rang in her pocket.

After a look at the number Sandy smiled a nasty smile and reached for the duct tape.

I heard a cry and then a thud. My hands and feet bound, I propped myself up and twisted from one side to another on the tile floor then pushed on the swinging door and almost fell into the reception area. Destiny lay on the ground, blood streaming from her head. Sandy looked at me, the gun back in her hand. "I wish you hadn't seen me tonight, Kate," she said. "It's going to be a bitch hiring another relief vet on such short notice."

She pushed Destiny up, sat us together on the built in reception bench, then duct-taped around our hands and feet. Our accountant moaned, still acting a little out of it. Sandy, on the other hand, had never appeared more lucid.

I pushed against the duct tape, tried to stretch it as much as I could with my wrists and forearms. It barely budged. Keep her talking, I thought. "Why did you hit Destiny?"

"I've been wanting to do that for some time," she confessed and waved the gun in our direction.

"She's been stealing money," said Destiny in a weak voice. "This time I got to the numbers before she could change them."

"Yes, Miss Destiny here finally figured it out after how many years? I didn't want Doc to hire an accountant but he said I had enough to do. He wanted to make things easier for me." Sandy walked over to the window and looked out. "Easier, he made it ten times harder. Now I had to run two sets of numbers, two sets of books, and keep track of what I gave her."

I thought for a moment. "So you adjusted everything and gave Doc and Destiny a different set of numbers, after you skimmed some off the top."

"Yeah, just a little, on the average about five or six thousand a year, sometimes more, sometimes less. But I'm not ready to pack it in just yet. Doc being gone has been a godsend. By the time he gets back I'll be up at least another ten thousand or more."

The discrepancy between what Sandy said and Mari told me suddenly made sense. "You told me business was down but in reality it was way up."

"Bingo. Sorry to see you go, Kate. Really, I am."

Part of me wasn't ready to give up either. "Sandy, you don't have to do this. Take off now and disappear. Don't add murder to your list of crimes."

"Too late for that," she said. "It's way too late for that."

I struggled to sit straight up. The bench was unyielding. "What do you mean?"

"Nothing, now shut up and let me think." Destiny and I watched her pace back and forth muttering to herself. This was no calm and organized office manager now, this woman looked out of control and dangerous. If she was a dog I would have slapped one of our leather muzzles on her.

When she stopped and stared at us I knew a decision had been made. Before we could react Sandy pulled out another roll of duct tape and put us back to back. Then she wrapped it around our bodies and taped us together.

"Okay, Kate, I'm taking your advice. It's almost over. I disconnected the hospital phone and took both your cell phones." She held them up as if on display, then slid them into her purse. "I'll be back in a few minutes. I'm moving my truck away from the front of the hospital. Then if you both are good, I'll drive you to the park and leave you in Doc's truck. Someone will find you by the morning. That ought to be enough time for me to get out of here." She dropped Destiny's purse onto the floor.

As she started to leave I yelled, "There must be more to this. Tell me the truth this time. Did you have something to do with the Langthorne deaths?"

A look of disbelief came over her face. "Well, duh. I finally got rid of those pain-in-the asses."

"Did you shoot Maybelle?"

"That, I have to admit, was the fun part."

I had been wrong, wrong about everything. But there was one more piece to the puzzle. "Did Pippi help you?"

She wheeled around, her face contorted with rage. Now I saw what Thomas and Vivian must have seen that last day. "She didn't do anything. Leave her out of it."

Why was she trying to protect Pippi? What had Gramps said about crime? It's either love or money. Pippi being adopted. Sandy's family having red hair, her little niece Melody a dead ringer for Pippi. Suddenly everything became clear. "Did you do all this for your daughter?" I asked. "For Pippi?"

"Clever, clever Kate." In a sudden move she slapped me on the face. Her nails dug deep. "How did you discover that?"

A thin ribbon of blood dripped down my cheek. My wrists were chaffing but I kept pushing and stretching as much as I could. The longer she talked the more time I had to work on the tape. "It wasn't that hard. I put two and two together—her birth certificate, seeing your niece Melody, Vivian's age when Pippi was born. But I didn't know for certain until right now. Did the local doctor help out pregnant teens and infertile couples?"

"Help, some help. He said he'd find my baby a good home, but he sold her to them and falsified the birth certificate." Her pale face reddened with emotion. "A good home, that's a laugh. They loved those stupid dogs more than they loved my little girl. All I did was help her to get all the money she deserved. "

Destiny moaned. "Please make this looser. My hands are numb."

"You've got to be kidding? Why would I do that?" Buttoning her coat up she turned out the lights, walked out the front door, then locked it behind her. Only the blue security lights lit up the darkness.

I waited until I saw her turn on the headlights of her truck. We didn't have much time. "Destiny," I said, "how tight are the straps around your hands?"

"So tight I can't feel my fingers. Do you think she's going to let us go?" Her voice held a modicum of hope.

"No. Honestly I don't think so. I think she is going to kill us."

I could hear Destiny quietly sobbing next to me. The duct tape hadn't budged even after trying my best.

"Oh, Hookie baby, Mommy is so sorry."

I couldn't believe my ears. "Is Captain Hook with you?"

"Of course, he's all snuggled up."

"Is he inside your shirt?" I certainly hadn't noticed the parrot and I doubted Sandy did either.

"Yes. I've got him tucked in my blouse under my jacket."

"If you can tell Hookie to get your keys we can cut the tape with them." Adrenaline surged into my body. It wasn't over yet.

"Why didn't I think of that?" Destiny still sounded weak but reacted quickly. "Hookie," she said in a careful voice, "Go get Mommy's keys."

I heard the bird rather than saw him. His body plunked onto the floor followed by nails scraped across the tile. Next, vague sounds which I took to be searching her purse which Sandy had left lying next to the bench. Then I heard the jingle of keys, the sound of freedom.

In a few moments Destiny said, "I've got them. There's a small metal nail file on my key ring."

With both of us concentrating, I freed one of Destiny's wrists then passed the keys over to her. Quickly she sawed herself free then sliced my tape. "Go out the back exit and head through the woods." I told her. "Directly behind us about a quarter mile is a small housing development. Look for the lights. Have them call 9-1-1. I'm going to get Buddy then I'll move in the other direction. Don't stop for anything."

Purse flung across her shoulder, Destiny ran to the rear exit and quickly disappeared. It made no sense for us to stay together. If Sandy caught one of us the other would get away. With her scheme exposed maybe she would give up. I hurried over to my apartment, put a leash on Buddy, picked up my truck keys and silently walked out the back door onto the stone patio.

"Hold it." Sandy's voice had an edge to it. She must have walked around to the rear parking lot and caught me leaving. "Get into the truck." Buddy began a low growl, the first I ever heard from him.

"I said get in the damn truck." To emphasize her intent she stuck the gun in my ribs.

At least Destiny got away, I thought as I approached Doc's truck. "You drive," she said, pointing to the keys in my hand. I opened the cab door and told Buddy to jump up. When he did someone groaned in the back.

"Get in," Sandy yelled at me. Buddy growled louder than before. When I got into the driver's seat I saw Destiny in a pile on the floor, a blanket squished beneath her. Her sleek hair was dark with clotted blood. Captain Hook poked out of her top, squished under her arm.

Sandy settled herself in but twisted in the seat to check on Destiny. I buckled my seat belt extra tight and drove to the edge of the parking lot. "Where are we going?"

"Head down to Silver Lake road, then drive to the boat ramp." I knew her plan then. She wanted to drown us, make it appear like an accident. When I came to a stop before pulling out of the parking lot I looked to the right and left, taking notice that she hadn't attached her seat belt yet. A plan began to form in my mind. "Keep going. I'll tell you when to turn."

With no street lights anywhere the road was dark and the truck lights pointed down, leaving the shoulders dark. I slowed at each curve to give me more time. Although it was only a little after ten thirty few cars were out. This road skirted along the park land then looped to the lake. To my knowledge teenagers didn't use it for their romantic trysts since it tended to be well lit. Come to think of it, I wouldn't be surprised if the parking lot had security cameras. Was she so desperate she forgot? A moan in the back seat reminded me that now it was one on one. But we had the same odds. I had height, youth, strength, agility, and intelligence. She still had a gun.

"Are we going to the lake parking lot?"

She laughed, "Too public. We're taking a dirt road that skirts the far side of the lake."

So much for cameras.

"You're driving too slowly. Speed it up," she ordered.

"Destiny," I spoke very carefully. "Make sure you don't bounce around back there. You could hurt your head. Wrap yourself and Buddy in that blanket and brace yourself. This road can get bumpy."

Sandy glanced over at me suspiciously. "Don't try anything."

"Listen, I don't want her to suffer another head injury. You are letting us go once we get there, aren't you?" I tried to make her believe my plea.

"That's the plan, if you cooperate." The gun shone in her hand.

"We'll cooperate. Just don't hurt us," I put fear in my voice to keep her from being suspicious. We sped along the road, dark woods streaming by with the moon barely a glow in the sky.

"Turn right up here about a quarter of a mile."

"Okay."

There was no way in hell I was going down without a fight. I pretended to squint at the road and slowed down, looking for the turn. Then I gunned the truck and slammed the passenger side into the closest tree.

Without the protection of the seat belt, Sandy went flying, but not before reflexively firing a round that shattered the windshield. Glass fell like hail. The old truck only had a driver's side airbag that pushed me back into the seat. The jolt when we came to a stop made my teeth chatter. As the bag began to deflate I slid past and opened the driver's door. Quickly running around the back of the truck I looked down into the broken passenger side window. Dazed, with blood streaming down the side of her face and neck, Sandy had been wedged into the foot space between the seat and the engine. The door had caved in and there was a branch resting on the passenger seat. I reached through, clamped down on her wrist and pulled the gun out of her grasp.

"Destiny, are you all right?" Although the passenger side door was severely damaged, the smaller cab door looked intact. Realizing Sandy was trapped in the front seat for now I went back over to the driver's side and peered into the back seat. A wet nose nudged me from under the heavy blanket. Buddy seemed fine. Destiny pushed the cloth off her head and gave me a weak smile.

"Remind me not to let you borrow my car, Kate. Is Sandy…?"

"She's under control."

I helped Destiny out of the truck and had her sit on the ground with her back propped against a tree. We retrieved her cell phone from Sandy's purse and called 9-1-1. With Buddy at her side and Captain Hook squawking his displeasure I went back to the truck and reached across the front seat divider to check on the woman who had killed Thomas and Vivian Langthorne and almost killed me. Sandy lifted her head up and gazed at me with those familiar watery blue eyes.

"Give me an hour before you call the police," she pleaded. "All I need is an hour."

"No can do. You've probably got a concussion," I told her. "You're not going anywhere except to a hospital and then to jail."

She started to move, moaned, then grasped onto the seat and hauled herself up. I tried to help. She repaid me by pulling a knife from her coat pocket and stabbing it into my right arm. Moonlight reflected off the brutal looking blade. A trickle of blood began to drip down my arm. "Give me the truck keys, Kate, now," she insisted. In the distance I heard the blare of a siren.

With my left hand I started to dig into my pocket. Her eyes followed the movement. With my right hand I swung out and karate chopped her wrist, hard. Boy did that hurt. The knife dropped down and fell between the seats. Those self-defense classes Gramps insisted I take finally paid off. I backed off to wait for the police.

Despite her injuries Sandy pushed her way over to the driver's seat then desperately jumped out of the truck. Buddy came out of nowhere, lunged at her, and bit her in the calf. With my left leg I drop kicked her in the hip and knocked her to the ground. I'd never used my martial arts training for real. It felt good.

Headlights flashed through the trees and multiple sirens blared. Fighting the impulse to kick her again I sat on the still scrambling Sandy, pinning her to the ground. Car doors slammed behind me and I heard a familiar voice.

"Handcuffs might be easier, Kate."

"Thanks, Luke. I thought you guys would never get here."

He offered me a hand while Police Chief Garcia pulled Sandy up and handcuffed her. As he led her away he read her the Miranda rights.

"I finally figured it out, Luke." My head hurt and I had abrasions and blood all up and down my right side and arm. Except for the pain, I felt great. Across from me a pair of EMTs knelt down by Destiny and began their exam.

Buddy ran over to me, tail wagging joyfully. Of all of us he had the least damage.

Luke gave him a pat on his head and then looked me over. "You should go to the hospital too." He lifted my hair to reveal a cut on my forehead I hadn't noticed.

"I'm fine," I insisted. "Did Destiny fill you in on what happened?"

He took my good arm and walked me to a police car. "The short version, I think. I couldn't tell you but we were keeping an eye on all the hospital employees, except you, for possible theft charges. Doc alerted us before he went on vacation because Destiny had become suspicious of discrepancies in the books. Last week we focused in on Sandy as the probable thief. We didn't think to connect her to the murders though."

"If it helps any, she confessed to Destiny and me before she abducted us. That alone should put her away for awhile. Did you know Pippi is her daughter?"

"No." He sounded surprised.

"My Gramps told me there are two motives for murder, love and money." I caught a glimpse of Sandy being loaded into the Fire Department ambulance with Police Chief Garcia at her side.

"I guess you could say this had both."

Chapter Thirty-two

"Surprise!" yelled the group of smiling faces waiting in ambush for me at Mari's house. I'd been invited to see Lucy's litter, but obviously Mari had something else up her sleeve for me.

I looked around and felt slightly guilty. There stood Henry James with a cake in his hands, the baking biker I cast as a killer for hire. Maybelle Guzzman, the woman I thought might be Pippi's boozy co-conspirator, lifted her martini glass. Miranda, the beautiful Astrid, and Joel Denny waved at me. Hopefully Joel would never find out I suspected him of sneaking back from Hollywood and offing the Langthornes so he wouldn't lose a ten million-dollar lawsuit. Lastly, standing in the back trying to chat up one of Mari's friends, Tube Depot Randy flirted away and showed absolutely no interest in me. Lucky as always, since he wasn't part of a murder-for-hire scheme. Absent of course, were Sandy, currently in custody and accused of multiple crimes, and Pippi, who had dodged the law but not a lawsuit from Hong Kong financier Charlie Too. A growing IRS investigation had frozen all her assets.

A chance remark plus lots of small clues helped me put two and two together, but even then I'd gotten it wrong. As an amateur detective I was a flop.

"Hey, everyone," Mari's voice cut through the crowd. "Let's toast to Kate's six-month anniversary, and an eventful six months it was." She passed out glasses of Prosecco, a sparkling white wine from Italy, and raised a glass in my direction.

"To Kate, we hope she stays at least another six months with us."

A thin high voice added, "To *Katerina*." I turned to see Mama G and Luke raising their glasses in the air. Cindy had let it slip at work that Dina and Luke's engagement might be off. Maybe that could be my next investigation.

Standing proudly in the front and looking significantly slimmer were Precious the beagle and owner, Brenda. Suitably attired in festive gear, Daffy and her Chihuahua, Little Man, wore matching blue pantsuits with baseball caps that read "We Love You, Dr. Kate" in rhinestones.

Destiny, with Captain Hook riding on her shoulder, pushed to the front of the group, gave me a hug and added, "I wouldn't be here without you, Kate"

"Thanks everyone," I said. "I value all of your friendships, just one thing, please…"

"Anything," Mari said.

I pushed my hair behind my ear then used my best Meryl Streep voice.

"Please. No more murders."

To receive a free catalog of Poisoned Pen Press titles, please
contact us in one of the following ways:

Phone: 1-800-421-3976
Facsimile: 1-480-949-1707
Email: info@poisonedpenpress.com
Website: www.poisonedpenpress.com

Poisoned Pen Press
6962 E. First Ave. Ste 103
Scottsdale, AZ 85251